DARK CHOICES

K. BOOZER

DARK CHOICES

K. BOOZER

AUTHORS NOTE

Your mental health matters to me.

This story explores dark themes and may contain content that some readers find distressing. If you prefer to dive into this book blind, please do so with the understanding that it is a dark romance. For those who would rather know what they're stepping into, a detailed list of potential triggers is provided below.

If you have any questions or concerns about the content, feel free to reach out to me at **authorkboozer@gmail.com**. If you are in need of support, please know that mental health resources and crisis lines are available, and I encourage you to seek help if needed—your safety and well-being comes first.

Trigger Warnings include but are not limited to: Graphic violence (including torture, murder, and death), explicit sexual content (including but not limited to: rough sex, spanking, praise, choking, exhibitionism, voyeurism), threat of sexual assault, human/sex trafficking, kidnapping, parental loss (off-page), mental and physical abuse (not between main characters), strong language, pregnancy, drug and alcohol use.

This is a work of fiction. I do not condone or support the actions or situations depicted between characters. That said... I hope you **enjoy the ride**.

Interested in listening to the songs that inspired this story?
Check out this playlist.

This one's for you, Mom. It might not be what you envisioned I would end up writing, but I hope there are books up in heaven and that I've still made you proud.

This one is also for the badass bitches out there who sometimes just want a tall, dark, and handsome man to take control and be called his "good fucking girl". 🫠

1

MICHAEL

"Please cheer up, Michael. Your grumpy face scares away the ladies."

I fixate my eyes on my brother and imagine what it would be like not to have an identical twin before pointing out the obvious. "We have the same face."

"Yet somehow, I'm still better looking than you."

We share the same light hazel eyes and olive skin tone inherited from our Italian ancestry. I keep my hair short on the sides and longer on top, while Raphael styles his hair longer until the ends curl around his ears. Tattoos cover his arms and extend to his chest, whereas I have a massive design of angel wings that spans my entire back.

Raphael snatches a pair of vodka shots from the tray on the table in front of us. He holds one out to me, but I wave it away. "I don't need that."

"No. Probably not," Raphael pushes, "but it will help you be more pleasant." He wiggles the alcohol in my face. When I don't take the bait, his face grows solemn. "I know what you're thinking, brother, but tonight is not about that."

No. Tonight is all about how to irritate Michael the quickest, apparently. Right now, it's a toss-up between the pounding music making my head ache, the blinding strobe lights, and the nauseating stench of sweat hanging in the air.

If it wasn't for our thirty-second birthday today, I wouldn't be here at all. Birthdays are meant to be celebrated, and I haven't felt like doing much of that lately. Months have passed, and I still struggle with the news that struck a match and burned my life to ashes.

Sterile.

That single word took away more than just my chance of having a family. It took away my future.

I've always known what my life will look like. It has been set in stone for me since birth. As the eldest son and heir of Dante DiAngelo, the don of the Italian Mafia in Miami, I would one day take his place at the head of the High Table; a trio of crime families that oversees all illegal operations in the city.

A role I've been groomed for and prepared for, the one thing I have ever known. Until it wasn't.

All because of the Law of Blood.

A law that requires the leader of the High Table to be married and have a blood heir. Two years ago, I fulfilled half of that condition when I married Sophia Mikhailov, the only child of Sergei Mikhailov, leader of the Russian Bratva. A power marriage concocted by our fathers to unite two of the High Table families. It would have worked. But after our first year of marriage with no child, I grew concerned. And by the second, I knew there was a problem.

It should be noted that our difficulty wasn't due to a lack of effort. In all manner of speaking, Sophia is a beautiful woman. She's tall, blond, and blue-eyed, with a body most women pay thousands to achieve. But sex with Sophia was never about love. It was a necessary means to an end.

Thinking about it makes my head hurt, and I want to feel numb right now.

I snatch the glass from my brother and toss the alcohol back. The burn of the liquid down my throat is over far too soon, leaving me parched for more. I slam back two more glasses in quick succession, leaving me to wonder how much alcohol it would take to drown my sorrows. Five? Maybe ten? Eager to test my theory, I raise my hand to signal our server to bring more alcohol.

"Tell me, Raphael. What is tonight about, then?" I level my younger brother with a look. "I have nothing to celebrate. I will be as sterile tomorrow as I am today. No number of birthday wishes will make any difference."

Exhaling hard, Raphael tosses back his shot and snaps, "Fine, then. Go drown your sorrows in bottles of alcohol tonight or go find a piece of ass to bury your angry cock in. Hell, go blow up another Triad supply house. I don't care what you decide, Michael, but please do something other than sit there and ruin my good buzz."

Anybody else and their tongue would be on the ground for talking like that to me. But it's Raphael's birthday too, and here I am, taking my anger out on my brother when he has every reason to be just as miserable as I am. The ink wasn't even dry on my divorce papers before Dad announced Raphael as his new heir—a title he never wanted or expected to have. A mere five minutes is all that separates us in age, but it's enough for me to be considered the oldest.

You'd think I'd feel animosity toward Raphael for taking what was rightfully mine since birth, but I don't because he's more than just my twin and brother. He's my closest confidant and my best friend. He has my back, and I have his. Always. There is no one I trust more, and he shares the same sentiment.

I reach for another pair of shot glasses and hand one to Raphael as an apology, which he accepts without comment.

My headache fades into a nice, numb feeling as I make a dent in my theory with another two shots. I survey the crowd with some interest from our private booth at the back of the club. Maybe I should consider Raphael's second suggestion. The packed dance floor has an assortment of beautiful women ripe for the picking, just as it does every night. But as my eyes scan the selection, no one does it for me. Instead, their beauty fades until all I see is the gleam of sweat covering their bodies as they continue to grind against one another like a pack of feral animals in heat.

Sinners is only one of several clubs owned by my family, but it's by far my favorite. Barely an inch of space is available on the dance floor or at the bar. Every VIP section is reserved weeks in advance, and the tables and private booths are never empty for long. I'm pleased with how busy the club is tonight. It's good for business. Just how I like it.

Organized crime operated in the shadows for so long, but that no longer works. In recent years, our family has focused on investing in various companies, including construction, accounting, security services, and high-end clubs and casinos. Each business is legitimate on the outside but also serves as a front to launder money and move products. The era of racketeering is over. Appearing as genuine businessmen has never been more important. I could walk past the director of the FBI tomorrow in a three-piece charcoal suit, and he wouldn't look at me twice. As far as the government is concerned, we're no different from any other law-abiding taxpayer. On the money they know of, at least.

Our cousin, Dominic Moretti, saunters to our table just as a pleasant buzz settles over me. A pretty brunette in a dress that barely covers her nipples hangs off his arm. From the look of her smeared red lipstick, her slightly tousled hair, and the way the strap of her dress hangs off her shoulder, it doesn't take a genius to know exactly what they've been doing for the past twenty minutes.

"Are you joining us, Dom?" I ask as I sink back into the luxurious leather couch. Only the best for the club.

Dominic tosses a wink my way before he leans down to whisper in the brunette's ear. Whatever he says makes her giggle like a teenage girl. And to be honest, from the look of her, she's probably barely legal as it is.

She runs a hand down Dom's chest, lower and lower, until she grazes his crotch. I raise a brow in silent approval at her boldness. Dominic grips her wrist, spins her around, and then slaps her ass. She squeals before disappearing back into the crowd. He flops down on the couch across the table, runs one hand over his short blond hair, and stretches the other along the back of the seat. "That was Kandy, and yes, that's with a k."

Our server returns, officially becoming my favorite person of the night. She lines a row of shot glasses out and quickly fills each with the best vodka money can buy. My head's fuzzy, but I think I'm up to six shots now. Another four and my theory will be complete. Maybe after, I'll go for another ten. Because fuck it. What else do I have to lose? My sanity? That shit's already on its way out along with every fuck I have left to give.

"She's gone to find a few more friends to help us celebrate your birthday properly," Dominic continues. "Unless you'd rather continue looking like someone kicked your puppy, Michael?"

He's smiling with unnecessary glee that I want to smack right off his face. I narrow my eyes at the smug bastard, my mind envisioning the very thing. But I promised Raphael I would behave tonight, and beating on my cousin is more trouble than it's worth.

Dominic brushes aside the murderous intent in my eyes and hands me another. "Here, you homicidal grump. I was only joking."

I hesitate to take the shot because doing so will admit that I am grumpy and feeling homicidal. But fuck it. No use in denying I am both of those things. I take the shot and slam it back. A few more and maybe this night will finally be over.

Dominic glances around before his face grows serious. He leans forward, resting his elbows on his knees. "I heard from Enzo. Our men at the downtown construction site caught a rat."

His words earn my attention, slicing through my alcohol-muddled brain.

"Shit," Raphael curses under his breath.

"Triad?" I guess.

"Yeah." Dominic signals to a server, who hands him a beer when she comes over.

"Is the rat still alive?" I'm sobering up quickly at the idea of getting my hands on a fucking Triad member.

In the weeks following my life-changing news, I went on a rampage through the streets of Miami fueled by pure, unhindered anger. My violent actions drove our enemies to hide from the storm I brought down on their heads. But while they cowered, the Triads took advantage, set up shop, and have been nothing but trouble since. A welcomed distraction from the shitty turn my life took, but now? Now they're just a giant pain in the ass.

"The boys beat him up pretty good." Dominic takes a long sip of his beer. "But yeah. The fucker is still alive."

Raphael chuckles. "What a great birthday present, Dom. You shouldn't have."

I have to agree. "Enzo's bringing him here?"

Dominic nods before checking his watch. "He should be here within the hour."

"Happy fucking birthday indeed." I grin.

I consider taking the final two shots in preparation when Kandy returns with two of her friends. The fake blonde claims my brother, climbing on his lap when he invites her to join him. The one closest to me has curly black hair with light brown skin and matching dark eyes.

"Hi there, sweetie," she coos, leaning down and forward enough to push her breasts level with my eyes. "My name's Sugar."

Sugar.

Right. Of course. What do I expect from the friend of a girl named Kandy?

"Michael."

"Oh, I know who you are." She smiles coyly, like she has a secret, but in my drunken haze, she just looks slightly constipated. Like a happy constipated, if that's even a thing. The thought makes me chuckle.

Sugar takes that as an invitation and perches on my lap, her little black dress rising enough for me to see that she's bare beneath it. Not a big surprise there since she wears the dress like it's a second skin. Sugar catches me looking and leans forward. "I heard it's your birthday," she whispers, her breath a little too warm and damp against my ear. "Did you make a wish?"

I pull my head away from her mouth. "Not a damn thing." I don't believe in wishes or fairy tales or magic. It's all just a fake attempt at trying to make something good come from something bad. Well, news flash. Life is cruel. No amount of blowing out candles or wishing on a faraway star will ever change that.

Sugar leans back with a pout. Now she just looks sad constipated. "Not a single thing?"

I shake my head.

She continues when it's clear I have nothing to say. "Well, that's really sad. A handsome man like you deserves to have all his birthday wishes come true."

I don't deserve a damn thing, and clearly, the big guy upstairs feels the same. Not that I'm much of a religious man either these days. My sins are of the darkest kind, and I doubt a man like me will earn enough forgiveness to secure a place in heaven. I'm confident there's a seat waiting for me in hell with my name on it. Probably the throne because even my soul is too dark for the devil to control.

"Well, maybe I can cheer you up at least." Sugar's lips twist up, and now we're back to happy constipated again.

Fuck. I need another shot.

I must say that out loud because the next thing I know, Sugar reaches behind her and grabs two glasses. She holds one up to me, and I accept it. She swings hers back before she leans forward again. I see the kiss coming even in my buzzed state and move my head at the last second so that instead of my lips, she gets my cheek. I don't care much for kissing. It feels too intimate and often gives the girl the wrong idea when all I need is her mouth on my cock or my cock in her cunt.

She presses her alcohol-wet lips to my cheek as one of her hands moves to pop open the buttons of my shirt while the other fumbles with my belt buckle. She awkwardly rocks against my lap as she struggles with my clothes. I lean my head back against the couch cushion, close my eyes, and sigh, content to just let Sugar take the lead. I am the birthday boy after all, right?

Suddenly, a wave of heat flashes across my body, but it's not because of Sugar and her desperate grinding. No. This is from something else. It's like that sixth sense that tells you someone is watching you.

I raise my head, open my eyes, and stare into the most captivating pair of emerald-green eyes. The strobe lights highlight the soft waves of her red hair, making the strands look like a waterfall of fire flowing down her back. Her dress falls off one shoulder, revealing the smooth curve of her neck and hugging the rest of her body in a way that's impossible to ignore. Lost in the throes of the music, she moves with an effortless grace, her body an extension of the melody.

My eyes move down her body, lingering on her supple chest and long, toned legs. I know beautiful women. They surround me daily. But even the most gorgeous women pale compared to her. She possesses a beauty beyond this world that I've never seen before.

I've always been so certain of my beliefs. But seeing her at this moment makes me question each one. That maybe magic, and fairy tales, and birthday wishes are real after all because an angel stands before me. Sent down from heaven to save my tortured soul from the darkness that holds it hostage. I'm ready for my rapture.

2

ROSE

As far as prisons go, Miami is a pretty one.

The depressing thought leaves me missing Ireland's wild, rolling green hills even more. At least in the Dublin countryside, I was free amid the vastness of nature—the rich forests, the bubbling creeks and rushing rivers, and the jagged cliffs that drop off right into the ocean.

The car slows and turns off the main road. Security barely has the gates open before we're driving through them. Once we pass through the heavy tree-lined and guarded entrance, the driveway opens up to the property's meticulously maintained green front acreage. We round a slight bend, and the O'Leary estate comes into view in all its majestic glory.

The two-story mansion wraps around a circular plot to accommodate the massive house. Inside are eight bedrooms, twelve bathrooms, a luxurious kitchen, a state-of-the-art gym, and a movie theater. Outdoors, the estate boasts an infinity swimming pool that overlooks Biscayne Bay.

If Miami is my prison, then this house is my cell.

The driver pulls around to the front of the house and parks. A guard approaches and opens my door, but I stay rooted to my seat. Because I know the moment I step out, the reality of being back in Miami after ten years away will hit me as hard as the humidity that hangs in the air, even in January.

"Miss O'Leary?" The guard ventures curiously. "Would you like help?"

I close my eyes to resist rolling them because no, I don't need help. Ignoring his outstretched hand, I slide out of the car and walk beneath the stone arch that leads to the front door. As soon as I look up the marble steps, a true smile stretches across my face when I see the beautiful woman in her mid-twenties standing in the open doorway. Waves of dark hair cascade around her shoulders, and her brown eyes sparkle as brightly as her smile. I jog up the last few steps and am greeted with the warm embrace of my big sister.

"Grace." I whisper her name like it's hard for me to accept that I'm finally holding her in my arms. Video calls can only ease the pain for so long before the physical ache becomes too much.

"I've missed you so much," Grace whispers softly into my hair as she squeezes me tighter. "I can't believe I'm hugging you again."

"I missed you too."

The trauma from the car accident ten years ago, which took our mother and little brother but spared me, left an ever-lasting wound on my soul that will never fully heal. A wound that, for a time after I first left, haunted me with a fear that I would never see my sister again, let alone ever hold her in my arms.

I experienced what all the therapists I saw following the accident called survivor's guilt. I know the accident wasn't my fault. I didn't cause the other driver to drink and drive. I didn't make him run that red light. I didn't ask him to hit our car so hard that it rolled several times, making it nearly impossible for the first responders to get us out.

Still, I struggled with depression for years. Plagued by the same terrible thoughts and questions.

Why did they have to die?

Why take Aiden, only ten years old, with the rest of his life ahead of him?

Why spare me?

But don't pity the dead. Pity the living, right?

Grace pulls away, and blinds me with her megawatt smile, which we both got from our mother. She has our father's dark hair and eyes, whereas I am a carbon copy of our mother. Aiden, too. Red hair and green eyes, with a splash of freckles across my cheeks that only appear after a bit of time spent in the sun.

"I'll need all the help I can get to have this wedding planned in time for April."

Yes. The reason I'm home after ten years away.

The wedding of Grace O'Leary and Connor Fraser.

Our uncle James, the boss of the Irish mob in Dublin, sent Connor to help our father after the car accident left him lost. He was young but experienced and quickly earned our dad's respect, becoming his right-hand man in a few short years.

His engagement to Grace was surprising but not entirely unexpected. By marrying his eldest daughter to his most trusted man, he essentially secured Connor's loyalty for life. And with the absence of a direct male heir, Dad was forced to keep power within the family. It was a smart move. I'd almost be impressed if I wasn't so angry with my father.

When Grace told me the news and shared how happy she was, I was honestly shocked. I didn't even know she liked Connor because she never spoke about him when we talked. That was when Grace let me in on a little secret of hers. When she returned home from university, she developed a huge crush on Connor. She once made a pass at him after drinking too much champagne at an event. But being a total gentleman, Connor shut it down fast despite liking her back. He said our dad would kill him if he even laid a finger on her. Which, to be fair, was true.

"I am at your disposal." I move to link our arms together. "Use and abuse me."

With my sister's help, the eight suitcases containing the past ten years of my life are unpacked and organized in my old childhood home. We spend the afternoon going over wedding details, including cake tastings and a recent disagreement she had with Connor about seating arrangements.

"Now that you're home, I can set up an appointment to have you try on different styles of dresses and get you fitted."

I grab a bottle of water and curl up on the couch in the sitting room attached to my suite of rooms. "I can't wait. Your wedding will be a gorgeous affair. I even saw it on one of those gossip sites."

Grace joins me on the couch with an exaggerated huff. "I know. It's unbelievable how interested they are in a simple wedding."

I snort. "Your wedding is anything but simple. It's the event of the season. Talk of the town even!"

Grace playfully shoves at my shoulder before we fall into a fit of laughter. The energy shifts before she whispers, "I'm really happy you're here. I know you don't want to be—"

"No, I don't," I snap, harsher than I mean.

Grace drops her eyes to her glass as if she still feels responsible.

"I'm sorry." A wave of shame washes over me. My frustration about being in Miami is not her fault. "I didn't mean—"

"You have nothing to apologize for, Rose," Grace says, using Mom's nickname for me to comfort us both. "You didn't leave on purpose. Dad gave you no choice. He can say all day long that it was for your education, but we all know why he really did it."

I squeeze my eyes shut as the memories of the accident crash over me like a wave. The sound of metal crunching, the terrified screams, the burning smell of—

Grace's hand on my arm breaks through the dark thoughts swirling in my mind. "Looking like Mom is not an excuse to send your daughter away. It's like he forgets you were in the accident, too."

"Trust me. He hasn't forgotten."

My sister has never blamed me for the accident that claimed the lives of our mother and brother because she has compassion and love and plain common sense. Dad, on the other hand, has never said it out loud, but in the months following the accident, I saw the words plain as day in his eyes. If the devil gave him the chance to make a deal, he wouldn't hesitate to trade my life for theirs. After all, what's a girl's worth in the grand scheme of our world? Aiden was his heir and Isabelle his wife. I'm nothing but a constant reminder of everything he's lost. A spare daughter.

"I remember how scared you were." Grace swallows hard before continuing in a choked voice. "I didn't want you to go. I fought with Dad, but he wouldn't listen to me." She reaches for my free hand and squeezes it hard. Sometimes I forget that Grace was only eighteen when Mom died. Older but still a child too young to lose her mother. "Please, don't take this the wrong way, but as terrible as it was to have you gone, you bloomed over there, Rosaleen. Who knows what ten years of living here with Dad would have done to who you are as a person now? Mom would be proud of the incredible young woman you've grown to be. I know I am."

My sister's words make my eyes burn with unshed tears.

"Dad can think he was punishing you when he sent you away," Grace points out, "but I think it was the best thing he could have done for you, and he doesn't even realize it."

Tears stream down our faces as we embrace each other tightly; two sisters who have finally found our way back to each other.

CONNOR WAITS by the table when we walk in for dinner later that night. He quickly wraps his arm around Grace's waist and places a kiss on the crown of her head. "Hello, beautiful."

My father's second is no longer the lean young man I remember. He's filled out, his chest and shoulders broader and more defined. His reddish-blond hair is longer than it was in the past, and his facial hair has grown out, which adds to his overall Irish charm. He stares down at Grace like she's the very air he breathes, his blue eyes twinkling with love. It's my first time seeing them together, and it's clear as day that they're genuinely happy. Something that makes me happy too.

Placing her hand on Connor's chest, Grace smiles up at him before turning to face me. "You remember Rosaleen?"

Connor shifts his attention to me and smiles. "Of course, I do. It's good to have you back in time for the wedding."

"I'm happy to be back." Liar, liar, pants on fire.

Connor takes a seat beside Grace as I sit across the table from her. My eyes slide unwillingly to the front of the table, where Dad's chair remains empty. My stomach twists in apprehension at the idea of being back in the same room as him… breathing the same air. Before I can give the dreadful feeling another thought, the familiar tap of Dad's shoes on the tile floor echoes from outside the dining room. The conversation dies at the table as Patrick O'Leary strides into the dining room like the mob boss he is. I'm tempted to drop my eyes as he approaches, but I've grown a spine in the past ten years. Enough of one not to feel immediately threatened by his presence.

Patrick sits and acknowledges his future son-in-law. "Connor, how wonderful of you to join us tonight as we welcome back our little Rosaleen."

At my name, our eyes lock, and I watch his dark eyes shift from painful longing to anger. It only takes a second, and I doubt anyone else sees it, but it tells me enough. Grace is right. It bothers him how much I looked like our mother as a child and even more now as a grown woman. My lips involuntarily twitch at the thought. Maybe if I play my cards right, I'll be back on a plane to Ireland tonight.

Time has not been kind to Dad otherwise. For the first time in ten years, I'm looking at the man through the eyes of an adult and not those of a lost child. His face is heavily lined, his once dark hair streaked with gray. Although still a large man, his posture is different from what I remember. His shoulders have a slight slump, like his back is no longer capable of holding up his weight. Maybe it's simply the result of growing older, or maybe I just no longer see him as a man to fear.

I adjust my posture, sitting taller in my chair with my spine straight and my shoulders square. "Hello, Dad."

Dad grunts his greeting, then leans forward and shovels

food on his plate from the dishes before him. "I trust your trip home was uneventful."

I resist the urge to roll my eyes. We both know that the staff kept him well informed of every second during my trip.

"Yes, it was."

Dad pauses with his fork in midair and looks directly at me as if he's waiting for me to continue.

Oh, right. Manners. Of course. How silly of me to forget. "Thank you for sending the jet."

He firmly nods and then motions with his fork to the plate of chicken. "Eat." His eyes roam over my figure before he frowns and redirects his fork to the salad. "It appears your uncle allowed you to indulge too much while staying with him. You'll need to go on a diet now that you're home."

And now I resist the urge to throw my plate at his head. I'm not runway model skinny, but I'm not overweight either. I was on my school's cross-country team and rode horses at my uncle's estate. I'm fit with a healthy level of muscle, not fat.

Grace softly kicks my ankle beneath the table, and I meet her pleading eyes. She looks at the salad bowl and then back at me, her silent request obvious. I take a deep breath and reach for the tongs in the salad bowl. She's right. This is one battle not worth fighting. I can always sneak down to the kitchen later and raid the fridge for something other than rabbit food.

"Rosaleen was telling me about the cross-country meets where she placed first several times. It's all very impressive," Grace says conversationally, and I almost wish she hadn't.

Dad nods. "Yes, I suppose it is." I doubt he means that, so I sit quietly, waiting for the other shoe to drop. "Although, I wondered if the extracurricular activities were the reason your sister did not graduate with honors from university."

And there it is.

"I didn't graduate with honors because I didn't care about the stupid business degree you forced me to get." I know the moment the words slip from my mouth that it's a mistake, but my anger's itching for a fight tonight. My time away may have built me a backbone, but no filter for my mouth to go with it. "You didn't listen to me or ask me what I wanted to study. I don't want to work for you or the family. Ever. I wanted to study—"

Dad's fist slams down on the table, causing the plates to rattle and water to spill from the glasses. Even Grace and Connor freeze. "You will quit this attitude at once, Rosaleen."

"What attitude? It's the truth," I challenge.

Dad snarls and stares at me with twin dark pools of fury. I should be afraid, but I'm no longer a twelve-year-old girl desperate for her father's love or attention. "I was concerned that sending you away so young would be a mistake." His voice is calm, his words calculated and precise as he speaks slowly, but I know the anger lurks beneath the surface. "Clearly, I was right. You've returned a selfish, self-centered, ungrateful child who thinks the world owes her something. I should have married you off the moment you turned eighteen instead of listening to your uncle, who insisted you attend university. It was obviously a waste of time and money."

I want to argue back, but I know there's no point. Instead, I snap my mouth close, toss my fork down, and lean back in my seat, crossing my arms over my chest. I've officially lost my appetite. Fuck etiquette. And fuck him.

"How are the wedding preparations coming?" Dad directs his question to Connor even though Grace is handling nearly every detail.

I don't miss the way Connor reaches for Grace's free hand on the table and squeezes it as a silent show of support. "It's going very well. We've narrowed our honeymoon choice and selected our wedding cake this week."

"That's excellent. It will be important for Rosaleen to be included in the planning."

"Of course, Dad." Grace speaks up, agreeing with the tyrant. "After all, helping me is why she's home."

"Yes. She'll also need to learn so she can start her own preparations." He carries on.

That earns my attention. My eyes snap up in confusion as I struggle to understand where he's going with this. I glance between Grace and Connor. My sister shrugs. She's just as lost as I am, and Connor shakes his head like he doesn't know either.

"My own preparations? What does that mean?" I whisper, afraid of the answer.

Dad pins me with a look so cold I can't stop my body from shivering. His lips twist into a smile that holds no love or warmth, and I know. I just know that whatever he's about to say will change the course of my life forever.

"In six months' time, you will marry Igor Mikhailov of the Russian Bratva."

3

ROSE

I study my reflection in the glass partition of the car. My hair is down in full, thick waves around my shoulders. I'm wearing only a little mascara and eye shadow, just enough to enhance the green of my eyes. I tug at the short hemline of my favorite little white dress that falls off one shoulder and molds to my curves in the most delicious of ways. Not bad for a rushed job.

My phone beeps, and I click on the text message thread with my best friend.

> Evelyn: Are you there yet?

> Me: Pulling up now.

> Evelyn: And you're wearing that little white number, right? Because I LOVE that dress on you. You're banging hot when you wear it.

Evelyn's words make me smile even though they are unbecoming of a lady. Her family is practically English royalty, which makes Evelyn an actual lady by title, but it makes no difference to her. She's as wild as the Irish countryside we both love, and there's no changing her.

Leaving her behind was one of the hardest things I have ever done, and I moved to a foreign country at twelve years old.

We met on the first day of school. I was hiding in the bathroom, wanting nothing to do with anyone, when she found me and took me under her wing. The rest, as they say, is history. She knows all my secrets, even the ones she's taken part in encouraging, and is as close to me as my actual sister.

I never had to tell Evelyn about my family and our ties to the Irish mob. When your uncle practically owns the city, the truth isn't much of a secret. Thankfully, Evelyn didn't let my family history stop her from being friends with me.

I click on the post she originally sent, and an image fills the phone screen. A social media influencer I follow stands outside a club called Sinners. Her bright blue hair shines in the club's neon lights as she poses with some friends. In the caption, she says the club is celebrating the owner's birthday and offering your first drink free.

After the bombshell dropped at dinner earlier this week, I needed out of the house. I had to get out. Not even a week back and I already want to escape to Ireland.

The car's speaker system turns on, and the driver's voice comes through. "We're here, Miss O'Leary."

I instruct him to drop me off at the corner of the street Sinners is on. Of course, none of this has been cleared by my dad. The only way I could leave without his approval at all is because he was locked away in a meeting. Sure, there'll be hell to pay for my actions, but what more can he do to me? He's already sold me to the Russians by arranging a marriage to that perverted old man, and nothing can be worse than a future tied to that bastard. I still remember how he acted at my mom's funeral. I was twelve, a child, and he looked at me like I was some kind of prize to be won. If Dad thinks I'm going to lie down and accept my fate, he can think again. I will strike a match and burn everything down before I succumb to my father's wishes. And something tells me the first match will be lit tonight.

The music in the club hits me the moment I walk in. It vibrates through my body and fills me with electric energy. The shadows in the dark club are broken only by the occasional beam of neon lights, but the focus is on the dance floor placed in the center of the main floor. I lean against the black iron railing and watch the mesmerizing scene unfold below. A mass of bodies moves in unison with the music and the lights. Their quick movements make it seem like time is being sliced into pieces. The erotic and enticing sight sends a shiver down my spine, and I feel the sudden need to join them.

The bar is busy when I approach, but I still grab the attention of one of the bartenders and order a cranberry whiskey. With my drink in hand, I find a spot close to the dance floor and lean against a stone pillar.

My gaze roams the couples on the dance floor until a pair catches my eye. Every stroke of the man's hands over the woman's body is confident and possessive. It's clear in the way she surrenders to him, giving him every ounce of trust she has, that she feels safe in his arms.

I enjoy observing people. I like to create these little stories about their lives in my head and watch it play out in my mind like a movie in real time. Like this couple. Maybe she's the daughter of his boss or his best friend's little sister, or maybe she's a stranger. The possibilities are endless, but one thing is for sure. Their love burns with a passion as hot as the fires of hell itself. The man isn't controlling her any more than she controls him. Their relationship is a give and take, a push and pull, an attraction similar to what the moon and ocean share. They live for one another.

God, how I want that. To be craved, to be wanted...to be loved.

My hand instinctively moves down the column of my throat as the sight of them sends a rush of heat through my body. Normally, I would turn away, but the shadows in the club keep me hidden from sight, leaving me free to watch and imagine and give in to the desire they provoke in my blood.

Two drinks later, I feel confident enough to step onto the dance floor. The warmth of the crowd and the alcohol in my system merge to create a blissful state where all my worries are replaced by the music. The song shifts to a slow, deep bass beat with lyrics of desire, dominance, and complete surrender.

Something whispers to open my eyes, and I listen. My breath catches as a pair of intense hazel eyes snare me. He has the most handsome face I've ever seen. The dark stubble on his sun-kissed face emphasizes his sharp and well-defined jawline. His dark hair frames his chiseled face perfectly, and I long to run my fingers through it.

A girl on his lap is trying her hardest to please him, but he's only looking at me. I don't know why I do it, but I raise a single finger and beckon with a sly smile. An air of confidence surrounds him, a captivating presence about him that I want to explore, and something tells me he'd be happy to let me.

I practically snort when he promptly shoves the girl off his lap, ignoring her cries of protest as he rises to his full height. His eyes remain fixed on me as he says something to his companions, but he doesn't wait for them to reply. I'm so captivated by the wet dream walking toward me that I don't bother sparing them a look either.

Even with my heels on, he towers over me, his height at least a foot taller than my five-four frame. His shirtsleeves are rolled up, baring the sinewy muscles of his arms. I trace the path upward, lingering on his broad chest that begs to be touched. This man knows how to entice a woman's sinful thoughts, drawing out her deepest, darkest desires.

The stranger stops in front of me, and without a moment of hesitation, he reaches out, wraps his hand around my waist, and pulls me flush against his hard chest. I gasp at the dominating movement and silently approve.

When I raise my face to his, he lifts his other hand to trace the side of my cheek with the back of his fingers. His touch is gentle despite his size, and I turn toward him, chasing the feeling. His eyes flash with a heated emotion that leaves me clenching my thighs in response. A shiver runs down my spine as he explores further, tracing a path down my neck to my collarbone and back up to the nape of my neck before burying his fingers in my hair.

Up close, his eyes are even more overwhelming. The intensity in his gold gaze is so strong. It feels like I'm standing too close to a blazing fire. And if I'm not careful, I'm likely to burn.

"Who are you?" His deep voice is smooth, like melted chocolate. "What's your name?"

"Is it important?" I breathe back, fighting to suppress a groan when his hand on my waist slips to rest on the curve of my ass.

He squeezes ever so gently before he leans down to whisper in my ear, "Yes because I need to know what to whisper against your skin when you're moaning beneath me."

His hot breath brushes along the sensitive skin of my neck, and this time, I don't stop the groan from slipping free. His hand tightens in my hair, forcing my face up. He levels me with a heated look, and I meet the challenge with one of my own.

"That's mighty presumptuous of you, don't you think?"

His sun-kissed orbs search my face before his smile turns

predatory. "The blush on your cheeks, your dilated eyes, and your racing heart tell me you want it, sweetheart. I bet that if I stick my hand under your pretty little dress, I'll find you soaking wet."

He raises a brow in a silent dare, and I rub my thighs together because he's right. If he makes good on his bet, he will find my panties soaked.

I draw my bottom lip between my teeth and watch his eyes darken with desire and something like hunger. He lets go of my hair, bringing his hand to my face, and uses his thumb to free my bottom lip. I think he's about to kiss me for a moment, but then he releases my lip and cups my face.

"Tell me I'm wrong." Challenge lines his voice, demanding an answer.

I meet his heated gaze. "You're not wrong."

"I didn't think so."

My admittance seems to be all the permission he needs. He pulls me into his arms and presses his mouth to my neck with a need I can't deny. His lips are like steel velvet against my skin, unyielding and soft. His hot breath tickles my neck as he kisses his way up to my jawbone, lingering just centimeters away from my lips.

The air between us feels charged, like we're sharing something sacred. I catch his eyes, and there's a question there, unspoken but clear. Despite his dominating nature, he waits patiently for me to make the choice that will change everything. Like a true gentleman, even though I can tell he is anything but.

My mom once told me that life is made of choices, and the consequences of those choices shape the path our lives will take. Good or bad, each decision is as important as the one before because a single one has the power to change your life forever.

If life is the sum of our choices, then my past has only consisted of ones my father has made for me. And if he thinks he can control my future—he's wrong. Because right here, right now, I'm choosing myself.

Consequences be damned.

"Kiss me."

4

MICHAEL

I didn't intend to kiss her. Given how against it I am, but her sassy mouth practically dared me to do it. If only to give her something to do with her mouth until she's down on her knees in front of me.

My lips crash down, claiming hers with a ferocity that makes her moan into my mouth, and I swallow the sound. I need more, and so does she. She buries her hand in my hair as she meets every swipe of my tongue, exploring my mouth in tandem with hers.

Each brush is like an electrical shock straight to my cock, and I growl, pressing forward into her soft body. And when the little vixen lifts her leg to encircle my hip, brushing her core against me, I just about die.

Playfully nipping at her bottom lip, I warn her, "You're playing with fire."

She meets my eyes, and the dark, sensual desire swirling in those green depths of her eyes calls to me. I haven't felt this kind of heat, this uncontrollable need, this intense desire in months. The only thing I can compare to it is the rush I get when I put a bullet between the eyes of an enemy. Her touch makes me feel alive again after being numb for so long.

"Last warning."

If she sees the fire dancing in my eyes, she's not afraid of it. She should be, though. She should run as fast and as far as she can from me because if she lets me, I will consume her until only ashes remain.

The red-haired angel wears a Cheshire cat smile as if hearing the dare in my tone excites her into dancing with the devil. "Then let me burn."

Her words make me spring into action, and I snatch her hand, escorting her off the dance floor. I lead her through the club and down a dimly lit hallway. No one stops us. They know better than to approach me. I'd like to take her upstairs to my office, but I don't have the time or patience right now. Instead, I push open the door to the employee bathroom and pull her inside.

She steps forward, and her eyes travel over the space, taking in the brown tones, gold accents, and frosted scone lighting. The music from the club is muffled, but the air inside is thick and so charged, it's as if a single spark will set off an explosion.

Meeting her eyes in the mirror hanging above the large marble slab counter, I flip the lock on the door and watch her visibly shiver with a thrill. I push off the door and cross the room in two large strides. Once I'm standing directly behind her, I brush my hands down the soft skin of her exposed arms.

I bury my face in her neck and inhale deep. The sweet smell of lavender and vanilla overwhelms my senses, and like the feral animal she makes me feel, I nip to see if she tastes as good as she smells. She gasps and jerks in my hold until she melts back against me as if begging for another nibble.

"Your name?" I ask, my voice a deep whisper along her skin. "Or the next thing I bite won't be your neck."

"Do you promise?" Goose bumps explode across her skin as if the idea of my mouth biting a dozen areas of her body, each one more erotic than the one before, is tempting.

I brush her hair away, revealing a bare shoulder. "Last chance."

"Laura."

No, it's not. A beautiful angel like her doesn't have a name as simple as *Laura*. But I understand her reluctance to provide her actual name since I'm a stranger to her as much as she is to me. I will have that name by the night's end, so I'll play along for now.

"Okay, Laura. My name is Michael." There's no use in lying to her since I'm not interested in hearing her call any other name out when I pull an orgasm free from her.

She squirms in my hold, grinding her ass against my crotch as if to ease the discomfort.

"Careful. You're playing with fire again."

She suddenly spins around, catching me by surprise. Intrigued, I let her take control, curious to see what she'll do next. She cups my face and pulls me down. Our mouths crash together like thunder in a storm, wild and unrestrained. My hand falls to her hip, gripping her tight while my free hand roams her figure, brushing against the side of her breast before squeezing. She pushes into my touch, needing more, seeking more. The way she responds to my touch is addicting.

My hands grip the back of her thighs, and I lift her, depositing her on the edge of the countertop. Finding the zipper on the back of her dress, I drag it down until the material falls off her shoulder and pools around her waist. With one flick of my wrist, the clasp holding her bra together snaps undone, and her ample breasts spill freely into my greedy hands.

"Fuck me," I groan at the sight, rolling one nipple between my fingers while my mouth descends over the other.

"I plan to." She throws her head back and arches her spine,

pushing her chest further into my face. If this is how I die, suffocated by these magnificent breasts, then what a fine fucking way to go.

She pushes against my shoulders, and I take a step back, momentarily annoyed before I realize what she's doing. When she slides off the counter, gravity takes over, and her dress pools around her feet.

My eyes run down her luscious figure, snagging on the lacy white thong and heels. Reaching out, I grab the front of the lace and tug, tearing the delicate fabric in one seamless movement. Bringing the destroyed lingerie to my nose, I take a deep breath and growl, "These are mine now," before slipping them into my pocket without waiting for the permission I don't need.

I can count on one hand the number of times I ever went down on Sophia during our marriage. I love eating a woman out; I just didn't enjoy doing it to her. But with "Laura," I can't wait to dive between her legs. I need to know if she tastes as good there as her mouth does.

Her back arches violently against the counter when I descend on her bare pussy, crying out when I run my tongue the length of her. I take my time licking and stroking, devouring her like a treat I've been denied. When I slide a single finger inside, she moans as her walls clamp down greedily with no intention of letting go. After adding another, I work with my mouth to quickly bring her to the edge. She shatters against my mouth, and I savor every drop as her orgasm works its way through her.

Rising with a crooked smile on my lips, I lick her juices away from the corner of my mouth and tell her, "I knew you'd taste sweet."

Without any hesitation, she pulls me close and kisses me,

not giving a single fuck that I still taste like her. When she moans, I know she likes it.

I unbutton my shirt and shrug it off, enjoying the way she drinks me in with a hungry look. I'm not gloating when I say I'm a handsome man. My daily workout includes a five-mile run, among other things like weightlifting and boxing, all of which have left me with a broad and powerful body.

Her eyes drop to my briefs. The tip of my cock pokes through the waistband, unable to be contained in the tight material. She pushes my briefs down, and my cock springs free, large and thick and powerful. Her mouth drops open in the cutest little O before she reaches out and strokes me from base to tip, drawing a deep groan from my mouth.

I reach forward, grab her waist, and spin her around before she can catch her breath.

"Look at us," I growl into her ear and raise my eyes to the mirror.

When she doesn't, I reach down and give her ass a good slap. She cries out from the surprise but not the pain. I follow it up with one hand to her breast, and the other slips between her slick folds, rubbing her clit in slow, firm circles until her cries transform into tiny moans.

"Look at us," I repeat with a nip between her shoulder blades.

Finally, she opens her orgasm-drunk eyes and meets mine in the mirror. My body engulfs her smaller one, my arms encasing her, making it hard to tell where she ends, and I begin.

"Good girl. Now, I'm going to fuck you until you forget your name and can only scream mine."

"Oh fuck. Yes, please," she moans as I push her down against the counter.

Something nags in the back of my mind, like I'm forgetting

a crucial detail, but I'm lost. I'm done thinking. I only want to feel now.

Gripping the base of my cock, I push in slowly, inch by brutal inch. I glance down and watch with a guttural groan as her pussy takes my cock like it was made for me. She's unbelievably tight, and the way she clenches around me causes sweat to bead on my forehead. "You're so tight. And so perfect. You take my cock like a good fucking girl."

"Holy..." she moans before shivering when I slide against that spot that steals her words for a moment. "Fuck—fuck me, Michael."

Leaning down, I nip her earlobe, loving the little shriek that escapes her throat. "Hold on to the counter, angel."

It's the only warning she gets before I pull out and thrust back in so deep and so quick that even I see stars. Placing one hand on the back of her neck, I hold her flush to the counter and slap her ass with the other. The countertop muffles her cries, but the sound only fuels me on. I do it again and again until I know she'll feel it every time she sits for the next week.

I pound into her, harder and faster than before, chasing my release, but not until she gives me one more orgasm. Gathering her hair in my hand, I use it to pull her upright against my chest. The change in angles is enough to drive her orgasm to the surface. Her walls spasm and clench around my cock, and I know she's close.

"Scream my name," I order.

One flick of my thumb over her hypersensitive clit is all it takes for her to erupt around me, shouting my name as she comes undone. Unable to hold on any longer, I spill myself inside her. Her walls milk every drop from my cock.

I rest my head in the crook of her neck, my heart racing, my breath coming in quick puffs of air. In a rare show of affection,

I turn my head and kiss her sweat-soaked neck before pulling out.

I slip my briefs back on before picking her dress up and handing it to her. She's sliding it up when she suddenly freezes, and I meet her panicked face.

"Oh my God. We didn't use a condom, and I'm—I'm not on birth control. What were we thinking? I'll need to get the morning-after pill, and what about diseases? I know I'm clean, but I don't—"

"Calm down."

"Don't tell me to calm down. This is serious, Michael."

Her sassy mouth is like heroin to my demons, and the little shits perk up; their interest is officially piqued once again. "I know, but you don't need to worry about anything."

She rubs her hands together like she's trying to relieve some of the stress clearly bothering her. "What does that mean?"

And I was having such a nice time. I would rather stick a knife into my stomach than have this conversation with her right now. But it's better to get it out of the way because she's panicking. She stares at me with glassy eyes, and an overwhelming need to comfort her fills me. I've never cared about a woman like this before, but something about this red-haired vixen angel has me feeling emotions that I've done a very good job of ignoring all my life.

Sighing, I close the distance between us, reaching out to trace her face. "First, I'm clean. I haven't been with anyone since the last time I was checked, which was a few months ago. That was also when I was told—"

A loud banging on the door fills the room, causing her to jump away from my touch, but I know who it is just by the rhythm of knocks.

"Hey, are you done in there? We need you," Raphael shouts.

"One moment," I holler back over my shoulder.

"Friend of yours?"

My lips twitch up. "You could say that."

The pounding resumes on the door, interrupting me again. "Let's go, Michael! We don't have all night. Enzo is waiting."

With a quick glance over my shoulder, I snap, "I'll be right there!" There's a frown on my face when I look back at her. "I have a little business to attend to, but will you stay?"

"I'm not staying in the bathroom," she jokes.

I smirk at her teasing tone, pleased to see some of the tension dissolve from her shoulders. "Of course not. Go to my table, and I'll meet you there."

"What about the group you were with? That girl?"

"You mean the girl I tossed off my lap the second I saw you?" I reach out and tap the tip of her nose playfully. "Jealousy looks cute on you."

"Well?" She raises one eyebrow, ignoring my comment and humor.

"No. She won't be there. The booth will be empty."

"Okay, but don't leave me waiting for long."

I'm halfway to the door when she calls from behind me, "Oh, and Michael?" I look over my shoulder. She has a coy smile on her lips, and I'm tempted to tell Raphael to fuck off and continue worshipping at this sinful angel's feet. "My name is Rose, not Laura. I lied."

I cross the room, pleased when she doesn't cower at my approach and happy to finally have her real name. Rose. It fits her. My lips come down on hers and own her mouth in a kiss that promises more passion to come because, like I said, I'm not done with her yet.

I nibble on her bottom lip, my tongue darting out to lick the pain away before demanding entrance. She opens for me, and I waste no time diving in to explore every inch I can. Deepening the kiss, I'm in complete control now and growl when she willingly surrenders. When I finally pull back, I rest my forehead on hers, our chests heaving for air in desperate unison.

"I'll see you soon...Rose."

5

MICHAEL

Raphael waits for me outside the bathroom. When he sees me, his lips twist up into a wicked grin.

"Don't you dare say a word," I warn him.

Raphael disregards my threat with a chuckle and shifts his gaze to the closed door behind me. "At least she's pretty."

"Careful, brother," I mock his condescending tone. "I may start to think you're into redheads."

Raphael shoves my shoulder as we start down the hallway. "The man gets laid for the first time in months, and suddenly, he's got jokes."

I glance over my shoulder before we turn the corner, hoping to catch sight of Rose. The disappointment that washes over me when the hall remains empty is unfamiliar. This intense need to own and possess her takes me by surprise. From the very first moment I saw her, I wanted her. Never once did I imagine I would end up kissing her, let alone have incredible sex in the bathroom tonight. But fuck. The girl is walking temptation in high heels, driving me to throw every one of my rules out the window.

For so long, a different desire has consumed my anger. A burning need to hunt and destroy and bury my enemies for no other reason than the need to feel something, anything other than the never-ending dark misery.

But being with Rose, I didn't feel all the guilt and anger of my past. When she looked at me, she saw the man beyond all that, beyond all the pain. And instead of running away from the fire burning in my eyes, she asked to burn in it. Her voice somehow quieted the demons in my mind and stirred a long-forgotten part of me buried deep inside.

I may not know what my life is anymore, but I do know one thing for certain now. One night with Rose will not be enough.

"THERE YOU TWO ARE!" Dominic exclaims when we walk through the steel door beneath the main club floor. "We've been itching to get started."

"Michael was busy enjoying himself with that pretty little redhead he ditched us for," Raphael discloses to the entire room.

I toss him a pointed look to shut the hell up, but it's too late. Dominic and Enzo latch on like two hungry dogs with a bone.

"A redhead, you say?" Enzo waggles his blond brow. "I like redheads. Want to share later?"

"Is this the same one I saw you tongue fucking on the dance floor before disappearing to the staff bathroom?" Dominic teases. "Couldn't you have at least taken her to your office? The bathroom just seems so belittling."

Says the guy who uses the same bathroom as his own den of inequity. I growl, "Fuck off, all of you." It only makes the three laugh harder.

"Well, happy birthday, guys. Hope you like your present," Dominic says after he composes himself.

"I brought him in, you asshole."

I turn my eyes to Enzo, my oldest friend and, by all means, a second brother to me. He shoves Dominic to the side, reaches into a big black bag on the table, and pulls out an assortment of knives.

"Dominic is trying to steal all the credit...as usual."

Enzo's father is Italian, but he takes after his fair-skinned and blue-eyed Swedish mother. Tattoos cover almost every inch of his body, and the swirl pattern shaved into the sides of his head matches. What remains of his blond hair is tied back in a high bun. He resembles a Viking straight from the history books, and the man fights like one, too. An expert in hand-to-hand combat, Enzo fights with an edge of viciousness and the brutality of a beast. The man is a force few dare to take on unless they have a death wish.

Dominic shrugs, not even bothering to deny Enzo's words.

An angry scream breaks our banter, and I look over at our present. A young Asian man with buzzed black hair is tied to the chair. I grab the back of another chair, swing it around, and straddle it backward, dropping down in front of our guest.

"Well, well, well," I drawl. "Who do we have here?"

The man thrashes against the steel cable ties that hold him securely to the chair. He leans forward and yells something I can't understand because of the gag currently stuffed in his mouth.

"I'm sorry. What was that?" I taunt, motioning to my ear like I'm having trouble hearing him. "Could you repeat that for me?"

The man collapses back in the chair with a huff and goes silent. He stares daggers at me, which I only find dull and not even the slightest bit threatening, given his current situation.

I take a moment to study his bruised and battered body. His skin glistens from sweat in the fluorescent light, which makes his already pale complexion appear sickly. A nasty wound bleeds on his forehead, along with several other minor cuts and abrasions spread across his naked chest and legs. My men gave him a good beating.

"Hold that thought, buddy." I slap the man's cheek a few times like we're old friends having a pleasant conversation. "I'll be right back with you."

He pulls his face from me but makes no further sound. Tossing him a smirk, I stand and turn back to the table.

"He was caught at the tower site downtown? What was he doing there?" I pick up a pair of knives and examine them in the room's light.

"Wouldn't tell us," Enzo answers. "The men found him in the parking garage."

That information makes me pause, and I glance up. "The parking garage?"

"Yeah."

"Did he have anything on him?"

Enzo shakes his head. "Nothing. No phone. No car keys. Not even a wallet."

Downtown Miami's newest high-rise luxury apartment building is only a few months away from completion. It's the latest venture in our family's expanding business portfolio, but it's more than that to me. Seeing how the top floor penthouse will be my future home, the Triads sniffing around the construction site concerns me greatly.

But we aren't the only ones dealing with the Triads. The Irish and Russians have also reported trouble, which is not good for business. But every time we get close to catching one, they slip through our fingers.

What the hell are the Triads playing at? What are they after? Their attacks appear random and without reason. I've never been a fan of the unknown, and it leaves me feeling unsettled. I'm tired of being left in the dark and want answers.

From my experience, torture is more about mental manipulation than physical pain. The right words can bring a man to his knees and break his willpower. But whether they reveal the information you want before succumbing to the Reaper depends entirely on the physical torture technique used.

I take the knives and a blowtorch and return to our guest. "I assume you've heard of the term 'death by a thousand cuts'?"

The man reluctantly nods, eyeing what I hold with growing dread.

"The problem with the technique has always been that death came too quickly." I flip the torch on. The fire is immediate as the roaring sound fills the quiet air. I stare into the heart of the flame and watch my demons dance with anticipation in the reflecting light. "The victims bleed out before saying anything of value." I run the blade through the fire until the steel glows a bright red. "I learned that if you use a hot knife when you make your cuts, the wound cauterizes almost immediately. It's all very—"

The man yells against his gag, interrupting me, and I immediately stab the burning hot knife in his thigh. The blade slides through his skin and muscle like soft butter, and the vomit-inducing smell of charred flesh fills the air. Our guest screams in agony, throwing his head back and thrashing against his bindings, trying hard to escape.

"It's rude to interrupt someone when they're talking. Didn't your mother teach you any manners?" I tell him. "Now, listen closely because this part is important. If I twist that knife, it will nick your femoral artery, and you'll bleed out and die within thirty seconds."

The man's breathing comes in desperate heaves of pain as he struggles to focus on me.

"So here's how tonight is going to go." I reach for a new blade and baptize it in the fire. "I ask you a question. You answer that question honestly, no cut. You don't answer that question and, well…" I twirl the hot knife in the air. "You get the point, I'm sure."

I motion with my hand. Enzo appears a moment later and pulls the gag free from our friend's mouth. "We'll start with an easy one. What's your name?"

"Why don't you ask your mother?" the Asian taunts with a bloodstained smile. "She was screaming it all last night."

"And here I thought we had an understanding."

I give him a moment to realize his mistake before I sweep the red-hot blade across his naked, pale chest, making a deep and long slice. Blood gushes from the wound as the skin bubbles and blisters from the heat.

"Go to hell, bastard!" he snaps, pain and anger fueling the words he spits at me. "You piece of shit asshole!"

I fake offense with a hand over my heart. "Language. Please."

The man pulls at his bonds again. "I'll kill you and every stupid Italian fucker in this room."

"Cute." I chuckle. "Your name."

When he stays quiet, I slice his chest again.

"Chang! My name is Chang."

Finally. Now we're getting somewhere. The first wall is always the hardest to break.

"What were you doing at my family's tower site, Chang?" I ask.

"Nothing."

"Wrong answer." Another slice, this time straight across his belly. "Try again."

Chang groans from the burning pain caused by my cuts. "I wasn't doing anything, man. I was out for a fucking walk, minding my own damn business, when your men kidnapped me for no reason."

I frown, narrowing my eyes. "Are you calling my men liars?"

"Fuck you, man!"

Another slice.

"Sorry. You're not my type. Let's try a different question. What have the Triads been doing at our warehouses and docks?"

"I'm not saying a fucking word."

"You didn't listen to the rules very well, Chang. I ask you a question; you answer. You don't answer, you get cut. It's a simple enough concept that even your pea-sized brain should be able to comprehend."

Chang hisses a string of curses in Chinese at me and then spits in my face. Enzo immediately slams his fist into Chang's jaw, snapping the man's head to the side.

From behind me, Dominic mumbles, "Shouldn't have done that."

I wipe my face clean on my jacket. My demons thrash at the clear disrespect, but I force their anger back. If I don't, I'm likely to kill the bastard now, and he's the first Triad member we've caught alive. I click the torch on and heat the knife again.

"Hold his head," I order my friend.

Chang tries to avoid Enzo's hands, but his attempt is pointless. He grabs Chang's head straight, making it impossible for him to move even an inch. Which is good because if he isn't still, he's likely to lose an eye. I drag the hot knife slowly across his forehead, down his temple, and over his cheek, stopping only when I reach his chin. This close, the stench of charred flesh is nauseating, but I push through the feeling.

I savor his screams and rephrase my question. "What are the Triads looking for?"

"Fuck off," Chang hisses.

Another slice, this time down his neck. "Do you have a death wish, Chang?"

"Better by your fucking hands than Xiao."

I pause. Xiao? Well, that's new information. "Who is Xiao?"

Shame fills Chang's expression. He likely wasn't supposed to say that.

Too late.

"What does this Xiao want? Money? Weapons? Drugs?" There's so little known about the Triads. Their organization is unorganized and chaotic. I assume there's a leader, there has to be, but with no witnesses to interrogate, the man's a fucking ghost. "Answer me, Chang."

"I'm a dead man if I do," Chang huffs, blood bubbling at the corners of his mouth. "Just like you are."

"I don't take kindly to threats."

"The boogeyman is coming for you." Chang's voice grows weaker, his words slurring, wet. Like he's drowning. One of my cuts must have sliced into his lungs. "Coming...for...all."

We won't get anything more out of him now. He has seconds left.

"Say hello to the devil for me." I grab the knife buried in his thigh and twist it, slicing through his femoral artery instantly.

The remaining light left in Chang's eyes fades, and in two heartbeats, he's gone.

"Fucking waste of time," Enzo growls, landing a swift kick to the dead man's leg.

I'm not so sure. I replay his words while I walk over to the table. Enzo gathers the used blades and torch while Dominic phones for a cleanup crew to come in. Noticing a bit of blood, I take off my jacket and shirt and pass them to Enzo to add to the bag. He hands me a clean black shirt before tying off the plastic bag of evidence.

"The damn rat didn't know shit," Enzo complains.

"Not true," Dominic says. "We know the leader's name now."

"Xiao?" Enzo snorts. "Never heard of him. You don't just come into power without others knowing who you are."

"Well, if he's this boogeyman he mentioned…" Dominic continues.

I tune my friend and cousin out and concentrate on our next steps. Though Chang was tight-lipped and didn't share much, his pieces are starting to fit with what we know.

I look at my twin, curious if he's thinking the same as I am. Raphael meets my eyes across the room and gives me a subtle nod.

Enzo and Dominic continue to bicker over the lore of this boogeyman when Raphael interrupts. "It sounds like the Triads are scouting High Table businesses for the best location to launch an attack."

I fold my arms across my chest and add, "We've long suspected the bombings on the Irish ships were Triad-related. This confirms that."

The O'Leary Irish mob has firm control over the docks, with an impressive number of import and export businesses fueling their wealth and influence. Patrick O'Leary is derailed enough to begin with, but he has become increasingly enraged with no one to blame.

I turn to Dominic. "Even if we're wrong, alert security across all businesses. Divert warehouse deliveries and question any new hires in recent months. If anyone sees a single thing out of place, have them bring it to our attention immediately. The Triads may have help from outlier families. And if they're bringing their attacks inland, we need to be prepared for anything."

Dominic nods and then glances at Raphael for confirmation of the order. I ignore the small stab of pain the look causes in my chest. It's good that they check in with Raphael. He'll be their don soon, and while I'll serve as his underboss, Raphael's words will always come first and last. His decisions will be final. His word law. I know that, but it still hurts to watch.

"Cleanup crew is here," Enzo announces, which is our cue to leave.

As we walk up the stairs, the club's music grows in volume the closer we get to the door. The rush of adrenaline from Chang's interrogation left me aching to expel some of that energy, and I know of a certain red-haired, green-eyed beauty who can help with that.

We return to our booth only to find it empty. Maybe she's still in the bathroom. I check my phone. How long have I been downstairs? Surely long enough for her to clean up and return to the booth. But...no. Something feels off.

My chest tightens unpleasantly as I look around. I don't see her on the dance floor or at the bar. And as the minutes tick by, my worry only increases until the truth becomes clear. She left.

"Michael, you alright?" Raphael asks, and I turn my head to look at him. It's sometimes eerie looking at my twin because it's like peering into a mirror. And seeing my reflection is the last thing I need right now.

"She left," I mutter, feeling a rush of unknown emotion settle over me like a heavy fog. It's like I don't know what to do next or where to turn.

Raphael studies my face for a long moment before he blows out a breath like he has come to a decision. "Damn. You really liked this girl, huh?"

"Yes." As if that hasn't been clear enough for him.

"Then I guess we'll just have to find her," he suggests.

Something in me shifts. The fog lifts, and a new purpose appears. I'll find her, and if I have to burn the entire world to find her, then so be it. Let it all burn.

6

ROSE

The Mikhailov compound is terrifying. Dark and foreboding, nothing about the house is warm. I've never been to the home of the Bratva leader, yet so far, I'm not impressed.

Crossing my arms over my chest, I shiver against the chill, even in the Florida evening heat. The O'Leary estate is cold, but this gothic-style home makes ours seem like a tropical paradise.

"Welcome, Ms. O'Leary. This way, please." The butler greets me at the door and gestures for me to follow him into a grand foyer as frightening as the exterior. He shows me into an equally dark dining room. The candles on the table and the wall sconces are the only light sources. Apparently, they don't believe in using light bulbs. It must clash with the frightening vibe they're going for here.

"Ah! Ms. O'Leary, there you are."

I turn toward the voice. Standing in the shadows across the room at the end of the table is Sergei Mikhailov and his younger brother, Igor. Another man is with them, someone I've never seen before.

"Come, come." Sergei motions for me to approach the table.

I swallow down my urge to say hell no and force my legs to move forward.

The stranger catches my eye first. He's tall, lean, and incredibly fit by how well his dark gray dress shirt stretches across his chest, clinging to his broad shoulders. His black hair falls in shaggy waves around his chiseled, handsome face. He takes a sip from his glass of wine and meets my eyes for the first time over the rim. Blue eyes as bright as the color of the Caribbean Sea lock on me with an expression of curiosity and something else harder to identify. Pity? Guilt? Concern?

A hand on my arm pulls my attention away, and I glance down to find Sergei touching me. The contact makes my skin crawl, and I fight back the urge to slap him. Instead, I gently pull my arm away with a tense smile. Sergei's dark eyes follow the movement, but he says nothing before he steps back to get a good look at me. His eyes roam over my figure, a leery smile growing on his lips, and it makes me want to hide from him.

"You've grown into a gorgeous woman, Rosaleen." He admires me with an approving nod. "Wouldn't you agree, little brother?"

My eyes unwillingly slide to the other man in the room. Igor shares a similar look with his brother. They're both tall and bulky, with dark hair and dark eyes. Their age shows on their faces. Igor's nose is crooked, like it's been broken one too many times, and his hair shows signs of receding.

The way Sergei looks at me is disgusting, but Igor takes the creep factor up to a whole other level. He stares at me like he's undressing me piece by piece until I'm left naked under his gaze. It's demeaning and degrading, and I don't care for it one bit. It reminds me too much of how he looked at me ten years ago at my mother's funeral. Only this time, there's excitement because he's been told he can have me. Well, fuck that.

"Very much so. Such young...beauty."

Gross.

"And this is Dimitri Volkov," Sergei introduces the blue-eyed stranger.

Dimitri nods in my direction but says nothing. Strangely, though, he feels like the safest in the room despite his icy exterior.

Sergei walks toward the table. "Come sit. Dinner will be served soon."

I freeze when Igor's giant hand lands on my lower back, a little too close to my ass for comfort. My dress is modest, but it still has a plunging back. The nauseating scent of his cologne overwhelms me until it's all I can smell.

"A little flustered there, my dear?" Igor asks with a touch of humor. I snap my eyes open at the sound and look over my shoulder, catching the gleam in his eyes. Does he really think I enjoy his touch? That it turns me on somehow? I purposely move away from him and walk to the other side of the table, picking a random seat and sitting down.

Sergei chuckles as if he finds my actions amusing, but Igor does not. A dark shadow crosses his face. It's a look I'm familiar with. I'm certain his hands would be on me in a different way if I was still near him. Particularly around my neck or as a fist against my cheekbone.

Suddenly, Sergei claps his hands, and there's a flurry of motion as dinner is served. I can barely focus on the dishes as they're placed in front of me because each one makes me nauseous.

I try a few spoonsful of a cold soup I'm told is called Okroshka, but the smoked fish is all I can smell, and I nearly hurl all over the table. Instead, I concentrate on tearing off pieces of bread and manage to keep that down as conversation flows around me in Russian and English. For once, I'm happy to be ignored.

When dinner concludes, I'm anxious to leave and request my car be brought around. Sergei stands, buttoning his suit jacket, and looks at his brother. "I think tonight calls for a celebratory drink and cigar. Meet me in the parlor, brother, after you've said your goodbyes."

The Russian leader walks around the table and reaches down for my hand. With no choice, I let him raise my hand to his lips for a kiss. I hold my breath and go still when his lips touch my skin. "It was wonderful to meet you again, Rosaleen. I look forward to the union of our families."

I can only give him a tight-lipped fake smile in return. When he leaves, I'm immediately very much aware of how alone Igor and I are. From the look on his face, he knows it, too. He stands and comes to sit beside me. I reach for my water glass when his ogre hand falls heavy on my thigh. He doesn't waste any time moving it up, and I lose my grip on my water glass. Water spills all over the table, including my lap and his. I push back my chair quickly and stand, causing Igor's hand to fall away. I don't care that my dress gets wet. Anything is better than the touch of his hand on my body.

Igor stands as well. His eyes are dark with lust. "Oh, my dear, you got a little wet there."

I don't miss the innuendo hidden between his words, and I do nothing to stop the look of repulse from flashing across my face. If he sees it, he doesn't comment on it. Instead, Igor steps forward, and I step back automatically. He continues until my back hits the wall by the door. His cologne is so strong. It's all I can smell, making my eyes burn. Desperate for fresh air, I turn my head away.

Igor takes that as an invitation when it's not. He leans

down before I even know what's happening, and his lips are suddenly on my neck. I lift my hands to push back against his chest, but Igor is a mountain of a man, even in his older age, and won't move.

"Stop." I hate how small my voice sounds. I hate how weak and defenseless I feel.

"We'll be married soon." Igor presses into my body, trapping me between him and the unforgiving wall. He runs his hand up my leg, pulling my dress with it. "I think I'm owed a little taste of the goods before buying the whole cake."

Fear fills my body, and I freeze as a terrible realization takes root. I'm experiencing a glimpse of my future with him if I don't find a way to escape before then.

"Please. I said stop."

"I do like a woman who begs," he murmurs against my neck, his breath hot and wet. His other hand comes forward to squeeze my breast hard.

The pain is like a direct shot to my stomach, and I can't stop what happens next, even if I want to. My stomach churns, bile burning my throat as it rises. I turn my head, my body convulsing, and I heave, spewing vomit all over Igor.

7

ROSE

Worshipping the porcelain god before sunrise is not my idea of a good time. I groan as another wave of nausea washes over me, and I barely turn in time to heave what little is left in my stomach into the toilet. Which, by this point, is nothing more than bile.

I reach up to flush the evidence away, then lean against the wall, closing my eyes to concentrate on my breathing. My skin feels clammy, and I'm shivering even though I'm not cold. When several minutes pass without another episode, I grab my phone and check the time.

5:00 a.m.

Which means it's ten in London, and Evelyn will be up.

"Hey, you." Her voice is extra chipper when she answers. I never developed an accent while overseas, but Evelyn's accent is strong, having been born and raised in England before coming to Dublin for school.

"Hey."

Evelyn knows me well enough to sense when something is wrong by just my tone. "What is it? Wait, why are you calling me so early? Is everything okay?"

"Yes...no. I-I don't know."

"Talk to me, sweetie. Do we need to switch this to a video call?" She doesn't wait for my answer. "You know what? Yes, we are. I miss seeing your gorgeous face."

A moment later, my phone rings, and I accept the video call. My best friend is the very definition of what magazines call a rare beauty. With her long, natural blond hair, bright blue eyes, and flawless porcelain skin, she is gorgeous.

"Oh, my dear girl, that bedhead of yours."

Evelyn is the yin to my yang. Growing up, she pushed me to be outgoing when all I wanted to do was hide away. She encouraged me to be daring and question things.

But she's more than a pretty face. Evelyn is wicked smart with computers. Her university degree may be in business like mine, but her true passion rests in code and program development. The girl can hack her way into the police database in less than a minute. Not saying she's ever done that exact thing to erase a few parking tickets she got growing up...but she can.

"Still better looking than you," I joke lamely.

"Where—" She squints her eyes at the screen. "Are you in the loo?"

I glance around at the spacious room. "I might be."

"Are you sick, Rose? Oh my God, you are. What's wrong? Do you need me to call someone?"

I chuckle as she rambles on until I finally interrupt. "Evelyn. Evelyn, stop." She does as I ask after a moment, her cheeks pink from embarrassment and her eyes full of concern. "It's just a little nausea and vomiting."

"So it's a stomach bug?" She looks relieved.

"Maybe?"

Evelyn narrows her eyes, all relief gone, replaced by concern again. "Maybe?"

I sigh because my thoughts will not be easy to talk about. "Remember when I told you about Michael?"

Evelyn's the only person who knows about him and our time together that night. Not even Grace knows, which makes me feel like a terrible sister, but...if my suspicions are correct, I'm glad I kept it from her.

"Yes, of course. The handsome as hell stranger who shagged your brains out in the club loo. What about him?" In typical Evelyn fashion, she applauds my sexual escapade like a proud mother would for her child at a spelling bee.

"I didn't tell you this, but he didn't wear a condom." I hold my hand up when she opens her mouth to reprimand me, I'm sure. "It was stupid, I know, but I haven't been with anyone since my ex, and he was over a year ago. So I stopped taking those birth control pills. I didn't like how they made me feel, but I think..." I know I'm rambling out of a need to prepare myself to speak aloud the fear lurking in the back of my mind for the past week. Because once said, it makes the possibility of it more real. "I think I might be pregnant."

It's rare for Evelyn to be left speechless. I can count on one hand the number of times she has. The woman is a walking chatterbox. While I wait for her to process my news and gather her thoughts, I pull myself up and walk over to the sink. I grab a washcloth and run cold water over it before wiping my face and neck. The cool sensation feels amazing on my heated skin.

"Pregnant," she repeats, drawing the single word out. "Bloody hell. Are you certain?"

"Not yet. I need to grab a test, but you know me, Evie. I'm never sick, and I vomited all over Igor last night."

"It's not like the sick bastard didn't deserve it," Evelyn remarks.

I snort before swishing water around in my mouth to get rid of the vomit taste. I spit it out into the sink and lift my eyes to the phone screen. "What am I going to do if it's positive?"

"Well, the first question is, do you want to keep it?" Evelyn isn't asking out of judgment. She's gone into fact-collecting mode and is officially thinking through all the options available to me.

I glance at my reflection in the mirror, my eyes drifting to my flat stomach. I can't even imagine what it'll look like round from pregnancy.

Stop it, Rose.

There's no need to get my hopes up imagining a baby when I haven't even taken a test to confirm or deny its existence yet. But if there is one, the idea of giving up the baby or having an abortion sends my heart racing. I bow my head and lean against the counter as my breathing grows erratic.

"Rose." Evelyn notices the panic setting in. "Take a breath and count to ten with me."

I follow her instructions and slowly feel my body come back under control.

"I guess that answers my question." Evelyn raises a single brow and smiles knowingly.

"I guess so." Still, the problem remains. "What do I do if it's real?"

"We can revisit my offer to find Michael," Evelyn suggests.

Three months have passed since that fateful night. I wanted to wait for Michael, I really did, but the spell we wove inside was broken the moment I stepped outside the bathroom. Reality came crashing down on me like a bucket of ice-cold water, and I realized there was no point in waiting for him. Him and I? It couldn't go anywhere. As much as I wanted it to, it wouldn't be possible. As much as he continues to haunt my every waking moment and invade my dreams at night, it's too late.

Because if living in this pretty prison has taught me anything, it's that Michael is better off without me in his life. Besides, what if he's moved on by now? Men as handsome as him don't stay single for long. And if by some miracle he is, would he even want us? A girl on the run from her deadly father and a baby he didn't ask for? I'd only bring danger to his life.

"No. It's too dangerous for him. I told you that. If I am pregnant, I'll need to leave Miami as soon as possible." My marriage to Igor looms on the horizon, and something tells me he wouldn't take too kindly to a fiancée pregnant with another man's child. "Maybe one day, when it's safe, I can try to find him, but until then...this is best."

My heart breaks at the decision, but it's the only one I can make.

Evelyn chews on her perfectly manicured nail as she studies the resolve on my face. "I don't like it, but I understand. I'll start working on a plan, but we don't have much time, Rose. You have a banging figure, luv, but even you'll start to show soon."

I fiddle with the washcloth in my hands before placing a hand over my flat belly. It's way too early to feel anything, but I swear I feel butterflies take off beneath my touch, and I don't need a test to tell me what I already know.

I'm pregnant and completely fucked.

8

MICHAEL

What's the point of owning a multimillion-dollar security company with the best equipment on the market if it can't even help me find one woman?

It's unacceptable, and I'm furious. No. I'm beyond furious. I'm whatever comes after that where you're just angry with every single fucking thing.

I looked for Rose every night I spent at Sinners, waiting for her to walk back through those doors. I imagined her apologizing profusely for leaving. On her knees, of course. And I would forgive her, but only after I took my displeasure out on that sweet ass of hers.

The cameras proved to be a dead end. I watched them over and over, replaying the moment she left the bathroom and walked out of the club. Our cameras tracked her outside, where she turned a corner and disappeared from view.

The days blend, and my hope fades a little more each night she fails to appear. Until every night becomes just another night. I should move on, but I can't. Just the touch of another woman feels wrong, so I've stopped seeking them out entirely. Which has made for several long nights and even more cold showers than I care to count.

Instead, I've thrown myself into work. Between all the mundane work that comes with running our numerous businesses to overseeing our illegal operations and tracking down this mysterious Xiao character, my every waking hour has been consumed, and before I know it, months have passed.

Climbing out of the car, I eye the church with a growing sense of dread that collects in the bottom of my stomach. It isn't the gathering of the most powerful families in Miami under one roof for the O'Leary wedding that makes me uneasy. Something else in the air has me sitting on pins and needles, but I can't figure out what it is.

"Oh, I just love weddings," Dominic announces as he steps out next to me on the sidewalk.

"Says the man who had to be bribed to be in mine," I remind him.

Dom tugs at the lapels of his suit jacket with a grimace. "That's because you were marrying the ice bitch with no heart and soul."

It's safe to say that there's no love lost between my cousin and ex-wife. He hates the woman as much today as the day our engagement was announced. I never learned why, but it's also not hard to dislike Sophia.

"Think she'll be here today?"

"Undoubtedly," I answer. "Sophia's not one to ignore a chance to show off."

Dominic growls his agreement under his breath just as Raphael walks up. From the look on my twin's face, something's up already, and we've only just arrived.

"What is it?"

Raphael meets my cautiously curious eyes with a frown. "Dad wants us inside. Patrick O'Leary would like to talk before the wedding."

I have a small inkling about what it is too. Over the past month, the Triads have claimed responsibility for several attacks on High Table businesses. It feels like we're putting literal fires out every day with no end in sight as we chase a ghost.

Dad and Uncle Leo meet us inside and lead us down a hallway clear of wedding guests. Two Irish enforcers stand at the end of the hallway and open the door for us when we approach. The stench of cigar smoke and rich scotch overwhelms us. Sergei and his younger brother Igor sit at a table with Patrick O'Leary, Miami's Irish mob boss, and third seat at the High Table. His eldest daughter is getting married today, which is why we're here. At a noticeably less crowded table is Connor, the man of the hour, and Dimitri, the captain of the Mikhailov Bratva.

Patrick notices us first and gestures extravagantly at us, a little scotch spilling over the rim of his glass. The man is undeniably drunk. "Please! Sit and drink in celebration of my daughter's marriage."

Dad and Uncle Leo join them at their table while we join Connor and Dimitri at the other.

"How are renovations coming along at that club of yours?" Patrick asks Dad, his words slightly slurred.

Sinners suffered a fire last week that started in the storeroom. The official story is an unfortunate accident caused by an electrical malfunction, but the truth is arson courtesy of our Asian rat friends.

"We start rebuilding next week," Dad answers, keeping his reply short and to the point. Thankfully, we suffered no fatalities, but the damage was enough to warrant a shutdown.

Patrick nods. "That's excellent to hear. I like that little club of yours. May I suggest you add a little more flair during the rebuild? Sergei is on to something with that club of his. What's it called again?" He snaps his fingers several times before exclaiming, "Oh yes, the Playground. Now there's a club that knows how to cater to those with more...unique tastes."

I bristle at the blatant dig but say nothing. I've been to the Playground a handful of times and enjoyed the atmosphere, but it's too much work to keep up with. Let the Russians have their little havens of debauchery. It's the only line of successful businesses they have.

"And you are a well-valued member, dear friend." Sergei lifts his glass and clinks it with Patrick's before wisely changing the subject. "So one down, one to go, O'Leary."

The Irish mob boss downs his finger of scotch, and Igor, like the good lap dog he is, refills it right away. "Yes, and good riddance, I say. Let that foolish, youngest daughter of mine be someone else's problem. No offense to you, of course, Igor."

"None taken, old friend." Igor chuckles.

"I sometimes think sending her to Ireland was a mistake. She was given too much free rein over there by my brother. It filled her head with nonsense and bad ideas. Unlike my oldest. Now, that girl I raised to be an obedient wife. Provide heirs to your husband, and you will be taken care of for life. Be thankful for what you are given and never question the nights when your husband doesn't come to warm your bed. Grace understands the world she lives in."

Listening to Patrick speak about his daughters like they're nothing more than prized breeding mares has my back bristling uncomfortably. I glance at Connor, curious what he thinks of his boss and soon-to-be father-in-law's views. The Irish groom rolls his neck before he takes a long sip of his scotch. His silence tells me he doesn't share the same views.

Marriages in our world can go one of three ways. First,

there are the arranged marriages, the loveless marriages, where the wife is simply a womb and nothing more. Then there are the marriages that start as friends but develop into love. Finally, the third type of marriage is where the couple is already in love. Those are the lucky and rare ones.

Igor takes a deep drag of his cigar and exhales a cloud of smoke before he boasts, "I'll have that wife of mine broken in and pregnant by the end of the year. Mark my words, Patrick."

So it wasn't a rumor after all. Patrick O'Leary really is going to marry his youngest to Sergei's little brother, Igor. The strange thing is that Rosaleen O'Leary hasn't been seen in public since returning home from Ireland after ten years away. The reason for her absence is a sad story I remember well. Rosaleen was the sole survivor of a car accident that claimed the lives of her mother and little brother. Patrick was never the same after the death of his wife and heir. When I heard his daughter was the spitting image of her mother, it didn't surprise me when Patrick shipped the young girl off to Ireland. He may claim it was for her education, but we all know differently. And now she's home, but only to marry a man old enough to be her grandfather.

Patrick O'Leary, folks. Father of the year.

"Yes, I heard congratulations are in order," Dad acknowledges, pushing away the glass of scotch Sergei offers him. Never one to turn down good liquor, Dad's refusal now also has me ignoring my glass in front of me. Something has Dad on edge, and if he is, so am I. "I was not aware that you brought the girl home and entered into a marriage contract with the Mikhailovs."

Patrick shrugs, his disrespect as clear as his inebriation. "What can I say? Sergei made me an offer I couldn't refuse."

Sergei clears his throat but stays silent like he's uncomfortable with the serious turn in the conversation.

Dad looks back and forth between his fellow High Table leaders. His tone is conversational when he speaks, but an underlying trace of something dangerous can be heard. "Better than my offer?"

Either the alcohol has really gone to the Irish leader's head or he just doesn't care what he says anymore. Either path is stupid. "No offense, but I'm not about to marry my last daughter to the twin of a sterile man. I'm concerned there could be a shared genetic condition."

Silence falls hard over the room. I glance at Raphael, wondering where my brother's head is as I try to process the new information myself. Raphael meets my eyes and slowly shakes his head. The news that Dad had been actively trying to secure a marriage for Raphael with the youngest O'Leary girl is news to him, too. Another power move marriage.

"What exactly are you—" Dad starts.

The door to the room flies open, and a distressed Irish guard hurries in. "Boss!"

Patrick exhales roughly, turning his angry red face to the man. "What?"

The guard swallows hard, visibly nervous to speak. His face is sickeningly pale. Whatever news he has is not good, and he's afraid to say it. "It's Rosaleen. The lass...she's gone."

"What do you mean she's gone?" Patrick's voice is icy calm. An eerie change from the heat it carried just moments before.

"Miss Grace said she went to the bathroom. When she didn't return, she grew concerned and came to find me. We found the bathroom empty, except for her dress and heels. The guards did a sweep outside and found her phone broken out on the street."

Patrick slams his glass down on the table. "What about the cameras?"

"Disabled, sir."

Patrick stands quickly and, in one fluid motion, pulls his gun out, levels it on the guard, and pulls the trigger. The Irish man falls to his knees, crying out as he clutches his shoulder, blood seeping through his hands from the bullet wound there.

Connor stands and is at Patrick's side in an instant. He reaches for the gun and persuades Patrick to lower it. "Patrick. Now is not the time. It's your daughter's wedding day."

I glance at the guard. He's kneeling in a puddle of his blood on the floor. If he doesn't seek medical attention soon, he's bound to bleed out. But he's lucky to be alive as it is. Patrick is an excellent shot...when sober.

Connor motions for another guard to help the wounded man. "Get him to the doctor, and then make sure he stays out of sight until I come and find him."

Patrick growls his disapproval of the decision under his breath as the guard is collected off the floor and escorted out of the room.

"What did he mean by that, Patrick?" Igor is the first to question. "My fiancée is missing?"

"We don't know what happened," Connor snaps over his shoulder. "All we know is that she's not here in the church. She could have been taken."

Patrick scoffs. "She wasn't kidnapped. No one would dare do so today, of all days. No. The selfish brat ran off. And on her sister's wedding day. She has no shame."

Dad stands, buttoning his suit jacket as he says, "Well, I'll leave you to deal with this family matter, Patrick." The way Dad says the word family is not lost on the Irish boss. Had Rosaleen been Raphael's fiancée, we'd happily do everything we could to help find her. But that's not the case. Let the Mikhailovs help him.

If the news of Rosaleen's disappearance has circulated throughout the wedding guests, it doesn't show. Of course, our mother notices something is off when we sit beside her. Nothing gets past that woman.

After our birth mother passed away from unforeseen childbirth complications, Dad was lost, raising two infant sons. Alice entered our lives when we were barely three months old and never left. She's raised us and is our mother in every way that matters. Falling in love with our dad, though, wasn't a fairy tale in the slightest, but that's a story for another time.

"What is it?" she asks, concern filling her face. She's a beautiful woman, her Italian ancestry clear in her olive skin, dark brown eyes, and hair.

"It's nothing serious," Dad assures her with a smile.

Mom narrows her eyes at the sight. "Dante. Don't play coy with me. I know when you're hiding something."

"I'm not playing coy," he claims.

"But you are hiding something."

Ignoring his wife, Dad looks around, noting a strange absence. "Gabriella's not here yet?"

Ah. Yes. Our spoiled brat, pain-in-the-ass little sister.

Raphael and I love her, but the woman enjoys pushing our buttons to no end. The little hellion is a complete terror on the days that end with a "y." She's as beautiful as Queen Cleopatra with a mouth worse than a sailor's and is trouble incarnate. Once, Dad brought up the idea of marriage with a family in Italy. When the poor boy came for a visit, Gabriella scared him into tears after just one conversation. Dad hasn't tried since. Convincing Gabriella to do something she doesn't want to is like trying to bathe a cat, frustrating and fruitless, and everyone will leave soaked, clawed, and bloody.

"She sent me a text that her car was pulling up," Mom says. "Now, stop trying to change the subject."

Our sister is in her final clinical rotations to be a nurse practitioner. As stubborn and annoying as she is, Gabriella is also incredibly smart and has a kind heart and gentle soul.

Like a dog with a bone, Mom returns to her original question. "Michael, do you know?"

I shake my head, making a motion over my lips like they're sealed. Frustrated, Mom turns to her other son and repeats her question.

Twisting in my seat, I catch sight of my sister standing in the doorway and breathe a sigh of relief, only to frown a moment later when I notice her talking to Dimitri. What the hell? From their body language, it doesn't look like an argument, but it also doesn't look like what I expect to witness from two strangers. So how come it looks like Gabriella knows Dimitri pretty well?

Well enough to touch his arm...

What the fuck?

Dimitri looks down at her hand, and Gabriella withdraws it quickly, like she's been burned. The Russian says something, bows his head, and turns on his heel. From this angle, I can't see my sister's expression, but she waits long enough to watch him disappear.

I struggle to read her expression as she approaches. As open as my sister is with her feelings, she can also be very guarded, and when she is, it's like trying to read a foreign language in the dark.

Impossible.

Our sister is the perfect mini-me of Mom, right down to

the way she laughs and the way she walks. The only difference, the only thing that proves Dante is her father, is her light amber eyes. A family trait we all share. Her dark hair flows in soft, bouncy waves over her shoulders, pinned back from her face with an elegant clip. She's wearing a light blue dress with a pink floral design that falls in a skirt design, stopping just above her knees in the front and her ankles in the back. I glance around the church. Too many men and a few women are ogling my sister. Too many for comfort. She rarely goes unnoticed. A fact that Raphael and I constantly battle against.

"Hi, Dad, Uncle Leo." Gabriella leans down and kisses Dad and our uncle on the cheek before doing the same to Mom. "Hi, Mom."

"Hello, sweetheart." Dad smiles at his daughter. "You look beautiful."

"Thank you." She quickly hugs Dominic and Raphael before settling down next to me.

"Was that Dimitri Volkov I saw you talking to?" I whisper in my sister's ear.

"Yes," Gabriella replies with no hesitation or regret. I don't know why, but I expected her to lie.

Her honest answer rattles me. "What about?"

Gabriella huffs and settles her honey eyes on me. They flash in annoyance. A normal look I'm familiar with. "Does it matter?"

"Of course, it does." How can she ask me something like that? "What could you possibly have to talk to Dimitri about? How do you even know the man?"

With a roll of her eyes, Gabriella sits back in her chair with a straight spine and squared shoulders. "If you must know, it was about school. He knows I attend the University of Miami and had a question about the admissions process."

"He looked mad." Not really but I'm fishing here.

"Really, Michael?" Gabriella snaps before leveling me with a heated look. "What is with the third degree here? He didn't like what I had to say. That's all."

"Oh." I feel a little ridiculous that I jumped immediately to a negative conclusion. I must still be on edge from the intense moment earlier in the room with Patrick and the others.

"Yeah," Gabriella says, and I leave her alone.

The crowd quiets down as the wedding gets underway. It's a beautiful ceremony, but I'm on edge the entire event. Like there's a storm on the horizon, and I don't know how to prepare for the destruction it will bring when it hits.

9

ROSE

"**Y**our son will be the death of me," I groan as I collapse next to Michael on the outdoor couch.

Chuckling, he drapes his arm over my shoulders and tucks me into his side. I rest my head on his shoulder and watch our one-year-old son toddling around the backyard. His laughs are close to squeals of delight as he chases the bubbles Evelyn blows from a plastic wand. I tagged his godmother in when I became too winded to continue.

"I want another baby," Michael confesses suddenly.

His honest admission surprises me, and I lift my head to stare up at his profile. "What?"

Michael refuses to take his eyes off our son as the edge of his lips curls up into a small smile. "Another baby. Let's make one."

"Our son just turned one."

"Yes, he did. Very observant of you."

I shove his shoulder playfully. "I just meant that he's still young. He needs me, and having another baby too soon will divide my attention. It wouldn't be fair to him or the new baby."

Michael sighs and turns to look down at me. Like a moth to a flame, the gold fire burning in his irises draws me in. "Yes, he will always need you, but I want our children to be close in age. I want our son to have that kind of bond. A best friend for life."

"*What if it's a girl?*" I argue.

"*Makes no difference. He'll just be more protective of her but a best friend nonetheless. Besides, it would be nice to have a partner to keep the boys away from her.*"

It's growing hard to ignore the excitement the idea of another baby brings. I love being a mother, and seeing Michael be a dad is heartwarming and rewarding. "*I'd like that for him. It could take a while, though. To get pregnant, I mean.*"

Michael snorts. "*Please. I knocked you up the first time we slept together.*"

"*And I'll never forget it.*"

He chuckles. The sound vibrates deeply and sends a shiver of pleasure skirting down my spine. I will never get enough of his laughter. Michael pulls me against his chest, and I nuzzle closer before he turns his face to kiss the crown of my head and whispers, "*Me either.*"

The result of that fateful night is beautiful as he runs around the garden chasing bubbles. The energy he possesses is as limitless as his love of life. His pale cheeks are flushed red, making the splash of freckles he inherited from me stand out more.

"*You know,*" I start, my voice dropping an octave. Michael catches on to it like he always does and squeezes my shoulder a little tighter, eager to hear what I'm thinking. "*He's going to nap for at least a couple of hours after this playtime. We could, you know...spend that time working on baby number two.*"

Michael shifts and places a hand under my chin, tilting my face toward his. That fire from earlier is a burning inferno now. "*I believe he's ready for that nap right now. Don't you?*"

Our lips are a breath away from each other. "*I think so.*"

He captures my mouth and kisses me deeply, his tongue exploring every inch with a hunger that mirrors his actions in *bed, fucking my mouth until I'm left in a quivering, wet mess, ready to climb him like a damn tree.*

"Get me pregnant, Michael."

My eyes open to the gentle light of morning streaming through the windows. Lifting my hand to my eyes, I wipe away the tears that always come after the dream fades and reality pulls me awake. They started after all five pregnancy tests came back positive and have plagued me almost every night since.

I expected to panic when I saw the two pink lines, but I didn't. Instead, there was this rush of relief and a sudden overpowering urge to shield my innocent baby from the evils of the world.

Of course, the panic quickly set in once the surprise of the news faded. I knew if I didn't find a way to escape my upcoming nuptials and my father, this baby would never see the light of day. And I wasn't about to let that happen. I was a mother the moment I learned of its existence. And a mother protects her child with every fiber of her being.

Evelyn knew the moment she saw my face when I called her, and "Operation Set Rose Free" officially kicked into high gear. We made the plans in secret, only speaking of them on a video call in the bathroom with the shower on since it was the safest place to do so. Call it overkill or whatever, but there is no risk of being overheard or spied on in there.

My stomach, once flat, now has a slight curve to it. Like I had one too many slices of cake. It's hardly noticeable, and I can still wear my clothes without it looking suspicious, but not for long. I'm running out of time. Just last week, during the final dress fitting, the seamstress commented on needing to let out the waist seam a little. I laughed it off, but it was a very real reminder that it's now or never. I have to escape, and today's that day.

My sister's wedding day.

It's terribly cruel and feels like a betrayal. Because it is. I'm abandoning my sister on the most important day of her life. But despite how harsh it is, it's necessary. Yes, my absence will ruin her day, leaving her to always wonder where I am and whether I'm okay or even alive. Maybe one day, when Dad is six feet under the ground, I'll try to contact her. I just hope that when that day comes, she will understand why I left and forgive me.

———

By the time we arrive, the church is already in full swing. Beautiful flowers in shades of blue and white decorate the ends of the church pews. The white marble aisle is adorned with a scattering of petals, and blue and white fabric billows overhead like ocean waves. Fairy lights intertwine with the fabric, creating a dreamy, underwater-like ambience.

When I enter the bridal suite and see how stunning my sister looks in her wedding dress, a sliver of doubt worms its way in. How can I do this to her? There has to be another way. Maybe if I tell her, we can find it together. Maybe we don't need to be apart. Maybe...

My hand moves of its own accord, seeking out the gentle curve beneath my dress. Taking a deep breath, I remind myself that my little jellybean is the reason for all this. Evelyn and I have thought through every possible way, and this has the most chance of success. Dreaming of anything else is unrealistic, and I can't afford to fail now, not when the consequences are far worse.

"Hey." Grace catches my eye in the mirror. "I know I'm gorgeous, but don't go crying now. If you start, I will, and I can't have that. It took over an hour to apply all this makeup."

Her laughter is weak, as if she's actually close to tears herself, and she runs a hand down the front of her dress, keeping her hands busy and her mind distracted.

I want to remember her as she looks right now, ridiculously happy and beautiful as she prepares for the biggest adventure of her life. Connor is a lucky man, and I pray hard that Dad doesn't corrupt him in the years to follow. My sister deserves the very best, and I want her to have that when I'm gone.

"You are the most beautiful bride I have ever seen," I admire, coming to stand behind her so that we can see one another in the full-length mirror. I wrap my arms around her waist and gently rest my chin on her exposed shoulder. Her hands rise to grip me tightly.

"Thank you, Rose." She squeezes once, and I kiss her cheek, giggling when she squirms in my hold because of her makeup.

Stepping back, I catch sight of the clock on the wall as I let her go. I have half an hour before I'm due to climb out of the bathroom window and get into my Uber. I spend the remaining time laughing and smiling with my sister instead of wallowing in sadness. I want to create happy memories, memories that will bring us both comfort in the dark times to come.

As the clock approaches the thirty-minute mark, I stand and use cramps as an excuse to use the bathroom. I give her another big hug, savoring the feel of her in my arms before I turn away and grab my bag. At the door, I glance back at Grace. She meets my eyes in the mirror and smiles. I return the gesture, hoping the guilt that overwhelms me doesn't show on my face. As soon as I close the door, a sharp pain explodes in my chest. I press down hard over the area. It's as if my heart is being torn to shreds with every heartbeat. But I can't dwell. I'll see her again. I have to trust in that.

I pass a guard stationed at the end of the hall. He eyes me as I approach, so I hold up a tampon, shaking it in the air. "Nature calls."

That does the trick. The guard visibly swallows and looks away, embarrassed by my womanly matters.

The bathroom is at the end of the next hall. I slip inside and quickly flip the lock. Unzipping my bag, I pull out a battery-powered watch and check the time. So far, so good. I change out of the dress into leggings and a tunic shirt. I slip on a pair of Chucks, fold my dress, and place it and my heels on the small table in the corner. It really is a beautiful dress. I want to leave a note, but Evelyn convinced me against it last night. Leaving a note will point to only one story, and I need all the time I can get if they think I've been kidnapped.

Turning my attention to the sink and the window above, I get to work. The window is as old as the church itself, and who knows when it was last opened. The lock is a little stiff, but after a few seconds of jiggling it back and forth, it finally gives. I push the window up and peek outside. Once I ensure the coast is clear, I shove my bag through the small opening. We chose this window because it's hidden behind a line of bushes, which is a good thing when I have trouble squeezing myself through the window, cursing my curvy hips as I do. I take a few extra seconds to close the window behind me. Anything to keep them off my trail.

Shouldering my bag, I poke my head around the bush. Farther down the path, I spy a pair of guards watching the area. I know the schedule by heart after listening carefully when Dad and Connor discussed the security details one night at dinner. Any minute now, they'll split up. One will go around the corner, and the other will pass by the bushes I'm hiding behind before walking into the garden, leaving me in his blind spot.

It feels like forever before the guards finally split up. I crouch down and hold my breath as the guard walks past me, none the wiser of my presence. Dad should really think about hiring better security. I don't breathe again until he enters the blind spot, and I take my chance. It's now or never. I slip through a small opening in the bush, hiking my bag higher on my shoulder, and take off for the street as quickly and quietly as I can. I don't stop until I see my Uber idling farther down the street. I wave him down and hurry to slide inside the car. After I confirm my destination as Miami International, I take my phone out and send Evelyn a coded text message to let her know I'm on the way to the airport. It will be our last communication before I land in London.

Before the car pulls away from the curb, I turn my phone off and roll the window down just enough to toss it out. The driver either doesn't see or doesn't care enough to comment. Settling back in my seat, I send up a silent prayer that the remaining steps go just as smoothly as the first because there's no going back now.

It's time to disappear.

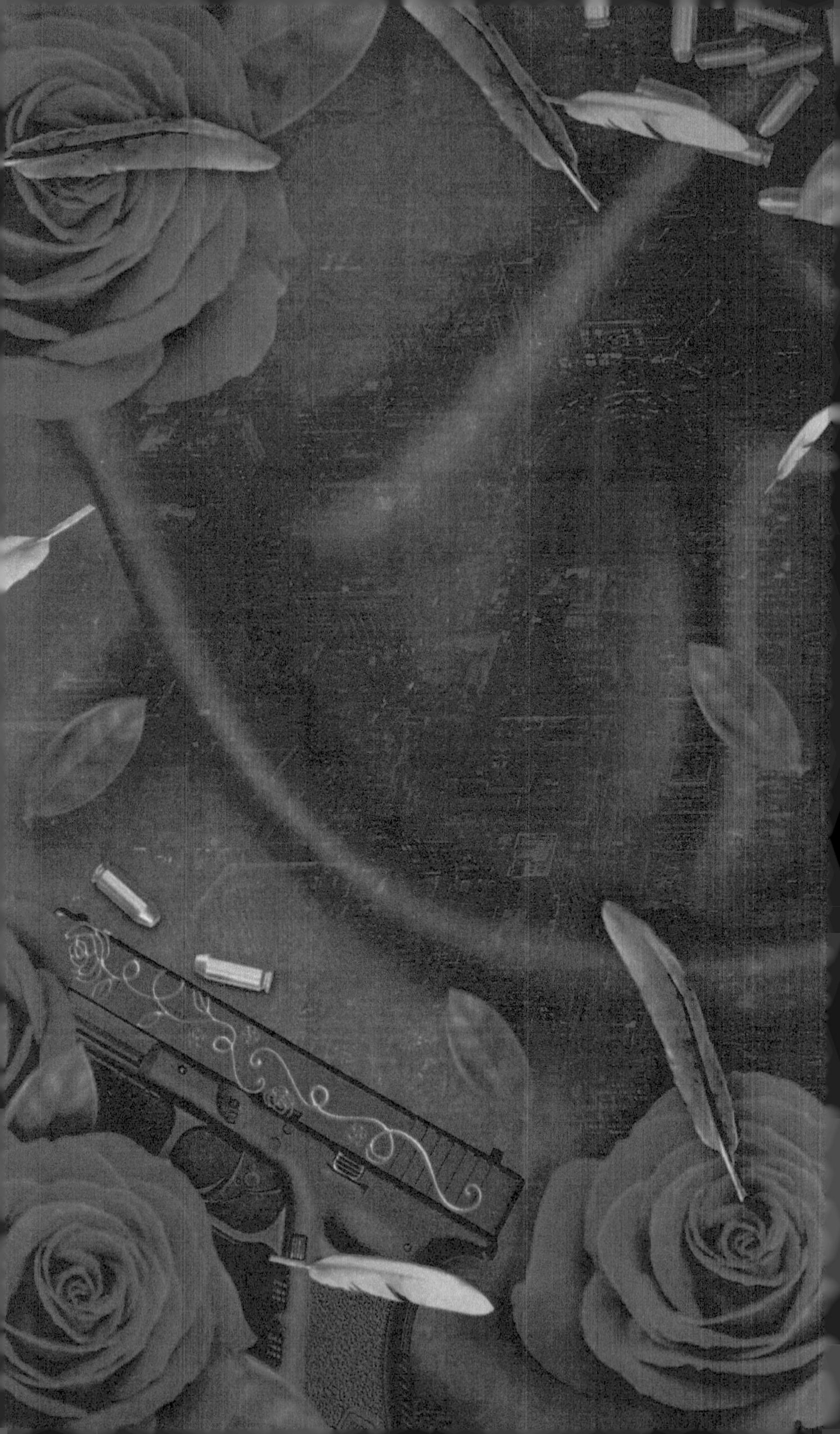

10

ROSE

Only after the plane takes off do I feel the tension in my chest ease enough to take a deep breath. Leaning back in my seat, I peer out the window and watch Miami fall away the higher the plane climbs. Every mile we travel is another mile farther away from my dad and another mile closer to freedom.

Placing a hand over my small baby bump, I rub the proof of life Michael and I created together with a content smile. Our escape isn't over, but for the next eight hours, I can rest easy. Every day is going to be a battle to stay hidden from my dad and his reach, but for the life of my baby, I will gladly run and keep running for as long as it takes.

I search my private space and find a fleece blanket, a small pillow, and a set of headphones tucked away in a storage area beneath my seat. Lowering the shade over the window, I press the button that maneuvers my seat into a bed-like position. I slip the headphones on and grab the remote to surf through the available movie and TV show options. Selecting the latest Disney movie, I settle in for the next eight hours of peace because my next fight begins once I land.

All too soon, the pilot announces over the intercom that we're starting our descent into London, and a sea of lights appears in the dark night below. A shiver of cold anxiety shoots down my spine. In the air, it's easy to push all my problems and fears to the side, but now, as the ground approaches, they all rush back in one fell swoop. Cool air fills the cabin once the plane stops at the gate and the heavy door is pulled open.

I tie my hair back in a low ponytail, pull my hoodie up so that it covers most of my face, and grab my bag from the overhead bin. Picking a pair of tall men, I hurry to walk behind them, using them to hide me. As we approach the end of the jetway, the airport gate terminal grows more visible, along with a group of tall, tattooed men who are unmistakably part of the Irish mob.

They study the group of passengers exiting for me. Fear seizes my heart, and I stop in my tracks, taking a few steps backward until I'm flush against the wall, my heart racing. A few passengers mumble their annoyance at my behavior but do their best to avoid bumping into me. I just ignore them.

Amid the sea of faces at the gate, I finally spot Evelyn. Seeing her gorgeous self is like a breath of fresh air. Leaning forward, I watch as she zeros in on the group of men others are giving a wide berth, pushes her shoulders back, marches straight across the crowded space, right up to the biggest of the five men, and slaps him across the face. Hard. My mouth falls open in surprise as the sound echoes, instantly drawing the attention of dozens of travelers.

Each of the men turns toward Evie as she faces off with the man she just slapped. He towers over her smaller frame, but she's not scared.

"So we share one hot, passionate night, and you don't even say goodbye?" Evelyn cries, dramatically flailing her arms about in the air. I guess all those elective theater classes have finally come in handy. When she said she had the distraction handled in case Dad sent men to collect me, I should have known this was what she had in mind. It's pretty badass.

The man raises his hands in front of him, like he's trying to ward off a rabid animal. Which, to be fair, fits my friend to the letter. "Look, lass—"

"Don't you dare lass me!" Evelyn interrupts. "I thought we had something special. How could you just leave me like that?"

She has the attention of the men. Now's my chance. I slip out and keep to the wall, moving quickly and quietly, trying hard to remain inconspicuous. Keeping my eyes fixed ahead, I don't dare risk looking at Evelyn.

A loud crash echoes through the terminal, and I freeze. A second later, Evelyn yells, "Don't you dare try to walk away from me, you Irish wanker! Explain yourself. Tell me why I woke up alone in bed. I even let you do that little kinky shit you wanted. Was I not good enough for you? Is that it?"

"That's enough now, lass," the large man growls, reaching out to grab her arms.

Evelyn reels back and slaps him again before he can stop her. "Don't you bloody dare touch me! You lost that right when you walked out after fucking me like some common whore."

"Ye 'ave me confused with someone else, lass. I 'ave never seen ye before."

Evelyn's grip on the conversation is slipping. I have maybe seconds left before they turn around and see me. Spotting the family bathroom we agreed to meet in, with an out-of-order sign hanging on the door courtesy of Evelyn, I slip inside and lock the door behind me. I lean heavily against the door, taking several long and deep breaths to try to slow my pounding heart as hot tears prick in the corner of my eyes. A rhythmic knock on the door has me freezing before a soft voice follows. "Rose?"

My hands fumble with the lock on the door before the mechanism finally slides open. Evelyn steps inside and locks the door behind her. In the very next breath, I fling myself at my best friend. She laughs at my enthusiasm but hugs me back just as hard.

"I've missed you so much, Evie," I sob into her shoulder.

"Not as much as I've missed you." Evelyn pulls back but keeps her hands on my shoulders as if she knows I can't bear the idea of being separated. Her blue gaze focuses down on my stomach. "How's the little jelly bean?"

I reach down and raise my hoodie and T-shirt to expose my small baby bump. "Growing."

Evelyn squeals as she steps back to admire my slight but prominent pregnant belly. "That is the most adorable baby bump I have ever seen."

"Makes everything seem more real, huh?" I worry my bottom lip as the gravity of my situation threatens to drown me.

Evelyn takes my face between her hands and forces me to look at her. Her blue eyes are firm but full of love. "Now you listen to me, Rose. Are you listening?"

I nod and sniff. "Yes."

"Good. Now, you may not have asked for this child, but like it or not, he or she will be here in only a few short months. And I know you're scared. You should be, honey. Honestly, I would be worried if you weren't. But you'll be an amazing mum. The most badass mum the world has ever known."

"How do you know?"

"Because you already are," she says simply. "This entire plan was made with that baby in mind. You have put them first since the moment you discovered they existed. That's called being a mother."

I wipe my eyes with the sleeve of my hoodie. She's right. Annoyingly so, but right all the same. "Thanks, Evie."

My eyes drop to the suitcase she brought in and the duffel bag beside it. The sight of them brings me full circle back to our current predicament. The men my dad sent are more than likely still waiting outside for me. I won't be safe until I'm in Italy, and even then, I'll never really be safe, not until my dad is six feet under.

"How long do we have?" I ask, my tone mournful.

Evelyn checks her watch. "Your plane leaves in less than an hour. We have maybe twenty minutes before they start boarding."

I frown, my voice small as I admit, "I don't want to say goodbye. It's too soon. I'm not ready."

"I don't want to either, but we can't risk you sticking around here any longer than you need to."

Evelyn turns to the duffel bag and rifles through the front pocket. A moment later, she hands me a brand-new iPhone. "It's clean and fully loaded, and I've already programmed my number in it, too. I want you to call me the moment you land in Italy and again when you make it to the safe house. We'll check in once a month until it's safer, but I'll have an eye on you. Both of you."

I accept the phone, happy to have a way to communicate safely with Evelyn. Kneeling in front of the suitcase, I drag the bag I brought from Miami over, take out the few mementos I packed, and move them to the suitcase.

"Okay, so here is everything you need to start your new life." Evelyn pulls a manila envelope out from another pocket. She opens it and digs out a passport and a slim wallet.

"Rose Bennett." In all our research, choosing a familiar name is the best option because you're less likely to ignore it. I give the picture an approving once-over. "You did a great job."

She photoshopped my hair blond so well that it actually looks real in the portrait.

"I also had a background created for authenticity. You graduated from the University of London with a degree in creative writing. When you got pregnant, you settled down in a small town outside of Venice to concentrate on your writing and commit to raising your child. The father of your baby passed away, and you have no other family."

"Wow, you really went all out."

"If all your family is dead, strangers tend to avoid asking questions. Death makes people uncomfortable."

"Isn't that the truth?" I mutter as Evelyn continues.

"The house is in your new name, and the code to the door is written on a piece of paper in this wallet. Memorize it and then destroy it. The house is completely furnished and stocked, and I left you a surprise, but you'll have to wait to see it. There's also a car to use when the baby comes because you can't cart the little jelly bean around on a bike. As cute as that would be. Also, I've set you up with a bank account. I know you want to find a job, but there's a big enough cushion in there that you won't have to for some time, even after the baby is born."

"You didn't have to do that." I know exactly what Evelyn considers a "cushion," and the money in that account won't even make a dent in the wealth tied to Evelyn's name.

Evelyn waves off my concern like she hasn't just given me the equivalent of lottery winnings. "Nonsense."

Overwhelmed with emotion, I lean forward and pull Evelyn in for another tight hug. "I really can't thank you enough for all of this. For all your help. I don't know what I would have done without you."

Evelyn rubs her hand up and down my back. "You never

have to. You're more than a best friend to me, Rose. You're the sister I never had."

"But this is just so much more than you needed to do." I wipe a stray tear from my eye as I step back. "I would have been happy with some shack in the wine country."

"Hell no. You will not live in some bloody shack, and you will not raise my niece or nephew there either." Evelyn takes my hand in hers and stares down at our clasped hands for a long moment. Finally, she says in a soft voice lined with sadness, "I will never understand the pain you felt when you lost your mum and brother. And although your father's behavior afterward was dreadful, I can't help but feel a little grateful because it brought you to me. Still, I hope I never meet the man because if I do, I'm pretty sure I'll commit murder, and I'm far too pretty for prison."

I choke out a small sob, emotion filling my chest again.

"What I'm trying to say through all of that is I admire your resilience and your courage. Anyone else would have turned to drugs or alcohol to escape the pain. Instead, you took all that anger and sadness and turned it into something beautiful and powerful. You are a force of nature no one can control or stop, and it is a sight to behold. You are a sight to behold, Rose. And if there is anything I could do to help you, it's this. I can at least make sure that you want for nothing while you finally achieve a little peace and quiet. Because you deserve it."

The tears are back tenfold, and I'm sobbing like a hormonal idiot again. Evelyn's words trigger a flood of memories and emotions that I thought were long buried. She holds me for a long while as we cry together, neither one of us saying a word because we don't have to.

Evelyn leans back and checks her watch before grimacing.

"Okay, we're cutting it really close. Come on, let's get you dressed."

I change into a pair of skinny jeans, a simple white T-shirt with a gray cardigan, and slip my shoes back on. Next up, Evelyn helps tie my hair back in a low bun so she can slip a blond wig over my head.

"I am a terrible-looking blond," I point out as I study my reflection. "Why couldn't you make me a brunette?"

I catch Evelyn's smile in the mirror. "Because I think you look great as a blond. We could be twins."

"Sure, except for your stunning blue eyes and curves for days."

"You have the same curves for days, baby, believe me. And you have that pregnancy glow going on, too. You're hot as fuck right now," Evelyn says as she finishes pinning the wig in place.

"Yeah, a real hot single pregnant lady right here, gentlemen. Come on down," I joke with a dry laugh.

"If you put that out in the universe, you'll have all the Italian men in that tiny town lining up outside your door." Evelyn wiggles her eyebrows at me, choosing to ignore my dry humor.

"Stop." I playfully shove her.

Evelyn just laughs and steps back. "There. You're perfect."

I glance at the girl in the mirror. The girl staring back is me...but not me. It's an odd feeling, like looking into a carnival fun mirror.

Evelyn finishes re-packing the suitcase, and then it's all too soon for us to say our goodbyes.

"You have your ticket and passport?" she asks.

I hold up the long rectangular piece of paper and passport. "Yes."

Without thinking, we both reach out at the same time and

hug one another tightly, savoring the moment because it will be quite a while before we see each other in person again.

"Remember to call me the second you land, okay?" Evelyn commands.

"Of course. The very moment I can."

"Be safe, you hear me? If anything looks out of place or suspicious, you get the hell out of there, and we meet in Milan like we talked about."

"I will. You need to be safe, too." My father won't just let me disappear. There will be heat on everyone I know, and if Dad convinces my uncle to help search for me, Evelyn is the first person he'll go to.

Evelyn snorts. "A little stalking is nothing new to me. Comes with the status."

I chuckle. It's true, but still. "Promise me, please."

"Okay, fine. I promise."

Evelyn leaves the bathroom first and will text when the coast is clear. Silence falls around me, and I grow anxious, staring at my phone as I wait. I'm worried something has gone wrong. That Dad's men will come barreling into the bathroom any second. Finally, a little notification lights up the screen, and the relief is sudden.

> Evelyn: All clear. Love you!

I send back a heart emoji before stowing the phone in the pocket of my cardigan.

Glancing down at my baby bump, I whisper, "Let's go, jelly bean."

With a deep breath, I grab my suitcase handle, open the door, and step into the airport. No longer Rosaleen O'Leary but Rose Bennett.

11

ROSE

Italy is a beautiful country.

I once joined Evelyn on a summer vacation to the country when we were sixteen. I was instantly enchanted with its miles of rolling hills, white sandy beaches, clear blue waters, and beautiful architecture. The culture was deeply steeped in art, family, music, and food, and reminded me of the Miami of my childhood. If I'm going to be anywhere, I'm glad it's Italy.

The single-story home Evelyn arranged for me is a cute, modest house with a comfortable, open floor plan. Floor-to-ceiling windows run the length of the backside of the house, providing an amazing view of the gardens and the Adriatic Sea in the distance. Evelyn's surprise was a beautiful nursery with everything I would ever need and more for my baby.

When I first arrived, one of my top priorities was setting up care with an OB-GYN. Seeing my baby and hearing their heartbeat for the first time had me in tears for days. Watching a tiny little blob grow into a baby with fingers and toes, a little nose, and a big personality was surreal.

Being a single mother never felt more pressing than the day my son was born. I made every decision that day alone with no idea if any of it was the right one. I want to be a good mother. I hope I will be. Because my son already won't have his father, but he will have me, and I'll shower him with twice the amount of love and affection to make up for it.

As if he knows I'm thinking about him, I hear my son making his usual fussy morning noises from the baby monitor beside the bed. Sure enough, when I turn my head, he's waving his little arms and kicking his legs in his crib on the small screen. I get up and dressed while he's being relatively quiet before walking into his nursery.

"Good morning, Liam."

At just a little over a month old, he's starting to notice and focus on things more, and when he sees me, he lights up. I scoop him up, savoring the feel of his solid, warm body in my arms as I take a deep breath of his special baby smell.

Before he came, the loneliness was deep and overwhelming. I missed Grace and Evelyn so much. Contact with my sister was impossible, and I only heard from Evelyn once a month. Being watched by my dad and uncle meant she had to act like the worried best friend who knew nothing. It was hard on both of us, but those phone calls were my only tie to the life I left behind.

Unsurprisingly, Dad was livid when he learned that my disappearance was my plan. Not because he loved me. No. Because I'm a large payday that went missing. He tried everything he could to find me, but Evie is good at what she does. After some time, I quit looking over my shoulder when I went outside. I stopped jumping at every creak and sound in the house and finally slept through the night. Life became repetitive, but it was peaceful, quiet, and free, exactly as Evelyn had wished.

Liam is an incredibly good baby with an old soul. He rarely cries unless it's for food, a clean diaper, or snuggles. He's easily entertained and has the sweetest laugh and smile I've ever seen. Liam has Michael's unique light hazel eyes and my red hair. I wasn't sure at first, but as he's grown older, I'm certain now. He's the perfect blend of us, and the love I have for him is more than life itself. The very moment the doctor placed him in my arms, I knew my heart was no longer mine.

Once I've dressed and fed Liam, we spend the morning baking a batch of muffins I plan on taking to the local bakery later today. The nice older lady who runs the shop fell in love with my pumpkin cream cheese muffins and commissioned me to bake a few dozen a week to sell. Not that I need the money, given the large nest egg Evelyn provided, but it's nice to do something.

While the muffins cool, Liam and I swing on the hammock outside. He falls into a milk coma, serenaded by the crashing sounds of distant waves and a full belly. As he naps, I take the chance to catch up on some reading, enjoying the brief escape from reality.

Once Liam wakes, I gather our things and the basket of fresh muffins and make the short drive into town.

"Ciao, bella signora," Anette greets me when I step inside the small shop carrying the basket and Liam's car seat.

"Ciao," I say back.

My Italian is rusty but getting better the more I speak it. Anette is sweet, though, and takes pity on my poor American self as she likes to call me and switches to English.

"Thank you so much for bringing more. I sold out again this morning."

I smile at the knowledge. "That's great to hear. Must be the change in weather."

"Sì." Anette takes the basket and removes the muffins. "They go great with the fall flavors."

Anette pours me a cup of the latest spice tea, and we share one of the muffins I brought in. She's been a sweet grandma figure and a comfort when I otherwise feel alone. Also, it helps that Liam loves her. Anyone that baby likes is good in my book. Not that it's hard to like him. The baby exudes charisma, much like his father.

My phone rings, and I see Evelyn's name on the screen when I pull it out of the diaper bag. Panic instantly seizes me. She's not due to call for another week. Something is off. I can feel it in the air, and the sensation sends an icy chill down my spine when I accept her call.

"Hey, everything okay?"

"Rose! Thank God." Evelyn's frantic over the line. I stand and motion to Anette that I'm stepping outside. Liam's so preoccupied with her silly noises that he won't even notice I'm gone.

"Evie, what is it?" I glance around by instinct. Night is falling. The street lamps have switched on to illuminate the town's main street, but it brings me little comfort.

"Run." From the sound of her harsh pants and hard breaths into the phone, it sounds like Evelyn is running herself. "Now. You need to run. He's there. In Italy. He found you."

He found you.

My father. Patrick O'Leary.

"How?" I ask, my voice pitched and tight.

"I don't know." Loud crashing sounds come from Evie's background like she's throwing things around in a hurry. "I set alerts in case your father left the country, and he triggered one when he booked his private plane to Italy. Where the fuck is it?" She mumbles under her breath, her attention divided. "Ah! There it is. Shit. Rose, he touched down outside of Venice not long ago. He's on his way to you. There's no other reason for him to be there."

"How much time do I have?" The house isn't far. No more than a five-minute drive.

Evelyn sobs, and the crashing sounds cease all at once. "I don't know. Oh my God, Rose. I'm so sorry. I didn't catch the warning in time. This is all my fault."

"No, it's not," I tell her firmly. It's silly to think my dad gave up looking for me by now. I hoped I meant so little to him, but in reality, he'll never stop. And I'll never be safe. We'll never be safe. Not until Patrick O'Leary is dead.

"I'm working on getting you out of Italy, but you need to run. Get to the train station and then get to Milan like we talked about. I'll find you there," Evelyn orders in a rush. "Stay safe."

"You too. I'll see you soon."

I spin around and reach for the doorknob before I pause. Inside, Liam and Anette sit unaware of the trouble coming our way. I need to get a few of our things and don't have a lot of time. If I leave Liam with Anette just long enough for me to drive back home and get what we need, I'll be faster than if he goes with me. I trust the older woman and know Liam will be safe with her. It's only for a few minutes anyway.

"Anette?" I call as I walk back inside and dig my keys out of the bag. "Will you watch Liam for a few minutes? I forgot a batch of muffins at home. Seems silly to load him in the car for such a quick trip."

"Sì. Yes, of course. I am happy to watch the piccolo." She smiles at the baby, waving his tiny fists around, trying to grab her white braid that swings in front of him. "Take as long as you need."

"Grazie." I lean down and kiss the crown of Liam's red

hair, savoring the moment before whispering, "Love you, little one. Be back soon."

From a distance, the house looks safe. The outdoor lights are on, and the living room window glows from the single lamp I always leave on so I never return to a dark house. The narrow street holds no strange cars or people. Nothing looks suspicious. If I have any time, it's precious and few.

I rush to the front door and force my hand to stop shaking long enough to punch the code. The door flings open, and I slam it shut behind me like someone is chasing me in the dark. Which they are. I just don't know from where or how close they are.

Leaning against the solid door, I close my eyes, relief crashing over me. I made it. I'm safe inside. But my relief is short-lived.

"Hello, Rosaleen."

12

ROSE

My eyes snap open just as beefy hands latch onto my arms. My reaction is immediate. I kick and shove with all my might, but the two men holding me continue to pull me forward. It's useless. They have the upper hand from the start. Still, I'm proud when I land a few frantic kicks to their bodies. Their responding grunts of pain are music to my ears.

Distracted by my satisfaction, I never see the hand coming before pain explodes across my face. Tears immediately spring to my eyes, and I freeze, looking up through wet eyelashes into the face of the very man I hoped to never see again.

"Quit your fighting this instant," Dad demands.

I should feel fear, but the pain from my face drives my mouth forward. "Like hell I will."

His muddy eyes flash with a hint of something dark before he spins on his heel and sits in the recliner across the room. He motions to his men, and I'm forced down on the couch opposite him. They release my arms and step back to take up position by the front door. I spy another pair of guards blocking the back door, which means there's no way to escape, and they know it, too.

My mind snaps to Liam, relief flooding me that I chose to leave him with Anette. He's safe with her. That's all that matters right now.

"You have caused quite a bit of trouble for me," Dad states. "Too much money, time, and resources have been wasted on this little manhunt to find you."

"Then you should have just stopped," I snap. "Saved us both the hassle."

Dad's eyes narrow at my sass. "Believe me, I wanted to. Why should I look for an ungrateful daughter who has been given everything she could ever want and then runs?"

"Everything I could ever want?" I snort. "I have only ever wanted my family, and you took that from me. You sent me away when I was a child. And for what? Because I looked too much like Mom?"

"I sent you away for your education. You were suffering in Miami—"

"I wasn't suffering. I was depressed. I was grieving. My mom and brother were dead, and you did nothing but turn your back on me. Just admit it! Admit you sent me away because I look like Mom, and you hate it."

"Like I said—"

"Admit it!"

"You will shut your mouth and listen, you—"

"Damn you! Just admit the fucking truth!"

"It's because you lived!" Dad roars.

And there it is. The truth. Out loud. Finally.

"Because I lived?" I repeat.

Dad levels me with a sinister look. "Yes. Is that what you want to hear? That I wish it had been you and not them? Fine. I do. My wife and my son were gone. And my youngest daughter is the only one who lives? I already had a daughter, but I only had one heir and one wife. And no, it's not because you look like her. That's just a frustrating inconvenience reminding me that you lived and your mother did not."

I always imagined I would feel some sort of grief when I finally heard the poisonous truth, but strangely, I only feel relief. His words cement my suspicions and bring closure to ten years of suffering and despair.

This man is not my father. A father loves their children unconditionally. A father doesn't blame his child for an accident that claimed two lives and destroyed a third. A father would comfort his surviving child. A father wouldn't be this cruel. It's more clear now than ever that my father died the same day my mother did.

"You know she was my mom, and he was my brother just as much as they were your wife and son, right? Don't you think I wish it had been me instead of them? I wished for that for so long, but I don't anymore. I want to do something with my life that would make Mom proud. And she would be so ashamed of you right now. Ashamed of how you turned your back on your youngest daughter when I needed you the most." I inhale deeply, refusing to look away from my dad's cold, dark eyes that grow angrier by the second. "I was twelve years old. We were on our way back from picking out a Christmas tree. It wasn't my fault, yet you sit there and blame me for living. But you don't get to be angry with me. I'm sorry you wish it had been me and not them. I really am. But I'm not sorry for living. I refuse to be."

Silence falls over the living room like a heavy weight. In my peripheral vision, I note my father's men grow anxious over the rising tension in the room. One strike and the whole place is likely to blow.

"You will return to Miami to fulfill your obligation to marry Igor Mikhailov." Dad's tone is sharp like a blade and just as deadly across my throat.

"I will not."

"This is not up for discussion."

"The hell it isn't. It's not my obligation to fulfill a promise you made for me without my consent. I won't marry that perverted old man. You don't have control over who I marry. I'm an adult."

"You are my daughter and—"

"Really? Your daughter? You wish I died. What kind of father wants that?"

"You will marry Igor. You have no choice in the matter."

It's like arguing with a brick wall. My words are going in one ear and out the other. "You can just let me be. No one needs to know I'm here. Leave Italy and return to Miami. Tell everyone I'm dead for all I care. Forget I exist. You want that so desperately, anyway."

"And what about Grace? You left her devastated on her wedding day."

The bastard knows just where to hit me. The depth of pain she must have felt that day haunts my dreams more often than his face does. "She'll understand." In time. The baby waiting for me back in town is reason enough.

"Unfortunately, I can't just let you be. There is a marriage contract between you and Igor."

"You bastard," I hiss. I know well enough what a marriage contract means. It's binding in our world, and as good as actually being married. "I won't—"

"Sir."

One of his men interrupts me, and all the blood rushes from my face when I see what he holds in his hands—a baby onesie from the laundry I hadn't put away just yet.

Dad waves the soldier over and takes the outfit from his outstretched hand. "Whose kid?"

"A neighbor I babysit for." The lie slips free before I can stop it.

The soldier clears his throat, and my heart plummets to my stomach. "We found something else when we searched the house."

"What?"

"There's a nursery down the hall and ultrasound photos on the fridge."

Dad examines the outfit before his eyes take in other baby items he overlooked when he first arrived. Like the baby blanket draped across the couch and the tummy mat rolled up beside the coffee table. Realization dawns on him. His jaw tightens as he studies me with cold and calculating eyes.

"You had a baby." There's no question in his words because there doesn't need to be one. The truth is obvious and clear as day.

Dad's face twists in anger, his eyes burning with restrained fury I've seen one too many times. And the first was when I snuck downstairs as a child and witnessed my dad kill a man for the first time.

"Get me Connor," Dad demands.

"Connor's here?" I ask foolishly. Of course, he's here. He's Dad's right-hand man. Where Dad goes, Connor goes.

Seconds later, my brother-in-law walks in, and if he's surprised to see me, he doesn't show it. I think I see a flicker of concern when his eyes land on me, but it must have been a trick of the light because his eyes are vacant of emotion a moment later.

"Yes, Boss?"

"I need you to get Jose on the phone immediately."

"What would you like me to tell him it's about?"

Dad looks at me once more and smiles. The sight fills me

with dread because there isn't an ounce of love or affection in it. Something in his expression tells me the wedding to Igor is no longer on the table, and it's been replaced by something far more sinister. "Tell him I have a girl to add to the roster."

What the fuck?

Connor straightens his back in surprise at the news, his eyes widening a fraction. "Sir?" He sounds confused.

"Is that a fucking problem, Connor?" Dad asks, venom lacing his words.

"No, sir." He nods, pulls his phone out, and steps outside. All without looking at me again.

Again, what the fuck?

Dad spins on his heel to face me. "Igor will not marry a slut for a bride, especially one who got herself knocked up. He wanted a virgin bride."

I snort. "Really? A virgin? I haven't been a virgin in quite some time. If you promised Igor that, he would have been wildly disappointed on our wedding night."

Dad's face grows dangerously red, bordering on purple, as he processes the news. "What?"

"I said I wasn't a virgin when I came back to Miami."

"That son of a bitch brother of mine," Dad growls. "He was supposed to ensure your innocence."

"Well, it's a good thing he didn't," I snap. "Uncle James didn't care who I fucked because he wasn't going to sell me off like some virgin cow at slaughter."

A guard walks in, and Dad looks at him. "Sir, the child is nowhere to be found in the house."

I fight hard to keep a straight face as Dad turns his hard gaze back on me. "Where is it?"

"I'll never tell you."

Dad's nostrils flare at my resistance. "With the father, perhaps?"

"Can't say I know who that is."

"Of course not. So no one will miss you, then."

"Miss me?" I frown.

"The Russians were going to pay me handsomely for you to marry Igor in return for our alliance. Now you've ruined any chance of that when you spread your legs like some common whore. So you'll just need to make me money some other way."

Connor re-enters the room and clears his throat. When his eyes dart to me this time, I catch his discomfort. Despite that, he still makes no move to help me. "Jose accepts."

"Excellent." Dad claps his hands, and I involuntarily jump at the sound. "I'll be glad to get rid of a whore for a daughter."

"At least that's one thing we can agree on." His insults mean nothing to me.

"You wanted to act like a slut? Well, now you'll get to be one for the rest of your miserable life."

I meet my dad's eyes. The ice in them hits me directly in my heart, spreading out until it threatens to consume me whole, freezing me to my seat. My heart beats fast, and I take shallow breaths. It's as if my body knows something my mind has yet to catch on to. With a strangled voice, I whisper, "What did you do?"

"You'll never see your bastard child again. Not after you're sold to the highest bidder at next week's auction."

13

MICHAEL

I toss the business report on the desk and pinch the bridge of my nose in frustration.

"How much did we lose?" I ask. I don't want to know because I really don't need this shit tonight, but I also need to know.

"Two dozen semi-automatic rifles, three dozen handguns, and two mixed crates of grenades and flash bangs," Raphael answers me solemnly.

I drop my hand, open my eyes, and gaze around the crowded office.

"Where the fuck were the guards? Where was Luke?" I demand. Luke is in charge of unloading all firearms at the docks when they arrive.

"Dead," Enzo growls. He's leaning against the bookcase with a brooding expression and his arms crossed. "He and a half dozen others, too. No survivors."

"Fuck." We lost good men and nothing to show for it. "You know the drill. Make sure we cover their funerals and set up funds for their families." What we do is dangerous. Those who follow us tempt death every day, and we pay our men handsomely for it. If they sacrifice their lives working for the family, we make sure their loved ones are taken care of afterward.

Raphael continues to be the bearer of bad news. "There's more. The dock we used to bring in the product is owned by the Irish. It was attacked too. I'm not clear on the exact number the Irish lost, but there were bodies on their end, too."

"How mad is Patrick?"

"On a scale of one to ten, where one is sunshine and rainbows and ten is murderous?" Raphael weighs the options with a tilt of his head. "I'd say he's at a twelve."

Awesome.

"And our father?"

"Pretty close to a fifteen," he answers.

Fuck.

"He's doing damage control, but I don't know what good it will do. It feels like we're on the cusp of starting another war when we haven't made a dent in the one we're currently fighting."

Enzo helps himself to my bar cart and pours a large drink. "Everything's out of control, Michael. There's no pattern to these attacks. Shitty time for Dominic to be overseas visiting his mom, if you ask me. When does he come home again?"

"In a couple of days." Dominic loves his mother, but it's hard for him to find time to get away to see her. She and Uncle Leo are still legally married, but neither take their vows seriously any longer. Aunt Mary moved back to Italy shortly after separating from our uncle when Dominic turned eighteen. I hate to think about ordering him home early, but if this shit show grows any bigger, I may be forced to.

"What do we do?" Raphael asks me, which reinforces just how serious this entire disaster is. I'm no longer the heir or boss, but since the fire at Sinners, the men have returned to treating me as their leader. None of us have tried to correct them either. Dad included.

I lean forward on the desk with my elbows, rest my chin on my clasped hands, and look directly at Enzo. "Send a team to wipe the warehouse and divert all incoming shipments to our dock on the north side. We own it, so we don't risk pissing off Patrick even more if it gets hit. We'll also need to clear some room in the airport warehouse to accommodate the additional load. Have Tony brought in to take point. Until it's decided who will inherit Luke's spot, he'll do." When Enzo nods, I ask. "Was the shipment claimed?"

"Thankfully, no."

I sigh in relief. "That's good." It's one less thing to worry about. Losing the supply is bad enough without the added trouble of an angry buyer.

Raphael's right, though. The fire at Sinners was retaliation for killing Chang, but everything else the Triads have done makes little sense. It's extremely unsettling fighting an enemy with no agenda. The recent attacks have been so random that it's as if they're simply drawing names and locations out of a damn hat.

I have a growing theory and can't shake the sour taste it leaves in my mouth. That maybe the Triads appear to act without reason because they're already getting exactly what they want. Tension building between the ruling High Table families. Anger and distrust tainting years of friendship and alliances that will eventually boil over into a war.

And if I'm right, our problems will be far worse than just stolen products and destroyed warehouses.

EVERY INCH of Sinners is covered in creepy decorations like cobwebs and skeletons, making it feel like a haunted house. The fog machine emits a cloud of smoke that billows and creeps along the ground, creating the illusion that the dancers are floating. Halloween tends to be our most popular night of the year, and this year is no different. Since we re-opened Sinners a few months ago, the club has never been busier.

Halloween is one of my favorite holidays. Something about the atmosphere of the night attracts me. It's the one time of the year when the world resembles the darkest parts of my mind, calling to me like a siren.

I lean forward, balancing my arms on the railing, and peer down at the eccentric crowd below. I wait to feel something. Anything. Desire. Temptation. But I feel nothing. And believe me, plenty of both can be found in Sinners tonight.

Rose disappeared months ago, but I can't seem to move on. After a while, I stopped searching relentlessly for her when there was nothing to be found. But even now, nearly ten months later, I can't bring myself to touch another woman, let alone have one touch me. And I've tried. Believe me. I've gone to the Playground a few times, hoping someone would tempt me, but not a single girl could compare to Rose. So I stopped going altogether, choosing instead to focus on the war at hand.

The damn temptress has a viselike grip on my cock without even knowing it. Sometimes it feels like she never even existed, but the panties tucked away in my nightstand prove otherwise.

PING

I dig my phone out of my suit jacket pocket and glance at the screen to see an email notification.

Subject line: Save her

All Hallows' Eve Auction

All ages, genders, and ethnicities are available

Midnight Halloween

96 Industrial Park

Masks are mandatory.

$100k admittance fee.

Holy shit. It's an invitation to a human trafficking auction.

Save her

The subject line makes a little more sense now. It's a plea to save someone, but I'm not sure who. Warning bells ring in my head. Red flags wave. My mind shouts that this is a bad idea, but my gut screams that if I don't go, I'll live to regret it. And I always trust my gut. It led me to Rose all those months ago, and that was hands down the best choice I've ever made.

I check my watch. It's a little after nine o'clock. There isn't much time.

Save her

Enzo flops into the chair in front of my desk. "What the hell, man? I was about to be balls deep in this girl dressed up as this spicy little devil. You would have loved her. She's with a friend dressed up as the sexiest angel I've ever seen, if you—"

"Shut up, Enzo."

The blond crosses his arms over his chest and pouts. "Okay, fine, Mr. Grumpy. What's so important then?"

I hand my phone to my friend. It's open to the email. I watch him scan the content not once or twice but three times before his eyes go wide with understanding. He passes the phone to Raphael, who hands it back to me after he reads the email.

"What have you gotten yourself into, Michael?" Enzo demands, all earlier humor now gone. "Human trafficking? We don't touch that shit with a ten-foot pole. None of the families do."

"Well, apparently, someone has." I glance at my phone. The elegant black and gold color scheme design could easily be an invitation to a ball, a stark reminder that even the most beautiful things can hide the darkest intentions imaginable.

Like Enzo said, human trafficking is an area of crime that the High Table refuses to get involved with. If you think the equestrian world is rich, the amount of money spent on the buying and selling of human beings would blow your mind. The business is a vicious and disgusting truth in the world. A cancer of the darkest kind that refuses to die. And this is coming from a man with more blood on his hands than most.

"We have to tell your dad," Enzo says with conviction.

"And then what? Ask his permission to go?" Raphael grunts. "For the sake of argument, let's say he gives us permission. We can't just go in there, guns blazing. We need to be smart about this. We'll fill him in afterward."

"If we want to kill this at the root before it spreads, we need to scout the auction. See if we can identify the ringleader," I add.

"You're seriously considering attending?" My friend looks at me in bewilderment.

I gesture at my phone. "I was invited. It would be rude not to go."

"It might be a trap," Raphael points out rather unhelpfully. I thought he was on my side here.

"Your brother's right," Enzo agrees. "You can't risk going. For all we know, this whole thing could be a setup, and there's no auction at all. It could just be a way for the Triads to get their hands on you."

"If it is, don't you think the invitation with the plea to 'save her' is going a little too far? Even Xiao isn't that smart."

Enzo mumbles, "Well, neither are you right now."

I snag Enzo with a narrowed-eye glare. "Watch it."

"I call it how I see it."

I growl out my only warning. It seems my friend is in a fighting mood this evening. Raphael steps in before I can throw something heavy like a stapler at Enzo's head.

"Michael." I turn my glare on my brother. He swallows hard at my icy look but pushes on. "Let one of us go in your place."

"No. I'm going, and that's final. I don't know who I'm supposed to save, but I'm sure it won't be anyone you two would know. Besides, it calls for a mask. No one will even know who I am."

Enzo sighs hard. "It's too risky. I don't like it."

"Then it's a good thing it's my decision and not yours," I fire back.

"Raphael, talk some sense into your brother," Enzo pleads.

Raphael snorts. "Are you joking?"

"Pull the heir card then," my stupid friend suggests, and I do pick up the stapler and throw it at him this time. It hits his shoulder...hard.

"Hey! You asshole!" He rubs at the sore spot as he scowls at me. "That fucking hurt."

"Good." I point my finger at my brother. "And don't you even think about ordering me to stand down or I'll throw the lamp next."

"I wasn't going to," Raphael assures me with a deep breath. "If you won't let one of us go in your place, then I guess I'm going with you. The invitation said you're allowed a plus-one."

"Oh, hell no!" Enzo shouts. "Sending you both in is not a good idea."

"Enough," Raphael cuts in. "We don't have the time to sit here and argue with each other. If Michael's set on attending to 'save her' or whatever the fuck this mysterious sender meant, then he's not going in alone."

"Great, it's decided. Raphael and I will go in," I say to Enzo before adding, "I'll need you to stay with the car in case shit hits the fan."

"You mean, when shit hits the fan," Enzo grumbles under his breath.

I ignore my friend's dig and glance at the clock on the wall. It's approaching ten o'clock, and the auction location is a solid forty-five minutes away on a good night. The time for discussion is over. I stand and grab my phone. "We need masks, Raphael. Go grab some from the employees and then work on the money. Enzo, get us an unmarked car that we can get rid of after."

As they leave to do as I ordered, I look back down at my phone and read the words for the hundredth time.

Save her

Who? Who's so important that someone would risk reaching out to me? The High Table's stance against human trafficking is common knowledge among Miami's criminal circles. The sender of the message must have known that if they were brave enough to contact me.

This is stupid. I'm stupid. I know this isn't a good idea, but my curiosity wins out in the end. No one deserves to be auctioned off like a piece of meat, doomed to spend their lives in pain and misery until they are finally given the sweet release of death. If there is even a slim chance that I know one girl there tonight and can save her from that kind of life...I'm going to try.

14

MICHAEL

Seeing the crowd gathered for the auction leaves me feeling tainted, like being in their mere presence makes me just as perverted and dirty as they are. Each one of these sick fuckers is incredibly lucky they're wearing masks and that I'm only here to observe. Because what I really want to do is put an end to every one of their miserable, disturbed existences.

Young women wearing only tiny thongs barely large enough to cover their bald mounds, walk around carrying black trays covered in flutes of gold champagne. One girl with a black bob approaches. One look and I quickly count her out as the one I was sent here to save. She offers the tray to us with a small and timid smile. Raphael and I each take a glass for show before she walks off to offer the same to another group of men. I watch as one large man grabs a handful of her bare ass, making the girl shriek as she struggles to keep her tray upright. Does she know what's going to happen here tonight? Maybe she's a part of it and will be sold off alongside the others? The thought has me clenching my jaw in silent rage.

Beside me, Raphael fidgets with his jacket sleeve, just as annoyed as I am. "I don't like this, brother," he comments over the rim of his glass, faking a sip as his eyes roam the crowd. "How many people do you think are here that we know?"

"One too many," I answer vaguely as I eye the men dressed

in sharp suits, their faces concealed by a sea of masks. What sends a shiver down my spine is not the idea that we may be surrounded by people we know, but the number of women accompanying them. How can they turn a blind eye to what is about to happen to other women, men...kids? They have to know what their husbands intend to buy them for. But maybe they enjoy it too. Women can be just as dark and twisted as men. Sometimes more.

A man's voice comes over the speaker, requesting us to take our seats as the auction is about to begin. Raphael and I find two empty seats in the back row where a pamphlet rests on the blood-red velvet cushion, alongside a numbered auction sign. I sit and open the trifold paper, immediately regretting it.

The different selections are listed out like options on a menu. The sick descriptions of each category send a frosty chill down my spine.

Preteen: A selection between the ages of 8 and 12. Guaranteed virgins.

Young: A selection between the ages of 16 and 21.

Adult: A unique selection of all genders above 21 years.

Who am I supposed to save? What category will she be in? Can't I just save them all and kill each sick motherfucker in the room, keeping future victims from their cruelty as well? And then I want to find the bastards behind the entire organization and kill them, too.

The lights dim over the crowd before a tall, thin man takes the stage. The resounding sound of applause is like nails on a chalkboard to my ears. With a huge smile stretched across his face, he bows to the crowd like he's about to put on a show.

"Welcome, welcome my friends, and thank you for attending. I do hope you enjoy the selection we have prepared for you tonight. As always, just a few rules to go over before we get started. Rule one, you are allowed only two purchases. Rule two, there are no returns, refunds, or exchanges. And rule three, no sampling of your purchase until payment has been received." He claps his hands, and the lights strobe, sweeping across the crowd like the start of a game show, before coming back together to highlight the stage.

"Without further ado. The preteens!"

It's exactly as terrible and gut-wrenching as I imagined it would be. One by one, young girls and boys are sold off to the highest bidder, their futures uncertain but horrible. Auction signs rise casually into the air like it's just another day for them. As the victims sob, I even spot some men around us shift uncomfortably, their hands moving to adjust their pants in a way that makes me feel dirty.

These are children. They're innocent. No matter how they came to be here at this auction, they are still someone's child and didn't deserve a single moment of this nightmare. Every time the gavel comes down with the word "Sold" shouted, it's like a judge delivering a death sentence. Because that's exactly what it is. The applause afterward drowns out the victims' sobs, which then turn into gut-wrenching wailing when they're pulled off stage and replaced with the next innocent.

There's a small break between sets, and I quickly stand, determined to move away from the main stage.

"Jesus Christ." Raphael joins me in an empty corner. "What the fuck is happening here? No less than five men were bidding on that young boy. That disgusting bastard is going to rape that child tonight and have him killed once he's had his fill and is no longer useful."

Only to attend the next auction and buy another innocent child. The terror in that boy's eyes when the horrifying realization of his future registered is something I'll never shake.

"I assume you didn't recognize any of them, then?" Raphael ventures.

I shake my head. "No. I want to burn this entire fucking building to the ground with everyone in it."

The auctioneer comes back over the speaker, and we take our seats once more. Somehow, I block out the next few sets, growing more angry and desperate with each slam of the gavel. I haven't recognized a single woman, man, or kid yet, and as the selections continue, a dark thought crosses my mind that maybe Dominic was right. Maybe this is all just an elaborate setup to get Raphael and me here? Because it sure is starting to look that way.

"And now for our adults. We'll start with the ladies, shall we?" The auctioneer motions for the first victim, and a loud commotion comes from behind the curtain. Two large men appear, dragging a woman between them. She's putting up a hell of a fight. Most have, but something about this woman is familiar, and I lean forward, suddenly anxious to see her face.

Finally, she's pulled onto the middle of the stage, and my heart slams to a stop. I would recognize this woman anywhere.

"Holy shit. Is that...?" Raphael whispers beside me.

"Rose."

15

ROSE

In my first year at university, I took an Introduction to Philosophy class where I learned all about Kübler-Ross and her model on the five stages of grief. It was initially created for people with terminal diseases to come to terms with their impending death, but since then, the idea has been adapted for those suffering from grief in general. The five stages are denial, anger, bargaining, depression, and finally acceptance. They can be experienced in any order, mixed, repeated, or, in my case, all at once.

On the first day of my journey back to Miami on this godforsaken piece of shit boat, I hover somewhere between denial and depression. That lasts until the first guard shows up with a tray of measly food and a bottle of water. I try to bargain with him, but he either doesn't speak English or doesn't care. Either way, his reluctance to talk to me shoves me straight into anger.

For hours, I curse my father's name until I'm blue in the face and my throat is raw. The bastard is dead to me. And then there's Connor. That the man my sister married is as corrupt and heartless as our father is my biggest fear coming true. I'm furious with him for doing nothing to stop my dad. But more than anything and anyone, I'm upset with myself for thinking I could get away. That I could ever be free from him.

Acceptance is a hard stage. Mostly because while I'm very

much aware of what's going on, I don't want to accept it. I've been sold into a human trafficking ring by my father like I'm nothing more than a piece of cattle waiting to go to market. I can wish the nightmare away all I want, but no matter how many times I close my eyes and dream otherwise, the reality remains.

The only silver lining, the only thing that keeps me from drowning in despair, is Liam. I can only imagine the terrible thoughts that went through Anette's head when I didn't return as promised. And what about Evelyn? We were supposed to meet in Milan. Would she go to the town and look for me? Would she risk collecting Liam?

Thinking of my son sends me spiraling through the five stages once more, but I linger on anger, refusing to accept that I'll never see him again. I'm determined to break free. I refuse to leave Liam alone without either of his parents so young. His life has only just begun.

I am his mother, and I owe it to him to keep fighting, to survive, and to find my way back to him. So I vow not to go down without a fight. No matter what, I will not become another statistic or forgotten face lost to the unknown.

"GET UP! LET'S GO, NOW."

I open my eyes to bright lights flashing in my face and men shouting at me. The next thing I know, I'm being pulled up, dragged out of my tiny room, and hauled off the ship onto a shipyard. The blinding lights illuminating the wide space feel like a thousand tiny needles piercing my skull, leaving me disoriented and dizzy after being in the dark for so long. Dozens of men, women, and children are pulled off the ship behind me, each one looking as frightened as I feel. Their confused and terrified cries echo through the night air.

Rough hands grab my wrists moments before handcuffs slap down on them. I wince at how tight the cold metal bites into my skin, so I don't see the other man coming until he's tying a cloth over my eyes.

"Hey!" I protest, fighting against the first man's hold. He tightens his grip, and my objection morphs into a cry of pain.

"Stop fighting and walk," the man grunts.

"Go to hell," I snap, throwing my weight back to dislodge his hold. It doesn't work.

"You're only going to make this harder on yourself if you don't walk."

"And you can fuck right off."

"Alright. That's enough of that," he states before the ground beneath my feet disappears, and before I can strike back, I'm thrown in the back of a vehicle, landing hard on my shoulder on the metal floor.

"Motherfucker!" I shout, hissing around the pain that radiates down my arm.

With my arms bound and my eyes covered, it's useless to fight back now. I know this, but like I said, I'm not going down without a fight. I kick out, my feet hitting nothing but air before doors slam shut, and my heel then connects with a solid door. And then we're moving.

I struggle to sit up and settle back on my knees, but it's hard with my equilibrium thrown off by the vehicle's movement. I'm not alone based on the sobbing sounds surrounding me. Several cry out in foreign languages I don't understand, but I have a feeling we're all wondering the same thing. *Where are we going? Why did this happen to us? What's going to happen to us?*

I don't know how long we drive, but it's long enough that we could be anywhere in Miami now. When the vehicle finally does stop, the back doors are flung open and hands are grabbing once again. I stumble out, falling to my knees on the gravel ground. The tiny rock pebbles tear into my bare skin, then I'm being pulled up and jerked away.

"Be careful with the merchandise, pendejo," a man warns with a heavy Spanish accent. "They're not worth as much money if they're damaged."

"I'm not merchandise, you asshole," I spit back in the general direction of the Spanish man.

His response is a deep laugh before he orders the man holding me, "Take her inside."

The floor beneath my feet changes to something hard, like concrete, and the crying of my fellow victims echoes all around me like we're somewhere large and empty.

I'm pushed against a wall, and my blindfold is pulled from my face. I blink rapidly and look around, trying to make sense of my surroundings while looking for any sign of an escape route.

We're in a large warehouse with a ceiling stretching high above the metal rafters and broken windows scattered along it. One by one, other women are shoved into similar positions, and my soul tears into pieces at the sight of children. I see Liam in each one of their scared faces, and all I want to do is pull them into my embrace and protect them from the horrors I know are coming.

I ache terribly for Liam, but seeing the children now, I'm glad he's back in Italy. At least with Anette, he has a chance at a normal life if I never see him again. Being an orphan is a better life than what awaits these children.

"Strip!" a man shouts. His single-word order sends waves

of terror through the room. His impatience grows when we don't comply fast enough. Snapping his fingers, he gestures to his men. A man with a scar cutting diagonally down his face approaches me with a crooked grin. He reaches out to touch me, but I'm quicker. I rip off my shirt and pants while keeping my eyes locked on his. Yes, I'm scared, but I refuse to give these disgusting excuses for men the satisfaction of seeing me cry.

There is a clap of hands, and an older woman wearing a cheetah-print skintight dress appears from behind a curtain. "Alright, ladies, let's get you dressed."

The cold, calculating way she examines us with her dark eyes tells me instantly that she isn't here to help us. Not in any way that matters, at least.

"Are you here to-to help us?" a young girl, barely a teenager, softly asks in broken English.

The woman snorts and turns her ice-cold gaze on the poor girl. "The sooner you realize no one is here to help you, the better off you'll be."

"Then why are you doing this? Why are you helping them? Don't you know what's going to happen to us?" I demand, unable to keep quiet after the poor girl bursts into tears.

"The same thing that happened to me," the woman spits toward me. "Now shut up and sit down. It is my job to prepare you so that you bring in the most money. The better you look, the higher the chance a good man will buy you."

"You're delusional if you think that. No good man buys a woman," I sneer. "And no good woman helps sell others either."

The woman says nothing more, and I know I struck a nerve by the deep frown on her face. She claps her hands rhythmically, and two more women appear around the curtain. One pushes a rack of dresses while the other carries a large box of makeup and accessories.

"We'll need to find a dress that covers the abrasions on her knees," the older woman comments as she circles me. She tuts like she found something she doesn't like. "We'll need to tell the auctioneer that she has a few stretch marks, but she's otherwise in excellent condition. Tell me, how long ago did you have a baby?"

"Go to hell," I hiss. I'm not about to tell her a damn thing about my baby.

"You would do well to shut your mouth and lose the attitude. No man wants a mouthy bitch," she warns me.

"Good."

The woman scowls but says nothing more before she leaves to inspect the work of the others.

In the end, I'm forced through a cold shower, strapped down to a chair, and waxed from head to toe before being dressed in a tight black velvet number with a keyhole back and a high halter neck. The front of the dress dips dangerously down, showcasing my supple breasts made more alluring and round from breastfeeding Liam. They ache from the number of days I've gone without pumping or feeding him. I did my best to relieve the pressure on the ship, but it's not the same as holding my baby to my breast.

"There," one girl says admiringly. "Now you're beautiful."

"Great."

The other girl sprays me with some kind of perfume that makes me want to vomit. "The higher the amount of money you fetch, the less likely they'll just use and abuse you. No one wants to spend thousands of dollars on something they're just going to destroy."

Something?

I stare at her in shock, unable to believe the words that just came out of her mouth. "Are you fucking serious right now? Do you even hear yourself? I am a human being. About to be sold. I'll probably be raped and tortured, and if I'm lucky, they'll kill me after they're finally done with me."

The girls share a somber look before one turns to push a body-length mirror on wheels over in front of me. They've transformed me into a glamorous doll, but all I see is a pig dressed for slaughter.

ONE BY ONE, the women and men and children ahead of me disappear around the curtain to go stand on the stage. The announcer describes each one like he's reading items off a menu rather than living beings. The bidding war is intense and disturbing as the dollar amount climbs rapidly until the auctioneer's voice finally rings out, going once, going twice, sold, followed by the sound of the gavel, signaling the ruin of another life. Once bought, the victims must be taken some-where else and prepared for the sick bastard who just bought them because they don't return.

"You're up." A man grabs my wrist over the handcuffs, causing the metal to bite down even harder into my already rubbed-raw wrists.

I hiss at the pain and keep my feet planted still. They'll have to drag me onto that stage, kicking and screaming, if they want me to go up there. Call it a last-ditch effort of desperation or whatever, but if there is even a chance I could break free right now, I'll fight for it.

The man tugs harder on my wrist. "Now, you slut."

"No." I attempt to yank my wrist back, but the man's

unyielding grip sends another wave of pain up my arms. "I'm not going up there."

The smile he throws me sends a shiver racing down my spine. "I like a good challenge as much as the next guy. Maybe I'll get to sample you before you're handed to your buyer. Wouldn't be the first time."

"Touch me and I will cut off your hand and shove it so far up your ass you'll taste it."

A man pops his head around the curtain, annoyance clear on his face. "What's the holdup, man?" His eyes flick between our faces. "Get her up here, man."

"She won't fucking budge. Help me out here. Grab her other arm."

The man starts toward me, triggering my fight-or-flight response into a second gear. "No! Let me go!"

They each grab an arm and practically pick me up, dragging me onto the stage. When they finally release me in the center, I stumble and nearly lose my footing. The stage lights are so intensely bright that it's difficult to see anything past the stage, but I can hear the murmured voices of the audience members lurking in the shadows. Taking a step back, I'm prepared to run when the second man appears at my elbow and warns in my ear, "Don't even think about it, girl. You won't get far if you try."

I tear away from him, tossing him a look that could kill. He's right, as much as I hate admitting it. Now isn't the time to run. My chance will come, and when it does, I'll find a phone and call Evelyn, the police, the fucking National Guard. Someone, anyone with the power to help me get free and return to Liam.

"Well, here she is. Lot number 71. And what a beauty she is. She's got quite a fiery temper, doesn't she, folks?"

I turn to face the auctioneer. "You're fucking disgusting," I spit at the weasel-looking man with his thin glasses and slicked-back hair. "You piece of shit, spineless, perverted little man. I will—"

My words are cut off when a strip of fabric is shoved into my mouth and tied behind my head...tight. But that doesn't stop me. I keep shouting through the cloth barrier and shoot daggers at the auctioneer.

"We'll start the bidding at two hundred thousand. Do I have three hundred thousand? Yes, sir. How about three hundred and fifty? Yes, to number fifteen. Do I have four? Excellent. Do I have four hundred and fifty? Yes, madam. How about five hundred? Thank you again, sir. We have a good bidding war going on here. Don't miss out on this lovely creature, ladies and gentlemen. If you're looking for a little fun, she won't disappoint you."

My heart races, pounding against my chest as my rushing blood fills my ears. Sweat breaks out on my skin, and I pant for air, struggling to catch my breath behind the fabric, and my chest tightens painfully from the lack of oxygen. I know the feeling of a panic attack all too well, and this feels like the start of one. Black spots appear in the corner of my vision. I close my eyes and bow my head. I'm on the verge of collapsing.

"Sold! To bidder number fourteen for five hundred thousand. Thank you, sir. Congratulations and do enjoy."

All the air leaves my body as I fall to my knees.

I've just been sold.

16

MICHAEL

"**M**ichael, don't move," Raphael warns me just as I move to stand. He grabs my jacket sleeve to keep me down before anyone notices. "I'm serious. You can't make a scene."

"But it's Rose," I argue as if those words are enough of a reason for me to unleash my demons and lay waste to this entire den of perversion and abuse. It's taking every ounce of my strength to remain seated and not rush to the stage.

"I know it is. But we are unarmed and outmanned. We have to save her some other way."

Save her.

She's the one the anonymous email sender meant. I knew it the moment I saw her. And if by some chance she isn't...well, she is now. Because after spending over half a year looking for my beautiful flower, here she is. At a human auction, of all places. What the fuck?

She's fucking radiant. Even after all these months, my attraction to this woman has not faded, not even in the slightest. I thought that if I ever saw her again, I would realize that the insane allure she had over me was nothing more than the result of a heated night of far too much alcohol. But no. One look now, and I want more. Just like that night.

Her gorgeous red hair is shorter than I remember, but her

green eyes still burn bright with the same intense fire that has haunted my dreams for months. Her black dress hugs every one of her curves in the most delicious ways, leaving me with the sudden desire to reacquaint myself with each one.

My eyes widen at Rose's outburst. It's followed quickly by a burst of pure fury when a guard steps forward and sticks a gag in her mouth. It doesn't stop her from trying to yell, though, and pride flares in my chest at her fight.

"Well, isn't she going to be a fun one to tame?" The auctioneer laughs, but I catch how the weasel watches Rose with a touch of uncertainty. Good. He should fear her. Not because of what she said but because of me. I'm the devil on her shoulder. The dark to her light. The monster under her bed. And I will turn my demons loose on every fucking person who harmed her, laying their heads at her feet.

Raphael leans over, humor in his voice as he says, "I can see why you like her so much. She's got a mouth as filthy as yours."

I smirk. "And she knows how to use it."

"What do you want to do?" Raphael asks as the bids continue to climb in number.

"I don't know." I honestly don't. I have to do something, but what?

I move to lift my sign, prepared to damn my soul even more to hell, when the auctioneer shouts, "Sold!"

The gavel coming down is like a jolt of electricity directly to my brain, forcing me into action.

"Let's go." I commit to memory the number and appearance of the man who just bought Rose. A plan forms in my mind as we stand and head for the door.

Enzo waits for us by the car he borrowed—with no intention of returning—from the long-term parking garage at the airport. He's wearing a simple black mask to shield his identity, which helps him blend in well with the other drivers and guards. Leaning against the driver's side door, his blue eyes scan the area until he sees us approaching.

"How's the auction going?" he asks when we reach him. "Did you find the girl you were asked to save?"

"Yes." I cross my arms and stare at the door at the far end of the warehouse where the buyers were instructed to collect their purchases.

"Well, who is it?" Enzo asks.

"It's Rose."

The blond man cocks his head as he thinks back. "Rose? That's the girl from the club on your birthday, right? The one you ran around Miami looking for?"

I nod solemnly. "That's the one."

Enzo curses. "How the hell did she get caught up in a human trafficking ring?"

"That's what I would like to find out."

He steps around the front of the car. "So what's the plan here? Did you buy her, or are we raiding the auction?"

"Neither."

Enzo shares a look with Raphael. I ignore them, monitoring the door instead.

After a long moment, Enzo ventures, "Do you have a plan?"

"Yes."

"Okay, Mr. One Syllable." My friend's sarcasm isn't hard to miss. "Would you like to share it with the rest of the class?"

That earns him a quick glare before I resume my watch. "Any moment, the bastard who bought her will walk out, collect Rose at the back door, get in his car, and then leave. When he does, we follow him and rescue her."

Enzo grunts. "Oh. Is that all?"

"We've done more with less," Raphael points out.

"A dozen things can go wrong," Enzo fires back. "The plan is too vague. We haven't thought this through."

"Enough," I snap, sparing a quick look at my friend with enough venom behind it that he lowers his gaze in response before I return my attention to the building. Finally, the door opens, and the fat fuck appears. "There he is."

Rage consumes me like the licks of hell's fire have arrived to reclaim my demons and drag my dark soul back down with them. I haven't felt this kind of anger since my diagnosis last year. And the result then was a rampage the likes our city has never seen, resulting in the start of our war with the Triads.

The short man gestures for his car to be brought around as he waits at the back door to receive Rose. A moment later, the door flies open, and Rose is dragged out, kicking and screaming, the handcuffs doing nothing to stop her from putting up a strong fight. She cries out in pain when one man grabs her hair, yanking her head back hard enough to cause whiplash, and I see red.

Without a second thought, I grab Enzo's gun holstered on his hip and cock the chamber back with a bullet. My only goal is to empty the entire clip into the bastard's body.

"Shit!" Enzo shouts, reaching for me. "He's got my gun."

I smack his hand away and take another two steps before he catches me around my waist. On any other day, my friend is a worthy sparring partner. But right now? Right now, my demons are in control, and Enzo is no match for the strength they bring to my body.

"A little help?" He grunts, struggling to hold me back.

Raphael steps directly in front of me, the only man who is not afraid to do so right then. The only man capable of calming my demons down when they break free to the surface. In the dark days following the news of my infertility, only Raphael could talk me off the cliff I often found myself on. Because if anyone understands how I felt, it's my twin.

"You need to stop." He sets his hands on my shoulders and leans forward until he's right in my face. He blocks my view of Rose, and I growl at him, trying to peer around his annoying face. "And we need to go. Now. We're drawing attention." His eyes flick over my shoulder at the guards stationed outside the warehouse. He swings his gaze back at me. "Take a breath and get your shit under control so we can go rescue your girl. You hear me, brother?"

Slowly, the dark recedes, and I do as he commands. Only when I finally concede with a nod, letting him know I'm back in control, does Enzo release me and step back, taking his gun back when he does. Over Raphael's shoulder, I watch as Rose is shoved into the car, and the fat bastard follows her.

"They're on the move. Time to go," Enzo directs. He doesn't have to tell me twice.

I rip off my mask the moment we're clear of the warehouse. The others follow suit. There's no point keeping our identities a secret anymore because once we catch up to the vehicle carrying Rose, no survivors will be left besides her.

"We don't have a lot of time to intercept their car," Enzo warns. "Once they hit the freeway, there's no telling their destination."

The idea of losing Rose after just finding her again hurts worse than when the doctors flipped my world on its axis last year.

"There's a bridge coming up that I know has no cameras, and the lights are shit. It's a tight space, but we can do it," Raphael chimes in from the back seat as he hands me my gun.

Enzo nods. "I'm familiar with the spot. Hold on to something."

He lays down on the gas and takes several turns before the bridge looms ahead. Stopping in the middle of the dark, empty street, I climb out just as the soon-to-be dead fucker's car comes around the corner, and I take aim. Knowing Rose is inside makes me hesitate, but only for a second. Then I squeeze the trigger because there's no other way. I fire off two perfect shots, taking out each front tire in quick succession. The driver slams on the brakes immediately, but it does little to stop the car from spinning out of control. My heart squeezes painfully at the sight, and I pray to whatever God will listen that Rose is safely buckled inside.

The car slams into a broken light pole and comes to a sudden stop. A second later, the front doors open, and two men emerge. Enzo puts them down with no hesitation. Like I said, no witnesses tonight. We descend on the car, and I keep my gun raised as Raphael pulls open the back door.

Curled up on the leather back seat is Rose. Her hands are still bound by the handcuffs in front of her. Her dress is torn from one shoulder, nearly exposing her breasts to the night air. The bottom is bunched up around her thighs, and I catch sight of red scratches marring her pale skin there. Her makeup is smudged, her nose is bleeding, and there's a red mark on her cheek that's definitely going to bruise. She blinks slowly as if coming out of a daze before her eyes focus on me.

Fear suddenly grips my chest. Will she remember me? The possibility never crossed my mind, and it hurts worse than the idea of her loving someone else. But then she does something that steals my breath. She smiles, and my heart soars at the sight.

"Michael," she whispers, and my heart fumbles at hearing my name from her mouth again.

Before I can say anything back, her eyes roll back in her head, and then she slumps against the leather seat, effectively passing out. Every inch of my body aches to reach out and gather her into my arms, but first, I have a piece of human scum to deal with.

I point my gun at the bastard crumpled on the floorboard. His hat and suit jacket are gone, and his shirt is unbuttoned, exposing a very hairy and pale gut. My eyes slide to his open pants, and I almost pull the trigger right then.

"Get out," I growl through clenched teeth. My demons pull at their chains, demanding to unleash their fury on the man who thought he could touch someone who never belonged to him. Rose is mine. She was mine from the very first moment I laid eyes on her.

"Who the hell do you think you are?" the man demands instead of doing as told.

"I said...get the fuck out," I repeat. He won't get a third chance.

"I'll have your head for this," the man spews as he finally clambers out of the car. He looks like a pig trying to roll over as he rises to his feet. In the dim light under the bridge, I study his face, and my demons purr at the three red scratches across his cheek. His neck boasts a matching set, deeper and bleeding. My girl put up a fight.

"Do you know who I am?"

I snort, like I give a damn, and repeat his question back to him. "Do you know who I am?"

"Looks like he's from Texas, boss," Enzo says as he examines the car's rental paperwork. "A Mr. John Casey from Houston. An oilman."

"You're far from home, Mr. Casey. What brings you to Miami? And don't tell me it was our beautiful beaches." I grab John's shirt and slam him against the car's unforgiving side. Fear flashes across his face as he realizes just how much danger he's in. His men are dead, and those responsible stand in front of him. "Or was it the auction? Tell me, Mr. Casey. Do you enjoy buying innocent women? Does it get you off? Is that sick power trip the only thing that gets your cock hard?"

"I don't know what you're talking about, man."

I tilt my head and examine the sack of shit. "Are you lying to me, Mr. Casey? I thought we were having an honest conversation here."

"I'm not lying, man. My girl and I—"

I bury my fist in his gut. He doubles over in a coughing fit, but we aren't done talking. Grabbing him by his throat, I shove him back against the car. I lean closer so that John can see the demons behind the fire in my eyes. "She's not your girl, and I don't like being lied to, Mr. Casey."

He struggles to breathe. "Please...man. Just let...let me go."

"I'm afraid that won't be happening. Because you see, you came into my city and hurt someone I care for. Now, the first grievance I could forgive, but the second? Sorry." Terror fills John's face as he finally understands his fate. Pleased with his reaction and officially done with him, I shove him toward Enzo. "Take care of this shit excuse for a human being, will you?"

"Gladly." Enzo pulls the pleading man toward the back of the car.

I turn my attention to the woman responsible for consuming my every thought. It's clear as day what the man planned to do to her, and if Enzo wasn't already dealing with him, I'd put a bullet in his skull this very second. As furious as I am at the terrifying thought that we were almost too late, I can't help but feel proud of how hard she fought back. Others might see a broken woman, but I see a beautiful warrior who refused to surrender.

I glance over my shoulder at Raphael. "Make sure the doctor meets us at my house immediately."

He nods, already pulling out his phone to type the message out.

A soft pop fills the silence. One problem down. A dozen more to go.

But first, Rose.

"It's done," Enzo says when he appears back at the door. "We should finish up and get out of here. I don't like that we're so exposed."

Gathering Rose in my arms is just as I remember. Soft and warm. The ache her absence has caused disappears, and it's like coming home. I kiss the crown of her head. She doesn't react, but that had been for me, not her.

Climbing back into our borrowed car isn't easy, but I manage without jostling Rose too much. Raphael helps secure the seat belt around us and then he leaves to help Enzo move the dead bodies back into the car before setting the entire thing on fire. Not our most subtle cleanup, but it's effective.

"Raphael, hand me the key for the cuffs," I ask once we're safely heading toward the tower.

My brother produces a small silver key that will unlock any standard-issue handcuff. Being mindful that her skin is raw from the metal, I unlock her wrists. Once free, I cradle Rose tight to my body.

She nuzzles closer against me, and a name slips free from her lips, so soft that I almost miss it if she hadn't been tucked up against me.

"Liam."

I stare down at her resting peacefully in my arms. Who the fuck is Liam?

Have I found her only to lose her all over again?

17

ROSE

The man's fingers dig into my neck, leaving me gasping for air. His breath is hot against my ear as he whispers all the deranged things he plans to do to me. He roughly squeezes my breast with his other hand, drawing a cry of pain from my choked throat. His elephant hand brushes over my thigh as he fumbles under my dress. One slip and he'll be there.

Terror seizes me, and I'm desperate to try anything that will help me break free. Reaching up, I scratch his neck, deep enough to draw blood. If I can reach his face, I'll claw that, too. He pulls away in a howl of pain, releasing me all at once. I take the chance to try to get away, but the space in the stretched car is minimal. I don't get far before he grabs my hair and yanks my head back hard enough that I lose my balance.

"You stupid fucking bitch," he roars in my face.

He shoves me face down onto the seat and places his hand on my back to keep me there. I try to scream, but I can't breathe, can't move. He surrounds me, suffocating me, crushing me, leaving me paralyzed and unable to fight back. I've never felt so weak, so powerless, so helpless. He's going to take what he wants, and I can do nothing to stop him. Tears fill my eyes, a sob catching in my throat, and the man just laughs. He's feeding off my pain and my fear. My desperation turns him on, and the proof of that brushes up against my backside.

"Rose!"

A distant voice yells my name, and my abuser grows angrier at the sound. His fingers roughly drag my panties down, and his hand is there, his fingers...

"La mia bella rosa. Wake up...please."

I open my eyes and blink. I'm no longer in the car, trapped and defenseless. My eyes focus on a face I thought I'd never see again. When I meet a pair of familiar bright hazel eyes, a rush of emotions consumes me, each one blending into the other until nothing but a whirlwind remains inside me. This man has lived in my dreams for so long that seeing him now feels almost surreal. It's like that hazy moment when you wake up and can't tell if you're still dreaming, where reality and fantasy overlap.

"Michael." My mouth is incredibly dry; it's like my tongue is stuck to the roof of my mouth, making my voice crack. I lick my lips and try to swallow, but it only worsens things. A sudden tickle in my throat triggers an uncontrollable cough.

"Here, drink this. It'll help." Michael holds out a glass. "It's just water, I promise."

My stiff shoulder protests a little as I reach for the glass, but it doesn't feel broken from being shoved forcefully into different vehicles...twice. I take small sips from the straw, and the cool water soothes my burning throat. Michael stares at me with concern, and I stare back. "It wasn't a dream. You're really here." My voice is still hoarse but a little better.

"I am." Michael takes the glass from me and then reaches for my hand. I let him take it. His touch is familiar and comforting as he rubs small, soothing circles over my knuckles. "How are you feeling?"

My eyes drift down to the white bandage standing out against my skin. An IV is taped to the top of my hand, and I follow the clear plastic line to a bag of fluids hanging from a hook on the bed canopy railing above.

"What happened?"

"You don't remember?"

Memories flood my mind, and the nightmare returns in full color. I swallow hard and raise my hand to trace my tender face down to my sore neck as I relive the terrifying moments in the car. "He slapped me and...choked me and—" A shuddering sob works its way through me. "He was going to–to rape me. I tried to fight back, I swear I tried...but he was—he was so strong, and I couldn't stop him."

Michael squeezes my hand gently, and I latch on to the comfort his touch offers. "You're safe, and you'll never have to worry about that man again."

"You were there. You saved me." It's not a question because the memory is clear in my mind. The fat bastard crumpled on the floorboard. Michael standing in the open car door...with a gun in his hand. And then...nothing. I must have passed out. "Is he dead?" Deep down, I already know the answer. The truth lingers in the air between us, but I have to hear it aloud. I need to know that he's gone and will never hurt me or anyone else ever again.

"Yes."

I'm relieved to hear that, but... "How?"

Michael raises a single brow, looking at me with a puzzled expression. "Do you really want to know the details?"

Not really. No. But I have to know one more thing.

"Did you kill him?"

"No."

"Then how did he die?"

"He didn't survive the accident."

Something about his short answers sounds very political and roundabout. My eyes take in every fancy and expensive feature of the room with a critical eye. From the four-poster canopy bed I rest on to the floor-to-ceiling windows and set of French doors leading to a large terrace with a stunning view of Miami's downtown skyline. It all screams money. A lot of money. And that annoying small voice in the back of my mind starts waving every red flag in the damn book. I look back at the man who saved me, the father of my son, and I'm suddenly afraid that I may have swapped one nightmare for another.

"Who are you, Michael?" I whisper.

Michael frowns and tilts his head, as if trying to understand my question. "I don't follow."

"What's your last name?"

"Gallo," he says after a long second. The unfamiliar name eases my anxiety a bit. "Yours?"

"Bennett." The last name I've been using slips out before I can stop it. Not that I'm about to tell him my real last name, anyway. I'm not ready to open that can of worms. If ever. "How did you find me? Were you there tonight? At that auction? Were you...going to buy someone?"

"No. Of course not. I own several businesses, and one of them is a security firm. We received an email about a human auction and attended to gather evidence. For the police of course." He seems to tack on that last bit as more of an afterthought. "When I saw you up on that stage...I couldn't let anything bad happen to you, Rose."

I suck in my bottom lip, and before the confidence can leave me, I lean forward and press my lips to his cheek. It's a quick kiss, more like an innocent peck of appreciation for saving me, but the next thing I know, Michael's hand cups my chin, and his mouth is on mine.

"Sorry," Michael groans when he pulls away before I even register the kiss. "I didn't mean to do that. You're hurt, and I didn't—"

I reach up and stroke his cheek, savoring the small sound he makes when he nuzzles into my touch. I should have agreed with him. But the words that set everything in motion all those months ago come out instead.

"Kiss me."

Without a moment's delay, Michael presses his mouth to mine again. His hunger is all-consuming and all too familiar. His kiss leaves me breathless, and only his mouth can breathe life back into me. He draws back only far enough to nibble on my bottom lip, seeking permission, and I happily part for him. His tongue eagerly explores my mouth, entwining with mine in a dance as old as time. His hand caresses down my spine, urging me closer.

I swing my legs out from under the covers and move to climb onto his lap when a loud knock echoes throughout the room. I pull away quickly, embarrassed when I realize just how out of control we were about to become. But a single touch from him is all it took to erase every painful minute we spent apart these past ten months.

Michael stands and winks at me even as he adjusts his pants shamelessly. He walks to the door and opens it to reveal an elderly man wearing a white coat and carrying a worn brown leather bag.

"Rose, this is Dr. Gonzalez. He's here to check on you now that you're awake."

The doctor reminds me immediately of Evelyn's grandfather. He was a nice older man who always carried those little butterscotch candies in his pocket. Dr. Gonzalez goes through a standard exam. He checks my blood pressure, listens to my heart, and asks me to take a deep breath, which induces another coughing fit. Michael's quick to offer me water, and I thank him with a small smile that he returns with another gentle yet firm hand squeeze.

All in all, I'm pretty banged up, but it could have been much worse. I know that. And if cuts and bruises are all I walk away with, then I'm luckier than the other victims last night.

The doctor hands Michael some antibiotic cream to put on my wrists, thighs, and knees abrasions. The bruises on my shoulder, face, and neck will just have to heal on their own.

After the doctor leaves, Michael shows me to the en suite bathroom for a shower. When I see my beaten and bruised reflection in the mirror, I'm suddenly embarrassed to strip in front of Michael when, less than thirty minutes ago, I was ready to climb him like a damn tree. Michael clears his throat and sets the stack of clothes he brought in on the counter.

"I'll leave you alone if you'd like."

I want to say no and ask him to stay, but I nod silently instead. As he turns to leave, I hold out my hand as if to stop him and say in a rush, "Could you..." He looks at me curiously over his shoulder, and I drop my gaze to the light gray tile floor. "Could you leave the door open and maybe...wait outside?"

"Of course." Michael crosses the elegant bathroom in two strides. He cups the back of my head gently, aware of how sore I am, and leans down to kiss the crown of my head. "Call if you need anything."

I raise my eyes only after he leaves, then purposely ignoring my reflection, I strip out of the tattered and ruined dress, watching it crumple to the floor. I have the sudden urge to burn the damn thing, but I settle for tossing it in the trash can instead.

The shower's hot water stings my cuts and abrasions, but it's not enough. I need to scrub every inch of my body free of that bastard's disgusting touch. Only when my skin is red and raw do I feel a little more like myself. I know it will take more than a single shower to cleanse my soul clean of the man, but I'm alive, and he's not, so that's a good starting point, in my opinion. Knowing he is no longer out there capable of hurting any more women is enough for now.

I'm no stranger to pain or misery at all. Waking up to the sight of your dead brother's small hand stretched out to you and your mom's blood-covered face is enough to haunt a girl for life. The memories never go away completely, but in time, they fade enough to a point where you can lock them inside a little box tucked away in the very back corner of your mind.

Even with the door open, the bathroom is clouded in steam, covering the giant mirror, much to my delight. I apply the cream the doctor left, then dress in a pair of Michael's sweatpants and shirt. He even left a pair of socks that swallow my feet, forcing me to roll the top several times, and I chuckle at the sight.

Michael waits for me outside the bathroom. He sits on the edge of the bed, his elbows on his knees as he rests his chin on his clasped hands. He looks lost in thought, and it takes a moment for him to realize I'm standing in the doorway. He runs his eyes over my outfit, making me blush. I know he's just checking me over for signs of more injury, but his eyes leave a trail of heat behind as well.

"How do you feel?" he asks.

"Better," I answer honestly. "Thank you for the shower and the clothes."

Michael nods before he stands, taking a deep breath as he looks at me with conflicted emotions in eyes that resemble our son's so much. "I need to know something, Rose. Who is Liam?"

18

MICHAEL

"I need to know something, Rose. Who is Liam?"

The name's been bothering me all night, ever since she said it in the car. I've invented a dozen different possibilities of his identity. Maybe he's her brother or her cousin. I hope he is because the idea that he could be her lover sends a rush of furious jealousy down my spine. He can cut himself right out for all I care. And if she has a problem with that, then too bad because I won't let her slip through my fingers again. If that means locking her away in my dark castle forever, then so be it. She can be the beauty to my beast.

Rose stares at me like a deer caught in headlights. "How do you know that name?"

"You said it when we rescued you." She looks like she doesn't believe me, so I add, "You were unconscious."

Rose visibly swallows hard, and I prepare myself for her answer. It's clear by her hesitancy that I won't like it.

"Liam," she starts, her voice soft but clear. "Liam is my son."

She has a kid? "How old is he?"

"He's six weeks old now."

Wait. What? "You were pregnant when we met?"

She looks at me puzzled, like she doesn't understand my question. "No. I got pregnant that night. You're his father."

I can count on one hand the number of times I've been

surprised into silence, shocked to the point where my mind blanks in response. Of all the possibilities, this was not one of them. In fact, the thought never even crossed my mind as an option. Because it's impossible.

"What?" A lame question, I know, because I heard her correctly the first time. It's just the only word that forms.

"Liam. He's your son," she explains before dropping her eyes to her clasped hands. She wrings her fingers together, a nervous habit I'm familiar with, and continues, "I'm sorry I didn't come find you to tell you about him before. I didn't know myself until it was too late, and I couldn't come back to tell you at that point because—"

"It's not possible." I cut off her rambling. My tone isn't harsh, but it isn't affectionate either.

She looks up and meets my hard eyes. She frowns when she registers what I said. "It very much is possible, Michael. We didn't use a condom, remember?"

"No, you don't understand. I can't be the father because —" I take a deep breath and scrub a hand down my face. I know I have to say it, but once I do, I can never take the words back. She's so certain that I'm the father of her child, and here I am about to shatter her belief and become the worst person in the world. Steadying my nerves, I admit my dark secret. "Because I'm sterile, Rose. I can't have kids."

"Sterile?"

"I was told it a few months before we met. It's why I said not to worry about the condom that night. I was going to tell you, but we didn't have time, and then you were gone."

Red creeps up her neck until her face is flushed. She levels me with a glare so hot even my demons flinch at the heat. "Then you were told wrong because you are the father."

"Rose, are you sure there wasn't someone—"

"Michael, if you are about to suggest that I spread my legs for another man the day after we had sex—"

"That's not—"

"I haven't slept with anyone since you, and before you ask, the last time I had sex was a year before I met you. I'm not lying. And if you think I'm that kind of girl, then maybe you shouldn't be in Liam's life at all. I would rather raise him on my own than with someone who thinks of his mother like that."

The air in the room is suddenly prime to explode, and being the stupid man I am, I strike the match. Don't ask me why I do. Maybe it's because of the way she manages to accuse me of being some deadbeat dad and a sorry excuse of a man all in one breath. Or maybe it's the months of pent-up frustration, sexually and otherwise, all because of this little spitfire temptress unconsciously cock-blocking me. Either way, I take the whole matchbox, soak it in gasoline, and throw it on the smoldering fire between us.

"Really? You're going to raise this baby on your own? For fuck's sake, Rose, I found you at a human sex trafficking auction. So tell me. How is that responsible parenting? If I hadn't found you, you would have been raped tonight, maybe even killed."

"How dare you," she hisses, her green eyes flashing a warning. "I was happy living my life far away from here. I didn't ask to be sold like a piece of meat at a fucking auction, Michael. I was kidnapped, you arrogant asshole. I've done nothing but give Liam the best life I could, and I will continue to do so, with or without his father."

"Speaking of, where is Liam then? Was he sold tonight as well?"

"No. Of course not. He's safe." Her voice is much softer now, and the pain on her face is raw and honest.

It's enough to bring my swirling anger to a brutal stop. Right as I'm about to ask more about her son, there's a knock on the door. I turn toward it. "What?"

A second later, my brother pokes his head inside. "Dad wants to see us at the house."

I catch Rose shift in the bathroom doorway and glance over at her. Her eyes bounce back and forth between Raphael and me, confusion and shock clear on her face. Oh right.

"Rose, this is my twin brother, Raphael. Raphael, meet Rose."

"Hi there," Raphael says with the same charming smile we're both known for.

"Hi," Rose mumbles, a small blush blooming on her cheeks.

Intense jealousy flares in my chest at the sight, and I suddenly want to throttle my brother. He doesn't have the right to smile at her like that, let alone make her blush. Maybe Rose needs to be reminded which brother she belongs to. Even if she's mad at said brother.

"Tell Dad I'll come to see him when I'm ready," I tell him, waving him away.

"Michael," Raphael warns me, ignoring my dismissal.

I level my brother with a look that tells him I'm not budging. "I'm not leaving Rose when she has just woken up."

"He was insistent."

"I don't fucking care. I am not leaving her—"

"Go." Rose's soft voice interrupts the rising heat between us, and I turn toward her. Standing in the doorway, she suddenly looks exhausted, and my anger fades a little. "I'll be fine. I could use some more sleep, anyway. That shower was really relaxing, and the pain meds are taking effect. I'm tired."

I've never known ibuprofen to make someone drowsy. But okay. I'll let her have her excuses if it makes her feel better. Either way, this conversation is far from over.

I stand and walk toward her. She watches me with guarded eyes but doesn't flinch when I reach for her hand and squeeze lightly. "We'll talk some more when I get back, okay?"

"Yeah."

I don't want to leave her. Not when I've just found her again, but I also haven't handled her confession well, so some time to process is a good idea for us both because while I'm confident she's confused, she's convinced she isn't, and continuing to argue about it right now isn't the best idea. "Please get some rest, Rose. You're safe here in my home, but don't leave. Alright? It's not safe out there."

"I won't leave," Rose assures me.

While I believe her, a faint memory tickles my mind, and I can't help but poke at it. "Do you promise to actually be here when I get back?"

The embarrassing blush that blooms across her face is adorable when she understands. "I promise."

My home is secure, but I still lock the penthouse down before we leave and station Enzo downstairs for added protection. No one else knows about Rose's presence in my home, but I'm not taking any chances.

I expect Raphael to say something the moment we step into the elevator, but surprisingly, he waits until we're in the car.

"Sounded like I interrupted a rather heated conversation."

I watch the city come alive as the beginnings of morning breaks outside the window. "It's fine."

"She seems lovely, brother," Raphael adds.

Lovely is just one way to describe her.

Stubborn, sassy, and headstrong are a few others.

As is beautiful, sweet, and...a mom.

Fuck.

I probably shouldn't have kissed her without talking first. But just like that night in the club, our passion is still there, burning hot and fierce. It's worth exploring, but how can we if she continues to swear I'm the father of her baby? Of this Liam kid? What kind of future can we build from that disillusion? How can we even entertain the idea when the real father of her son is out there somewhere? It's clear I have to find the father, as much as I hate the idea of seeing his bastard face. But only his identity will settle this argument between us before it festers into a wound that can't be healed.

DAD LEVELS RAPHAEL and me with a stern yet tired look from his seat behind his office desk. Uncle Leo stands behind him, leaning against the wall beside the bay window, nursing a coffee between big yawns.

"Do either of you want to explain why the chief of police woke me up before dawn about three dead bodies found in a burning car outside of the warehouse district?"

Dad isn't stupid. He knows we had something to do with it. I'm just annoyed that the police spoke to him before I could. "Do you want the short or the long version?"

Dad swings his eyes to me and narrows them. "I am in no mood for your sarcasm. I want the fucking truth, Michael."

Fair enough. "I received an email last night with an invitation to a human auction happening at midnight. The email was sent anonymously with the subject line save her."

"A human auction?" Dad frowns, sharing a look with his brother over his shoulder. "Let me see the email."

I pull my phone out, load the email, and hand the device over. He studies it for a long minute before handing my phone back.

"And I assume the girl you have resting in your penthouse is the one the email instructed you to save?"

Of course, he knows about her. I shoot my brother an annoyed look, and the bastard has the nerve to shrug. "She is."

"Did you buy her?"

"Of course not."

"Of course not, he says," Dad mocks with a scoff. "No. Instead, you ambushed and killed a well-respected businessman and his guards." His anger slips its leash an inch. "Do you honestly think his disappearance will go unnoticed?"

I glare at Dad, unable to believe what I'm hearing. Is he really defending a man who bought another human being? "Well-respected? The man bought her like he was ordering something off a fucking menu. What would you have done, Dad? Just let him get away with it?"

"I wouldn't have gone to the fucking auction to begin with!" he shouts, swinging his arm out and sweeping a stack of folders off his desk. They hover before fluttering to the ground in a jumbled mess. "You rushed into this, half-cocked and unprepared."

Perhaps it's sleep deprivation or the lingering memory of my argument with Rose, but his accusations cause an uncomfortable irritation to crawl under my skin, triggering a reflexive need to defend myself. "I disagree, Dad. We had to act quickly, and we thought everything through. We wore masks and took a vehicle that couldn't be traced back to us. We ambushed them under a bridge with no cameras and burned any evidence we may have left behind."

"A dozen different things could have gone wrong," Dad argues, sounding an awful lot like Enzo.

"But they didn't."

With a roar, Dad hurls his coffee cup at the wall. The porcelain shatters, filling the air with the heavy aroma of freshly brewed coffee.

"Do you feel any remorse at all, son? Do you not understand the gravity of how stupid your decision last night was? What could have happened if even one thing went wrong?"

"Yes, I do, but isn't human trafficking in Miami cause for alarm?"

"Of course it is!" Dad yells. "But that's not the point. It should have been an investigation approved by the High Table. The moment you received that email, you should have called me."

"There was no time, Dad."

"I doubt that." Dad takes several deep breaths to calm his rising blood pressure. "You're lucky. Absolutely fucking lucky that no one recognized your stupid, reckless asses. But that doesn't excuse your behavior with the oilman. What were you thinking? You should have brought him in. He might have known something we could have used to find out who's behind the entire thing."

He's right. Keeping the sad excuse of a man alive would have been the better option, but then I remember the dreadful sight in that car when I opened the door.

"He was about to rape her."

Dad studies my forlorn expression, and slowly, the anger leaves his face, softening his temper for a moment as realization dawns on him. "Is this the girl you've been exhausting resources trying to find for the past ten months?"

Of course, he knows about her and what I have done to look for her. Like I said, Dad knows everything.

"Yes."

"What do we know about this girl?"

"Her name is Rose Bennett. She woke up not long before Raphael came to collect me."

Dad ignores my passive-aggressive stab and digs deeper. "What else?"

"She has a six-week-old son named Liam. I don't know much about him except..." I pause, unsure if I should share this bit or not. Except a small, little damaged part of my soul pokes its stupid head up and forces the words from my mouth. "Except she claims he's my son."

Raphael tenses up beside me, surprise ebbing off him in waves since I didn't share this detail with him on the ride over. Uncle Leo releases a string of curses under his breath. The only one who doesn't react is Dad. He stares at me like I haven't just dropped a giant bombshell. After a long moment, he stands and strides over to the bar, pouring himself a finger of scotch. He swallows it and then pours another and another.

"That's impossible." Uncle Leo fills the silence, voicing the thoughts of everyone in the room and my exact words to Rose earlier.

My eyes stay trained on Dad, but I direct my words to my uncle. "That's what I told her, but she swears it's true."

"And you believe her?" Uncle Leo asks incredulously. "She's practically a stranger."

"Yes," I say without hesitation, that tormented part of my soul taking control of my mouth once again before I can speak rationally.

Uncle Leo scoffs at me like he sees me as some naive child. I hated when he did that as a kid and hated it even more as an adult. "Have you considered that she might be trying to trick you into thinking the kid is yours? That she sees how rich you are and is just after money?"

"That's what a paternity test is for," Raphael points out, earning a stern look from our uncle.

"But the doctor—" Uncle Leo tries.

"Enough." Dad's deep tone fills the office space, silencing the rest of us. He swallows two more glasses before returning to his chair. Leaning forward on his elbows, he rests his chin on top of his clasped hands and closes his eyes.

I watch him closely, desperately wanting to know his thoughts. Dad raised me and my siblings to be fair, to gather all the facts first, and to always listen with an open mind. It made him a well-respected and feared leader in a world that rarely acknowledges either trait. I just hope he's exercising those same virtues right now.

Taking a deep breath, Dad opens his eyes and exhales hard, like he's just made a heavy decision. "You'll need to be retested, Michael. And at a different facility this time. If, by some miracle, you're not sterile, we'll move forward with a paternity test."

Hearing Dad consider that the impossible might actually be possible gives that stupid little part of my soul hope. Hope I know will only be squished when the inevitable is proven true.

"I'll go today."

19

ROSE

I wasn't lying to Michael when I told him I was tired. Between the relaxing shower and the numbing effect of the pain meds, I'm fast asleep before long.

Liam fills my dreams, and I wake up in tears. The longing to embrace my son is so intense that I feel like I'm suffocating. He must be so scared and confused right now. I've been gone for at least a week now, and a lot can happen in that time. I trust Anette will watch him, but for how long? Will Evelyn risk traveling to the city to retrieve Liam? We never discussed the possibility because every scenario included him being with me if I had to run. But surely Dad's no longer having her watched now that he's essentially wiped his hands clean of me.

And then a terrifying thought suddenly seizes me. What if Dad returned to the town to find and take my son? What if he sold him into the same human trafficking ring he did to me?

I have to get to Liam. Somehow.

Bringing him here to Miami is dangerous, but leaving him there in Italy or with Evelyn is just as risky. Every single option in front of me sucks, and at this point, it's a matter of which one sucks the least.

With a goal in mind, I get out of bed and take care of business before I dare to leave the bedroom. I poke my head out the doorway and wait and listen. The low sound of a television playing floats down the hallway. Did Michael come home, and he just didn't want to wake me up? That's considerate of him, but now I'm awake and ready to revisit our conversation from earlier and then go collect my son.

I pad down the hallway, my steps slower than normal because even with the pain meds on board, every inch of my body is sore. Coming around the corner, I say before really looking at the figure on the couch, "Michael, can we talk?"

The man on the couch twists around, and I scream.

Because that's not Michael.

I spin and run, rather pathetically, back to Michael's room.

"Shit. Wait!" the man calls after me.

I don't listen because I don't know him, and that's enough for me.

Slamming the door behind me, I shove my back against it while I fumble with the lock. A second later, the stranger knocks on the door. It's not angry or demanding, but I back away from the door and stare at it like the Hulk is about to burst through anyway.

"Rose?"

I freeze. How does he know my name?

"Rose?" He tries again, his tone a little softer this time. "I guess Michael didn't tell you he was leaving me to keep guard?"

No. No, he did not.

The man chuckles when I remain quiet, like he finds this whole thing amusing. Something I do not. "Well, anyway, listen. My name is Enzo. I work with Michael." He pauses as if waiting for me to reply. "I'm really sorry I scared you." He finishes when I don't speak.

He sounds remorseful, and it pulls at my heartstrings for whatever reason. I blame the lingering hormones.

"How do I know you're not lying?" I'm proud at the confidence in my tone.

Enzo sighs loud and dramatically. "Oh, good. You are there. I thought maybe you were in the bathroom or the closet or something, and I was just talking to myself out here, like an idiot. To be honest with you, it happens a lot, but I was really hoping it wouldn't this time because, man, that was a seriously bad first impression I made in the living room."

His rambling is actually kind of cute, but I say nothing and just wait.

"Would it help if I called Michael to explain everything?"

"Yes."

"Great!" He sounds relieved, like I'd actually say no.

I hear him mess with his phone through the door, putting the device on speaker as it rings twice before Michael answers. "Enzo? Is everything okay?"

"Yeah, boss. Everything's fine. It's just that I'm here with Rose, and well, I'm actually outside your bedroom door because I may have scared her—"

"What?" Michael interrupts. "What did you do?"

"Nothing. I swear. She came out into the living room, and I think she was expecting you. Anyway, she ran off when it was my handsome face instead and locked herself in your room. I introduced myself and apologized, then offered to call you to confirm I was not lying. Also, you're on speaker."

Michael sighs into the phone. "Rose?"

I step closer to the door. "Yes?"

"I'm sorry I didn't tell you that I was leaving Enzo behind. I didn't realize I would be gone so long and hoped you would still be asleep when I returned. But I trust Enzo with my life and so can you, I promise." His deep voice calms my frayed nerves. "You did well, by the way, running from a stranger. I would too from Enzo. He is rather ugly," he adds on, which makes the stranger I now know as Enzo scoff in disbelief.

I raise my hand to the doorknob and twist, pulling the door open just enough to peek out at Enzo. Vivid blue eyes meet mine cautiously before he offers me a reassuring smile. He's an incredibly large man with tattoos covering every inch of visible skin. The sides of his head are shaved, showing off the swirls of intricate tattoos on his skull. What's left of his blond hair is pulled back into a high bun. He resembles a buffed, tattooed, modern-day Viking, completing the look with a long, clean beard tied off at the bottom. Looking at him now, he's rather intimidating but also good looking...in a gruff kind of way.

"Hi, Rose," he says. "Nice to meet you. Officially."

"Hi."

He offers his phone out to me, and I reach out for it.

"Michael?"

"Rose," he purrs, and a shiver skirts down my spine. "How are you feeling?"

"Better. I'm hungry, though."

"I'll bring you back some breakfast. Unfortunately, there isn't much in the kitchen, but I'll have it stocked right away."

"Breakfast is fine. I'm not picky, so whatever you like is fine. When will you be back?"

"I'm on my way."

"Okay."

"Listen, Rose. Enzo is a little strange—"

"Hey!" the Viking protests.

"But he means well. I wouldn't have left him with you if I didn't trust him completely."

"Aw, thanks, Boss. I didn't know you cared so much." Enzo wipes fake tears from his eyes before tossing me a wink when he catches the small smile on my lips at his antics.

"Shut up, Enzo, before I take it back," Michael snaps, but there's no heat in his voice. "I'll be home soon, Rose."

After saying our goodbyes, I hand Enzo back his phone, embarrassment washing over me. "I'm sorry for how I over-reacted."

Enzo pockets his phone and steps back. "You have nothing to be sorry for. It was just a misunderstanding is all."

I step into the hallway and follow Enzo as he leads the way back to the living room. Now that I won't be scared shitless by another stranger, I take in the main space of Michael's home with an admiring eye. Windows to my right stretch two stories high. Doors set in the center lead out to a large terrace, and from this angle, I catch the very edge of a pool nestled among the vegetation, like it's a secret space tucked away in an oasis. Directly to my left is a wood staircase that rises to the second floor, each step open to the air, so it gives the illusion that the stairs float in midair.

The living space stretches out in front, every little detail grabbing my attention. Abstract paintings adorn the walls that add to the tranquil and peaceful ambience the room strives for. The entire space carries a gray-and-white color scheme with steel blue accents. Sunken into the floor is an enormous sofa, which can be rearranged into different layouts, covered in various soft blankets and pillows. Directly across from the inviting sofa and above an electric fireplace hangs a TV nearly as long as the couch. The living space bleeds into an open kitchen with brand-new appliances and smooth marble countertops. Elegant pendant lights hang high above the large island, surrounded by stools. I'm curious to explore the other hallway on the other side of the living room, but it feels a little wrong to do that without Michael.

Instead, I claim a spot on the couch and wrap a throw

blanket around me. Enzo, very wisely, sits on the other end of the couch.

"So you're Rose, huh?" he asks with a sly smile, breaking the silence before it becomes too awkward.

Something in the way he says it has me asking, "You've heard about me?"

"Oh, yeah. Michael's been borderline obsessed, trying to find you ever since that night at the club in January."

"What? Really?" I didn't realize or even consider he might look for me.

"Yeah. When the trail went cold, he turned into a miserable bastard and has been one ever since. But now that he's found you, we can thank God for small miracles."

My mouth drops open, and I flounder like a fish out of water for a moment before I finally regain my composure. Barely. Because Enzo's words leave a lot to unpack. I remember our moment in the bedroom when we nearly got carried away. Clearly, our passion hasn't fizzled, and we share a son, despite his insistence otherwise, but in the craze of the last day, it never once crossed my mind that Michael may have been as haunted with longing as I have been since January.

"Why would he do that?"

Enzo's blue gaze is powerful and holds mine captive. "Why does the moon hold power over the tide? Why do flowers need the sun and water to grow? It's simple. He needs you. He still does."

"He barely knows me." It's a lame excuse but the truth.

"Time makes no difference when your soul finds its counterpart in another. These things just happen, Rose. There's no rhyme or reason to it, and every minute you spend thinking about it is just another minute wasted. And don't you think you've wasted enough time?" Enzo waits for me to digest his words, but I have nothing to say because he's right.

Michael and I spent the totality of an hour together, then suffered the next ten months apart, but it made no difference in the end. Because here we are together again, and it's like those months never happened. Sure, we have a lot to talk about and a son to retrieve, but something about Michael draws me to him. Whatever that feeling is was there in January. And it's still there now.

A chime echoes through the space, and I twist my head in the direction it came.

"Michael's home," Enzo announces, rising to his feet to meet Michael in a hallway beside the kitchen. It must lead to an elevator.

Michael appears, and the sight of him is like a breath of fresh air shot directly into my lungs. I haven't been able to take a real breath since he left. The realization of how intensely he affects me is overwhelming and eerily familiar because his son is the only other person who shares the same ability.

As soon as he smiles at me, I know I'm royally fucked because the man has me caught in his orbit, and I'm helpless to pull away.

20

MICHAEL

Enzo leaves shortly after I arrive home, but not before snagging a honey biscuit on his way out. Rose digs in before he even leaves. She's not shy at all about eating her fill, which is strangely attractive. She covers the biscuit in an obscene amount of grape jelly, and my eyes track a drop that falls down her chin. She reaches for a napkin, but my hand is on her chin before she can wipe it away. Rose stares at me with wide eyes as I swipe the drop from her chin with my thumb and then lick it clean, keeping my eyes on hers the entire time.

"Mmm. Tastes sweet." I wink, enjoying it immensely when a hard blush blossoms on her cheeks.

Rose clears her throat, pushing her plate away as she does. "Michael, I need to ask you something."

"Okay." Something tells me her question doesn't involve spreading jam on her breasts for me to lick off. Shame.

"I know you don't believe Liam is your son, but he is mine, and he's too young to be away from me." As she speaks, her voice cracks, and I notice tears beginning to gather in her eyes. "You found and rescued me. Will you help me get him?"

To avoid her starting to cry, I swiftly change the subject to focus on the facts. "You said he wasn't at the auction. So where is he?"

"Back in Italy. In a small town outside of Venice. I was dropping off muffins at a local bakery and left Liam with my friend there while I ran another errand really quick. That's when I was taken."

Italy, huh? No wonder I could never find her afterward. She wasn't even in the same damn country. Still, something tells me she's not telling me everything, but I get the sense that enough of it is the truth. Enough for me to let it go until her son is back by her side. "Do you think he's still with your friend?"

"I hope so," she says. "But what if he's not? What if he's been taken too? What if she just abandoned him on the steps of some church, and he's been adopted into a new family already? What if—"

I reach out and grip her shoulders. "Rose. Stop. And take a breath for me."

Her tears stream down her face freely now. So much for distracting her. Rose sniffles hard and listens, taking a few deep breaths. I hand her a napkin and wait as she wipes her face clean. She looks at me with bloodshot eyes and a blotchy face. She's a mess, but she's never been more beautiful because that fire is still there, burning bright and hot with determination. "Please, Michael. He's our son."

"I'll help you," I tell her, purposely avoiding the part about him being our son because that remains to be seen, and I'm not holding my breath that the fertility results have changed.

Unsurprisingly, Dominic is perplexed by my request but knows better than to question it. Although I'm sure he has several dozen he's aching to ask, and he's not alone. I have several dozen myself. It should be a simple task, a quick grab-and-go kind of situation, but nothing about any of this is simple.

We finish breakfast while we wait for Dominic to call back. He was still in Venice visiting his mom, so he wasn't far. When my phone finally rings with a FaceTime call, Rose practically jumps out of her skin in anticipation.

As soon as I swipe the green button, my cousin's angry and very annoyed face fills the screen. His dark eyes zero in on me before snapping, "Someone want to tell me why I just kidnapped a baby from a sweet old grandma? Oh, and a follow-up question. Why does said baby have your eyes, Michael?"

Rose grabs my hand and pulls the phone toward her. She's never met Dominic, but that doesn't stop her momma bear side from coming out when she demands, "You have him? You have Liam?"

"You know, even with your instructions, that woman still refused to hand him over? Honestly, it feels like I kidnapped the baby. I feel dirty somehow—"

"Do you have Liam?"

"Answer her, Dominic," I order out of video sight.

"Fine. Yes. I have the little rug rat." Dominic shifts the phone, and it's a long second of tumbling views before he centers the phone on a car seat and the baby resting inside. "Say hi, kid."

"Liam!" Rose cries, her eyes shining with tears. "Oh, my sweet boy. It's really you."

The baby blinks open his eyes, and the setting Italian sunlight catches the color. My heart slams to a stop as my entire focus shifts to the impossible child peering up at the camera with eyes the same shade as mine.

THE GENTLE BUZZING of my phone on the couch wakes me up. Honestly, I'm surprised I fell asleep at all with my mind so overwhelmed with questions and not enough answers. And of all my questions, my biggest one is how it's even possible that Rose's baby can be my son.

I look over at Rose, relieved to find her still sleeping, curled up beside me, using my lap as her personal pillow. She spent as long as she could on the phone with Liam, staring at his sleeping face until Dominic was forced to hang up when he boarded the private plane to bring them to Miami. Afterward, she passed out again, with a noticeably lighter air around her. Like seeing Liam was enough to ease some of the nightmares haunting her, and she could finally just sleep.

My phone buzzes once more, and I grab it before it wakes Rose up. She needs every minute of sleep she can get. I gently brush a lock of gorgeous red hair from her face before answering the phone without looking at the caller ID.

"Yes?"

"Mr. DiAngelo? It's Dr. Gonzalez. I have your preliminary results."

"And?"

"Sperm motility, morphology, and vitality are well within normal limits. A further analysis is being done at the lab, but everything looks good so far."

"What does that mean? Am I sterile or not?"

"Not in the slightest, Mr. DiAngelo."

I close my eyes and rest my head back on the couch. "Thank you, Doctor."

Hanging up, I blindly toss my phone to the side, then pinch the bridge of my nose. It feels like the world I know is unraveling into one giant storm, with Rose and Liam at the center of it.

Liam.

The boy has the same unique light hazel eyes the DiAngelo family is known for, and with proof of my fertility, there's no doubt in my mind now that Liam is my son. Which means that someone lied and that someone will pay dearly. With their life.

"Michael?"

I open my eyes and lift my head, meeting Rose's sleepy but curious gaze. She peers up at me from my lap, and I feel the sudden need to touch her. Raising a hand, I trace the side of her face that's not bruised and smile when she nuzzles further into my touch.

"Sleep well?" I ask her.

"I did," she answers honestly. "I didn't mean to overhear, but was that the doctor?"

"Yeah. Preliminary results show that I'm not sterile after all." It doesn't need repeating, but saying it aloud makes the whole thing even more real.

"I told you." She smiles up at me through her lashes. "So do you believe me now?"

I trace her cheekbone and down her jawline with my thumb. She shivers beneath my touch, her eyes fluttering closed briefly. "I do. And I owe you an apology for how I acted. For the things I said."

She shakes her head. "It's okay, Michael. You believed you were sterile. I can't fault you for that when you didn't know any different. And I apologize too for lashing out. I was hurt, but it was uncalled for."

I repeat the same route down the other side of her face being careful of her sore cheek. "Clean slate?"

"I'd like that." Rose's smile grows bigger dand more brilliant. The beautiful sight sends a sensation down my spine. Rose stretches and makes the cutest squeak when she does. As she resettles with her head on my lap, I'm acutely aware of her warmth and feel myself grow hard. I try to shift without making my discomfort evident, but of course, Rose notices.

Her eyes drop to the obvious bulge straining against my zipper, and the fiery temptress comes out to play. The one that calls to my demons like a siren at sea.

With a mischievous grin, she sits up and swings herself on my lap, wrapping her arms around my neck. My hands immediately find her hips, and I pull her snug against me, letting her feel the very thing she's responsible for. Her lips hover over mine as she rocks forward with a deep moan. I push up and capture her lips. Our tongues tangle as we each fight to control the kiss. One quick nibble on her bottom lip, and I win that battle. But not the war. Because the next thing I know, Rose's hands are on my zipper, and then her dainty hand dives in and wraps around my hard cock.

She swallows my groan with a devilish chuckle that has my demons purring in submission. This woman could ask for anything, and I'd give it to her without hesitation. She wants to burn the world? I'll strike the match for her. She wants to hunt down and kill those responsible for kidnapping her? I'll hand her the gun. She wants to claim my dark soul for her own? It's already hers.

My hands tighten, ready to throw her down on this couch and eat her pussy out until she sees stars when the elevator pings, the sound echoing through the penthouse like a fire alarm.

With a sudden jerk, Rose removes her hand from my pants as if there's a raging inferno there, which, to be fair, feels like there is. She tumbles off my lap, her face as red as a tomato, before she disappears beneath a blanket.

Her embarrassment is adorable. My innocent little angel with a devilish side. It makes me wonder if she'd enjoy a visit to the Playground, the Russian sex club, for a night of discovery and pleasure.

"Knock, knock!"

I barely rezip my pants before my sister flutters around the corner like a bird. Bird of prey, maybe. A second later, Raphael follows, his arms ladened with several large bags, and Enzo is on his heels carrying a tower of boxes.

"Yo, where can I put these boxes of diapers?"

"What?"

Rose pops up, tossing the blanket away, all embarrassment gone now. "Yeah, what?"

Gabriella points at the hallway that leads to the guest rooms. "First door on the right. It's a cute room with the best potential for a nursery. The windows face the east, so the sunrise will be beautiful in the morning."

"Wait," I call, but Enzo doesn't hear me. Or maybe he does but ignores me anyway to follow Gabriella's order instead.

I meet Rose's confused face and reach for her hand, giving it a reassuring squeeze before I stand and cross the living room to approach my sister.

"Gabriella, what the hell are you all doing here?" I demand.

My sister looks at me in exasperation, like I have the nerve to question her. "Bringing you the essentials for the baby. You have nothing here for him, Michael, and babies need a lot of things."

I can sense Rose's growing panic behind me. "How do you know about the baby?"

Gabriella gives her source away when her eyes flick to our brother. I turn on my twin, who at least has the decency to look a little ashamed this time, unlike earlier in Dad's office. "And how do you know the baby is coming here?" I answer my question the second after I ask it. "Dominic. The bastard. Can't keep a secret to save his damn life."

Raphael shrugs, then heads off to dump his bags in the

same room Enzo disappeared in. I turn back to my sister, ready to continue my questioning, only to find her gone.

"Hi, I'm Gabriella." She's sitting on the couch, facing a stunned Rose with her hand outstretched. "Michael and Raphael's little sister."

Jesus. The woman can fucking move like a damn ninja when she wants to. But then again, she has DiAngelo blood running through her veins, so it's not all that surprising. Just annoying and often highly inconvenient. Like right now.

"I'm Rose." With a brief hesitation, she takes Gabriella's hand and shakes it. "It's nice to meet you."

"Same," Gabriella chirps with a smile, then launches into a speech. "I couldn't believe it when I heard the news that Michael was hiding a beautiful redhead in his penthouse. I just had to meet you. And when Dominic called saying he was bringing her baby home from Italy, a baby with Michael's eyes, I realized my brother has nothing here for a baby. So Auntie Gabriella to the rescue!"

"Wow." Rose chuckles humorlessly, panic growing on her face.

Gabriella catches her mistake, and her smile drops instantly. "Oh, I'm sorry. I just got so excited when I heard everything, that's all. I didn't mean to offend you or upset you."

"It's okay. It's just been a lot over the last week. You caught me off guard is all."

Gabriella's eyes fall, and I know that she knows some, if not all, of the details of how Rose came to be here. Again. Raphael. "No woman should ever have to go through something as terrible as what you did. I'm glad my brothers found you and that you're here. And that your son is on his way here also."

"Me too." I can tell Rose means that. The tension in her shoulders relaxes as the conversation moves on to Liam.

I lean over the couch, and Rose turns her face toward me, her green eyes sparkling. "I'm going to go check on the disaster those two are probably making in the bedroom. Are you okay out here?"

She nods, and I kiss her cheek, groaning under my breath when my sister admires us with an immature "aw." The small giggle I hear from Rose as I walk away makes up for my sister's annoying behavior, though.

I hate to admit it, but Gabriella is right. This room will make a wonderful nursery. The window faces to the east with a beautiful view of the Atlantic Ocean in the morning.

Enzo and Raphael are currently arguing in the corner about how to organize the diapers and wipes in the best way.

"Don't you think this is something Rose might want to do?" I ask, breaking up the back-and-forth bickering.

"Yeah, you're right." Raphael sets the box in his hands back on the pile. "Hey. Have you heard from the doctor about your fertility test yet?"

"I did. Just before you three crashed into my place actually. Turns out I'm not sterile."

"Holy shit!" Enzo shouts. "That's insane."

"So the kid really is yours?" Raphael ventures with a lace of hope tracing his voice.

I nod. "Yeah."

"Congratulations, brother." Raphael slaps my back with a genuine smile. "Dominic sent a picture. He has the family eyes."

"I know."

A phone buzzes, and Raphael pulls his phone free from his pocket. "It's Dad," he says when he glances at the screen. "He wants us at the house. If I had to guess, he heard from the doctor too."

"He'll want a paternity test to be sure," Enzo says, dampening the mood in the soon-to-be nursery.

"And a background check, if he hasn't already done that," Raphael adds.

I have no doubt he already did that following this morning's interrogation. But I'm not ready to think about what the results of it might mean just yet.

Just then, I hear a shout followed by a crash. In a second, all three of us rush out of the room and hurry into the living room with our guns drawn. My penthouse is a fortress, but if someone has broken in, their life is now forfeit. But as soon as I see what's in front of me, I quickly holster my gun because there's no danger. Not unless you consider a little baby boy with red hair and light hazel eyes a threat.

21

ROSE

Gabriella is...a lot, but I still like her right away. I'm certain, given the chance, we could be great friends. Along with her abundant energy, she's also sweet and kind, with a witty humor that reminds me so much of my sister and my best friend. Thinking about them now makes my heart ache, and I feel guilty because I've had little time to think about the pair. My thoughts are consumed with Liam and Michael when I'm not sleeping, leaving little room for anything else.

Evie must be losing her mind trying to find me. But I also want to know why she didn't get Liam. Learning he was still with Anette has me worried that something may have happened to Evie that prevented her from retrieving Liam. And Grace? Who knows what lies our father has told her? It's hard knowing I'm back in Miami, so close to my sister, yet...so far away.

"So I have to know," Gabriella says, pulling me from my thoughts. "Did Michael really screw your brains out in the bathroom at Sinners?"

I'm taken aback by her bluntness, but I also admire her lack of beating around the bush. Still though, I nearly choke on my sip of tea when she asks it. With a small chuckle, I say, "Makes me sound a bit like a slut, huh?"

Gabriella laughs then and waves away my question. "Nonsense. I think it sounds rather romantic."

"How is any of that romantic?"

"How is it not? You two locked eyes across the dance floor and shared an instant connection of intense, fiery passion," Gabriella preaches with a wistful smile. "It's like something out of a movie."

"Well, when you put it that way."

The elevator pings, and we both turn toward the hallway.

"Who could that be?" Gabriella wonders out loud.

But I know. Call it mother's intuition or whatever you want, but somehow, I just know. I spring up, my teacup crashing to the floor before I run around the couch, ignoring my body's painful protests. The only medicine I need now is a ten-pound baby boy.

Just then, the man I met on FaceTime appears around the corner. He's carrying a car seat in one hand and a diaper bag in the other. Dominic has barely set the car seat down before I'm unbuckling the sleeping baby and scooping him into my arms. I know they say you should never wake a sleeping baby, but whoever said that must have never spent a week apart from their kid. So what do they know?

Liam opens his eyes and yawns really big, scrunching his face up before he notices me and giggles. If that's not the sweetest sound I've ever heard, then I don't know what is. My eyes scan him over, checking for any signs of bruises or cuts, but I find none. He looks perfectly fine, dressed in a sleep-and-play onesie decorated with little forest creatures. I remove the blue beanie covering his beautiful light red hair and lean down to kiss the soft locks, savoring his unique baby smell. Liam's warm and solid and safe back in my arms where he belongs.

"Is that him?" Michael asks from behind me. "Is that Liam?"

I turn, cradling my cooing, happy son to my chest, and meet Michael's curious and hesitant expression. Taking a step forward, I notice Michael tense up, but he doesn't retreat, which I count as a win. There's still uncertainty in his eyes, but I understand. The man has become a father practically overnight. That's a lot for anyone to process and accept.

"It is." I stop in front of him and wait. I don't want to push him. Instead, I shift Liam in my arms so that they can see each other.

Michael's eyes drop to the baby, and they just stare at one another for a long moment. Then Liam reaches out with a hand to his father, smiling and giggling as he does, and I watch the tension melt away from Michael's body.

"May I hold him?"

"Of course."

Liam looks so small in Michael's arms but also so right, and my heart threatens to burst at the sight. A sight I never thought I would get to see. Watching Michael interact with his son is extremely attractive and does something to my ovaries that has me telling the damn things to cool down.

"He's real," Michael breathes, staring down in wonder at the baby in his arms. "He's really real."

"Of course, he is. I had to deal with the angry mini-Michael all damn day, and let me tell you—" Dominic complains loud enough to break the endearing moment, which earns him a slap upside the head from Gabriella.

"Language, you big idiot."

Rubbing his head, Dominic turns on her and scowls. "He's a baby, Gabriella. He can't even speak yet."

"But he can hear, and babies are practically sponges," Gabriella argues.

"Better to get in the habit now, Dominic," Enzo advises as he peers over Michael's shoulder to get a good look at Liam.

"Says the one the baby should stay away from the most," Dominic grumbles before he walks toward me with the diaper bag. He hands it over to me and says, "We didn't get to talk much before I basically kidnapped your baby, but hi, I'm Dominic. Your baby daddy's cousin."

Dominic, similar to his cousins, is a tall man with a strong build, but unlike them, he has short blond hair and dark eyes. He's handsome, sure, but he's not Michael.

"Thank you, Dominic. Really, I'm incredibly grateful for your help." I mean every word and hope he sees my gratitude in my face.

"Yeah, well, it's the least I can do since I missed out on your rescue. I always miss the good stuff when I leave." He crosses his arms over his chest and frowns.

"I wouldn't call rescuing Rose from a man who bought her at a human auction a good time, you idiot," Raphael chastises him, which deflates Dominic's mood a little when he realizes exactly how his words sound.

"Sorry. Anyway, that Anette lady said you left that diaper bag behind, and she wants you to call her when you leave the hospital and get settled."

Michael and Dominic devised a clever cover story to explain my sudden disappearance and lack of communication. As far as Anette knows, I suffered a serious fall on the way back to the house and have spent the last week in and out of consciousness in a hospital in Venice, before being transferred back to the States. Dominic stepped in as a worried family member tasked with bringing Liam to me while I recovered back home.

Dominic turns to Michael. "Anything else, cousin? I'm exhausted and would really like to go home and sleep for the next week."

Michael doesn't look up from Liam as he answers, "Go ahead. Thank you, Dominic."

"You're welcome." He starts toward the elevator before he stops and turns. "Hey, I'd like to come see the rug rat after I've rested a bit. You know, just to check on him and make sure Michael's not being a total idiot when it comes to parenthood."

"Goodbye, Dominic," Michael says flatly.

"We should go too," Raphael suggests, his tone solemn.

Michael sighs and traces his big hand over Liam's fair red hair and down his face. Liam tries grabbing for his fingers but is too clumsy and awkward. "I know."

"Where are you going?" I ask, catching on that Raphael means Michael in that equation.

"Our dad wants to see us," Raphael answers.

"Again?" The question slips free before I can stop it. "Sorry, I didn't mean for it to sound like that."

"That's quite alright, Rose." Raphael smiles at me. It's eerie how he's identical to Michael...but also not. Michael keeps his hair longer on top and his sides shorter, whereas Raphael styles his hair long and messy around his face. Hairstyles aside, Michael carries himself a certain way that's just slightly different from Raphael.

Reluctantly, Michael hands Liam back to me. The baby fusses for a moment before settling into my arms. A finger lifts my chin, and I gaze into Michael's hooded eyes. He leans forward and whispers against my lips, "You look hot as fuck right now holding my son. Makes me want to impregnate you again."

And there go my ovaries. Only this time, my greedy pussy joins in, and I fight back the urge to rub my thighs together. I'm faintly aware we have an audience, but Michael has me trapped in his gravity.

He chuckles, his breath warm and delicious on my mouth before he kisses me. "I'll see you soon." He moves to my ear and whispers, "And I plan on revisiting what we started on that couch when I get back."

Fuck me. If I could get pregnant from just words, there's no doubt I would have right then and there.

22

ROSE

I wake up to the familiar feeling of muscular arms enveloping me in warmth. My eyes slowly open, gazing up at Michael's chiseled features. He hasn't realized I've woken up yet and is still speaking with Gabriella and Enzo, so I close my eyes again to respect their privacy.

"You need to go home, Gabriella," he says. His voice sounds as exhausted as my body feels, and I wonder what time it is. "Raphael shouldn't be alone right now. He stormed out and wouldn't talk to me when I followed him. Maybe you can get through to him."

"I'll go with her," Enzo offers. "Make sure he doesn't do anything stupid tonight."

"I can't believe Dad would do this to him." Gabriella's words are sharp, her tone angry. Very much unlike the woman I've enjoyed getting to know all night. "He doesn't even know the girl."

"We'll talk about it some more tomorrow. Nothing is set in stone. I'll find a way to get him out of it. For now, I just want to check on Liam and tuck Rose into bed."

After a long pause, Gabriella murmurs softly, "I like her, brother."

"Me too," Enzo agrees. It's easy to hear the smile in his voice.

My cheeks warm at hearing their praises. I like them both too.

"And I'm happy for you. After you-know-who, you deserve this, Michael. You deserve her and that precious baby boy," Gabriella continues.

You-know-who? Who's that?

My eyes pop open, and I squirm in Michael's arms, suddenly feeling the desire to get down. He peers down at me when he feels me moving.

"Time for you two to go," Michael instructs his sister and friend.

The two say their goodbyes and promise to visit again soon. Before the elevator doors even close, Michael turns away and walks toward his bedroom. He gently places me down on the bed, setting the brand-new baby video monitor beside me before he disappears into the closet to change. I glance at the video to make sure Liam is still fast asleep before turning back to the matter at hand.

"Did you have a good time?" he calls out. "Gabriella told me Liam fell asleep with no trouble and that he's settling in good."

My gaze fixes on the empty doorway with a frown. Does he actually expect me to ignore what I just heard? He has to know I heard the last part and is trying to distract me with Liam, but it won't work.

"Who were they talking about?" I ask before I lose my nerve. "Who was you-know-who?"

I count a total of five breaths before he reappears...and fuck. The man looks downright sinful. He's changed into a pair of light gray sweatpants that rest low on his hips. My eyes drink in the sight of his muscular chest and his cut arms, tracing his well-defined Apollo's belt that points down to a certain outlined part of his body that I've missed very much... and what did I ask again?

"How much did you hear?" He sounds tired, not angry, but he also doesn't seem thrilled to be having this conversation either.

"Are you married?"

Michael moves quickly then, sitting beside me on the bed before I can even move away. He gathers my hands and holds them tightly. Our clasped hands are the only thing I focus on, trying hard to ignore the burning behind my eyes. I was just thinking how safe I feel here, but now I'm worried that's not the case.

"I am not married. There is no girlfriend or anything of the sort. I promise."

Relief floods my system, and I let out a deep breath. Only for it to be ripped away by his next words.

"I do have an ex-wife, though."

"What?" My head snaps up. He looks at me like he's worried I'll run, which, to be fair, I'm considering...if I had somewhere to run.

"We were married for a few years and divorced a couple of months before I met you."

"Why?"

"I wanted kids."

"And?"

"And when it didn't happen, we got professional help. That was when I was told I was sterile."

"Then?"

I guess one-syllable questions are all I have in me to ask.

"Then we got divorced," he answers and pulls one of his

hands away, gently tracing down my cheekbone and across my jawline. His thumb caresses my bottom lip, his eyes growing darker as he watches the motion. "And then I met you, and my entire life changed in one night."

I lean into his touch, savoring the warmth of his hand on my skin and closing my eyes. I believe him. The sadness in his eyes as he relives the memories of his dream of a family being torn away are too real to be faked.

"I just have one question." I open my eyes and catch the spark of humor in his.

"So long as it's not another one-word question."

Snorting softly, I reach up and pull his hand away from my face. I keep hold of it and trace the back of his hand with my thumb. Taking a deep breath, I force myself to look into his eyes as I ask my question because I have to see if he's lying.

"Do you love her still?"

Horror fills his face, and I have my answer before he says a word. "No. I don't. I never did. Our marriage wasn't about love. It was a business arrangement. Something that benefited us both. That's all. I never felt once for her what I felt the first moment I laid eyes on you. There is no one else."

Overwhelmed, I lean in for a quick kiss, but as usual with us, it turns into something more. Michael buries his hand in my hair to maneuver my head just how he likes it to deepen the kiss. Michael pulls me onto his lap to straddle his hips without breaking our kiss. He wraps his arms around me and pulls me closer, his cock hard against my core, and I rock against it, both of us moaning at the contact.

Michael pulls back, his smile instant and predatory when he sees how much his kiss affects me. His eyes hold mine, and like a bee drawn to honey, I'm transported back to that night all those months ago when I locked eyes with a gorgeous man who whispered sweet temptations in my ear and showed me heaven with every touch.

"I want to strip you naked, lay you out on this bed, and feast on your body until it's fucking clear to everyone who you belong to." His whispered words are hot against my ear, and I shudder at the heat. "Who I belong to."

"So do it," I encourage him, completely lost in the moment.

He nibbles kisses down my neck, caressing the abused flesh afterward with his warm tongue that leaves me shivering in his arms at the sensation.

"You taste even better than I remember," he says, finding that soft spot behind my ear and kissing the space there.

"More, Michael. Please. I need more," I beg, digging my fingers into his back. The bite of my nails has him doubling down until I know I will have a mark behind my ear tomorrow morning. "You did promise we would revisit this when you got back."

Michael raises his face and studies my expression. We've teased this line twice now, and I'm hoping the third time is the charm, but I see the question in his eyes. The worry. The concern that I may regret going further than kissing like a pair of horny teenagers who only know how to dry hump.

"What are you asking, Rose? I need to hear you say it."

"Touch me, Michael. I need you to touch me and remind me how good this can feel. Please." Because while I know the man is dead and it's Michael holding me, that bastard lingers still. I want...no, I need Michael to erase every inch of that man from my skin and my soul.

I rock against his steel-like rod and enjoy the hiss that slips from his mouth. He leans in and bites the space where my neck and collarbone meet. I cry out, and he takes advantage, capturing my lips and swallowing the last bit of the air from my lungs. He shoves his tongue inside, and mine meets his with the same level of passion.

"Lie down, Rose," he orders.

I do as he says and smile up at him when he cages me in. His eyes are wary, like he's still uncertain. I reach up and cup his face. "I want this. I'm telling you it's okay."

"If at any point it's too much, you tell me."

I won't need a safe word because I don't plan on stopping. When I nod, he blinks, and all concern washes away. Michael makes quick work of my sweatpants, his eyes darkening when he remembers I have no underwear.

"Holy fuck, Rose. You're gorgeous. This makes me want to tell Gabriella to fuck off on buying you clothes. You should be naked in my bed, in my house all day, every day."

Unrealistic, but damn, he paints a pretty picture that I'm tempted to say yes to.

The heat of his breath on my bare pussy sets every one of my nerve endings on fire. I have ached for his touch for so long, dreamed of it for so long, but having him between my legs now is better than I remembered or imagined. He runs his tongue up the length of my pussy before his lips cover the sensitive bundle of nerves like a suction cup. I moan, arching up off the bed, as he slips one finger, then two inside me.

"Fuck me," he growls, his voice muffled. "I missed this. Missed you. Missed this magic pussy that is still so tight after having my baby. It's perfect. You're perfect."

If I had the breath in me to laugh, I would have, but every lick of his tongue, every thrust of his finger, steals every ounce of breath I have left in my lungs and narrows my mind until it's only focused on Michael and his touch, driving away the fear that haunts me. White heat gathers at the base of my spine. My muscles contract, building until the dam finally breaks, and the orgasm crashes over me like a wave, washing away all the darkness of that man until it's only Michael and me left behind in its wake.

23

MICHAEL

When we enter our family home, piano music greets us. I poke my head into the sitting room. The world outside is dark, and the mood in the room matches it. Mom sits at the grand piano with her back to us. Her hands fly across the keys as the familiar sounds of "Moonlight Sonata" by Beethoven fill the air. A somber melody I've heard her play for as long as I can remember. A melody she only plays when her heart and soul are heavy.

Raphael and I exchange a knowing glance. Whatever's bothering Mom is undoubtedly linked to our father. It almost always is. Mom loves our father deeply and without reserve, but the life of a Mafia don's wife is not always sunshine and rainbows. It's often exhausting to carry the burden of her husband's decisions, even when she doesn't agree with them herself.

The mood in Dad's office isn't much better.

He stands at the dark window with his back to us. Uncle Leo sits in his usual spot, his fingers tapping against the glass of whiskey he nurses, his gaze far off like he's deep in thought. I'm surprised to see Dominic here. I thought he went home after dropping Liam off. Judging by the grimace on his face and the extra tall coffee cup in his hands, he thought so, too.

After what seems like an eternity, Dad finally turns away from the window and sinks into his chair. His gaze finds mine. "I heard from Dr. Gonzalez. I'm assuming he called you too?"

"He did."

Uncle Leo curses under his breath before hissing, "This is an absolute shit show, Dante. Which doctor are we supposed to believe here?"

Three negative tests with one doctor and a single positive with another. Unless I somehow became magically fertile in less than a year, someone's lying, and my money is on the first doctor. Seeing as how I have no doubts now that Liam is my son.

"Bring me that first doctor, Leo, and we'll find out," Dad orders his brother, his temper slipping a fraction.

"Consider it done."

Dad heaves a deep sigh before he reaches for a manila folder and holds it out to me. "Rose's background check."

I snatch it from his hand immediately. "There was no need for a background check."

Dad huffs, settling back in his seat with his arms crossed over his chest. "You must be joking. A woman you fucked almost a year ago claims her son is yours after you found her at a human auction. Did you really think I wouldn't investigate her?"

I bite my tongue, holding back my retort because it should have been the first thing I did, but I can barely think logically when it comes to Rose. Even though his decision rubs me wrong in a dozen different ways, I know he means well and is just looking out for the family.

I thumb through the few documents inside. It's the standard items; a credit check, criminal report, her education records, and her employment history. Nothing alarming jumps out at me as I skim the details. She graduated with a degree in creative writing from the University of London before moving to Italy, where she owns a house outside of Venice. Several medical reports of visits to an OB-GYN clinic in Italy are included, along with Liam's birth certificate dated a little over six weeks ago. My eye twitches at the empty space listed for father. A mistake I'll need to correct immediately.

I move on to the family records and frown at the lack of information. Her parents died in a car accident when she was young. She spent the years afterward living with a family friend before going off to university. No siblings or extended family to speak of. She's completely on her own.

On paper, Rose Bennett is a lovely twenty-four-year-old girl from England...with no familial ties to a Mafia family.

Now I understand why the mood is so depressing in this damn house.

I close the report, toss it back on the desk, and sit back. "This changes nothing for me."

"It changes everything," Dad argues, knowing exactly where my mind is.

"The boy is mine, Dad. I know he is." I soften my tone, hoping it will soothe some of the anger in the room and talk sense into my old man. "He has my eyes."

Surprise flashes across his face at the news. He leans forward and rubs his temples like he has a growing headache. "A paternity test will still need to be done."

I resist the urge to roll my eyes. "It's unnecessary. But fine."

"So what now?" Dominic asks in the silence that follows.

"There's the marriage law to consider," his father answers.

"What about it? It just states the leader of the High Table needs to be married and produce an heir within three years—"

"With a member of another Mafia family," Raphael reminds our cousin of the small detail often overlooked because it's never been a concern.

According to the law, if I were to marry Rose, I could never reclaim my position because she's not related to a Mafia family. But I can't bring myself to care. I can't turn my back on Rose and our son because of a stupid law that only the leader of the High Table has to follow.

"Are you serious? You're really going to enforce that stupid part of the law?" Dominic asks.

"It's there to protect the ruling family, son," Uncle Leo says.

Dominic snorts, throwing his father a heated look. "That law is there to keep control over bloodlines in a world that no longer needs it."

"Enough." Dad slams his fist on the desk, breaking the growing tension between his brother and nephew.

I meet my dad's gaze with steely eyes. "Dominic is right, Dad. The law is outdated. I understand the reasoning behind it, I do, but surely you must understand the desire to marry for love."

"I loved your birth mother."

"I know you did." I pause. "But not in the same way that you love Alice."

"The High Table will not move against the marriage law—"

"You are the High Table—" I try to cut in but clamp my mouth shut when he raises his hand.

Sometimes it's easy to forget that Dad is the don of the Italian Mafia and sits at the head of the High Table. The name

DiAngelo is feared by many near and far. In his early years as Don, before he took over as the leader of the High Table, Dad was ruthless and cunning in growing his various family businesses. He earned the loyalty of his men by ensuring they were well-paid and looked after. Dad single-handedly organized Miami's criminal underworld, taking control and making our enemies think twice before crossing Dad or risk facing his brutality.

"If you insist on pursuing a relationship with this girl, then I have no objections." I wait for the "but" to come. "But." There it is. "If you do, you do so understanding that Raphael will remain the named heir of the family and future High Table leader. So what will it be, Michael?"

I glance at my brother, who sits silently fuming beside me. He's not mad *at* me. No. He's mad *for* me. It guts me that my happiness will come at the cost of his...again. Because if I pursue a relationship with Rose, then that's it for Raphael. He will remain heir, a title he doesn't want. But if I allow Dad to arrange an appropriate marriage for me now that I've been proven fertile, I could be the heir once more, but then I would lose Rose and any chance of a life with her and Liam.

It feels like I'm being forced to choose between Rose and Raphael. Between my new family and my current family. Because that's exactly what it is. Keep Rose and lose my birthright, trapping Raphael in a life he never considered. Or secure my birthright and lose Rose, but free Raphael.

Choices and consequences.

Damn them both.

Rose offers me everything I've ever dreamed of and wanted but never imagined I'd ever find.

Breaking a heart is inevitable, regardless of which choice I make. But I have to make one.

I open my mouth to answer when Raphael cuts me off. "I'll remain the heir. Allow Michael the chance to be happy with Rose and their son."

"Raphael," I breathe out his name. "Brother, please."

My twin turns to me, and my breath catches in my chest. In his eyes, I see the sacrifice he's willingly making for me and the acceptance of his decision. "It'll be okay, Michael. I want to do this. I need to do this."

Foolishly, I somehow thought Rose and Liam would release him from his obligation, had hoped that Dad would understand, but hearing him accept his fate out loud is like a punch to the gut.

Dad nods. "I'm pleased to hear this. The High Table has been growing restless with you in this position without a secured marriage contract. I've been discussing options with your uncle, and I believe we have found a suitable match for you."

"Who?" Raphael asks, his tone even like he's discussing business, which, in a way, he is.

"The youngest daughter of the Cosa Nostra family in Sicily. She's beautiful, kind, smart, well accomplished, and—"

"How old is she?" Raphael interrupts.

Dad presses his lips into a thin line, and it's clear we won't like the answer. "She just celebrated her eighteenth birthday last month."

Raphael stands so quickly the motion causes his chair to topple backward and crash to the floor. "Are you joking? I'm not marrying a child."

"She is not a child. She is a grown woman who—"

"She's younger than Gabriella. How would you feel about marrying her off to a man fifteen years her senior?"

"We're not discussing Gabriella's marriage prospects right

now," Dad replies, avoiding the question with ease. "This is not up for debate, Raphael. We need this right now. The High Table is too unstable as it is with the fucking Triads running us ragged."

"There has to be someone else. Someone older, at the very least."

"You will like her, son. I've met her over video conference, and she's a very nice young woman. She grew up in the life and is well aware of what being your wife entails. She'll give you children to carry on the family name," Dad explains. "And who knows? You may even grow to love her."

And now I understand why Mom was playing the piano when we arrived. She knew this conversation was coming. Family duty is a sore subject in this house. When my marriage to Sophia was in the planning stages, I remember quite vividly the dozens of arguments they shared. Some ended up with Dad sleeping on the couch for days on end. Mom hates everything to do with the idea of an arranged marriage, and now here we are again, coming full circle, ready to repeat the process with Raphael.

I watch my brother's face, a mirror image of my own, and see the range of emotion there. Anger, heartache, pain, and sadness crash together into a blend of emotional turmoil, and I know he's on the verge of erupting.

"Her name is Emilia. She will arrive before Christmas, and you will be married on New Year's Eve."

24

MICHAEL

Asmall hand slapping my face pulls me from my sleep. I open my eyes to find the same shade staring back at me with a curious expression.

Somehow, Liam ended up in bed with Rose and me last night. She must have brought him back with her after getting up in the middle of the night to feed him. While I understand her need to keep him close, I sure hope it doesn't become a thing because there's nothing like a baby in bed to kill the mood in the morning.

Liam reaches out again and latches onto my nose this time. The boy has a strong grip for an infant, leaving me impressed and highly proud.

He's so innocent and pure. His whole life stretches out before him. What kind of man will he grow up to be? Will he want to be in the life? Or keep to the edge? Will he prefer the logic of science, the freedom of art, or the strategy of battle? Whatever he chooses, though, I will give him the chance to discover his passion for himself and be there to support him when he does. It's funny how my priorities have shifted now that I'm no longer the heir of the family and able to give Liam that freedom that I wasn't awarded by my father.

Liam shifts his hand and sets his palm on my cheek, probably more by accident then intention. We lock eyes, and for a moment, I see the future I want for him, for us all. A future that includes more mornings like this with a few more siblings. The image sends an electric shock of protective emotion directly to my heart.

"Good morning." I keep my voice low to avoid waking Rose up.

Reaching out, I trace down his soft, chubby cheek, completely in awe of the little human we created. His hair is a lighter shade with hints of red, and his eyes are the same light hazel as mine. I may be biased, but he's a cute baby who will grow into a handsome man. A heartbreaker in the making. If our son is this perfect, I'm concerned about what our daughter could look like. I'll probably end up killing more than a dozen men just for looking at her wrong. Better yet, maybe I should just lock her up until she's thirty. Actually, I like that idea better.

My phone buzzes on the nightstand. I reach behind me and glance at the screen.

Dominic: My dad's got the doctor in the white room. Your dad wants you here.

Me: Excellent. I'll be there in an hour. Don't have too much fun without me.

Dominic: I can't make that promise. I didn't get much sleep last night and haven't had my coffee yet.

Rolling my eyes, I put my phone down and turn back to Liam and his mom. Rose peacefully sleeps with her mouth popped open in the cutest little O. The morning sunlight highlights her bruises, but I'm pleased they're starting to heal around the edges already. Although some bruises can't be seen, I hope those hidden ones continue to heal and fade until they're nothing more than a memory.

It'll be hard to leave her, but a skeleton in my closet needs burying before we can move forward. I need to know why the doctor lied last year. Not once, not twice, but three times. Once, I could write off as an accident, a false negative. But three times? No. Something more is happening here, and I intend to understand whatever it is.

Behind Liam, Rose takes a deep breath and blinks awake. Her eyes lock on Liam's wiggling body right away.

"Good morning."

She glances up and smiles at me softly. Rubbing the sleep from her eyes, she says, "Morning. Sorry if Liam woke you up. He was a little fussy last night, probably because of the time apart, and wouldn't let me put him down. So I brought him in here with every intention of taking him back when he fell asleep...but I guess I fell asleep instead."

I lean forward and kiss Liam's forehead, savoring the unique smell only a baby has. "That's alright. It was a nice surprise to wake up to you both. How did you sleep? Any nightmares?"

"Not a single one." Rose smiles.

"Are you saying I'm to thank?" I cock a brow and chuckle when she rolls her eyes at my question. After the marathon session of orgasms I gave her last night, she better have slept soundly.

"Don't let it go to your head."

"Too late."

She playfully shoves my shoulder before cuddling up around Liam. The baby makes a gurgling sound that I assume means he's happy, but I don't speak baby so it's hard to tell.

"What time is it?" she asks.

"A little before nine. There's an issue at work that needs my attention." Her responding frown is adorable. She chews on her bottom lip, and I move my thumb to pop the offending part from her teeth. The only one of us biting her lips will be me. "What is it?"

"The last time you left me alone..." She looks away, but I understand. The last time she was left with her thoughts, she suffered a panic attack. She's afraid it'll happen again without me here.

"Do you think Gabriella could come over?"

Now, that's a wonderful idea. "I'll ask her. I'm sure she would love to." I reach for my phone before I stop when a better idea strikes me. "Wait. I have an idea. I'll be right back." I carefully jump off the bed and hurry out of the room.

Swinging into my office, I grab what I need from my desk and return to find that she has moved to the edge of the bed with Liam nestled between pillows behind her. Rubbing the remnants of sleep from her eyes, she watches curiously as I hand her the rectangular black box.

"What is this?"

I eye the box in her hand and chuckle. "It's called a phone, sweetheart."

Rose shoots me a look that says it's too early for my humor. "I know that. I meant, what is this for?"

I take the box from her and open it to reveal a brand-new black iPhone. Turning it on, I program my number first and then the others. Handing it back, she carefully accepts it, almost like she's afraid it might break in her hand.

"I don't know if you want to call Anette or anyone else, but at least now you can if there is." She has no family to speak of, but she must have friends outside of Anette who are worried about her.

"Thank you," she whispers, her glassy eyes meeting mine with genuine gratitude, and my chest swells with pride at the sight.

Rose sets the phone on the bed, then throws herself into my arms. I barely catch her in time before her lips are on mine. My thoughts momentarily stumble, but I quickly regain my focus and take control of the kiss by pulling her closer.

"I'll call Gabriella and have her come over," she breathes.

***

DOMINIC IS HELPING his dad tie the good doctor to the chair in the center of the room when I walk in with Enzo behind me. With his arms crossed over his broad chest, my dad stands in front, intimidating the frightened man with his hard gaze.

"Where's Raphael?" I ask when I notice my twin's absence.

"Your brother decided to drink an entire bottle of Macallan last night," Dad answers, his eyes never leaving our guest.

Couldn't say I blame my brother for overindulging. Last night wasn't pleasant for any of us and if my brother wants to drown his sorrows, then who am I to stop him? Especially considering my decision to pursue a relationship with Rose is partly to blame for his sorrow. Well. Me and the crying doctor in front of us.

"Dr. Murphy," I greet the fertility specialist pleasantly, like this is just another conversation over a Sunday dinner.

The middle-aged man looks at me in confusion before recognition fills his face. "Mr.-Mr. DiAngelo?"

I slip my jacket off, revealing the pair of guns haltered at my chest, and enjoy the way his face pales. Handing Dominic my jacket, I roll up my sleeves and walk forward. Sliding my hands in my pockets, I gaze down at the man who delivered the worst news of my life. And certainly lied about it.

"Do you know why you're here?" I ask, starting out easy.

He shakes his head quickly. "No. What–what's happening?"

"Do you remember the last time you saw me?" I press on.

He shakes his head again, beads of sweat forming on his forehead. He's lying to me, and I hate being lied to.

"November of last year. Jog your memory yet?" I wait and watch as the doctor visibly swallows hard before I continue, "No? Well, allow me to remind you."

I jerk my head at Enzo. He steps forward and grabs the back of Dr. Murphy's head, his hand fisting what's left of the doctor's hair tight enough that it forces his face up. "My wife and I visited you because we were trying to have a child and weren't having any luck. So you ran some tests and assured me all would be fine. Only it wasn't. Was it?"

It's a rhetorical question that I don't need him to answer.

"Now, listen to me very carefully, Dr. Murphy, and try to answer truthfully, because your life depends on it." He stares up at me in terror, tears filling his dull brown eyes. Finally. Now we're getting somewhere. "Why did you tell me I was sterile when I am not?"

Enzo pushes the doctor's head forward with enough force to cause whiplash, then steps back, resting a hand on his gun's handle, ready to take aim and fire if necessary.

The doctor sobs, his voice frantic and uneven as he stammers, "I...I don't–I don't know. I—"

"Doctor." I reach for the knife I keep sheathed beside one of my guns. The light catches the silver blade, and the doctor thrashes against his bindings in panic at the sight. "Remember what I said. The truth. Please."

"I swear I didn't mean to do it," he cries out in a rush. "I was told...I was told to lie and say you were sterile."

I glance at my dad over my shoulder and watch his jaw lock

as he raises his chin at the news. He meets my eyes and nods for me to continue.

"Who told you to fake the results?"

The doctor shakes his head slowly from side to side as if spilling the truth is painful. "I can't. I can't say. He'll...he'll kill me if I do."

"He's not the one you should be worried about right now," I warn him. "Tell me who told you to lie."

The man wails, snot falling from his nostrils to mix with the tears streaming down his cheeks. He's a disgusting mess. "I never saw his face. We only ever talked over the phone, and his voice was always disguised."

"What did you get in exchange for lying?"

The doctor whimpers. "Five hundred thousand."

Dominic snorts behind me, and I have to agree with my cousin. Five hundred grand to ruin my life? That's all it took?

"Why?"

"I have kids in college, Mr. DiAngelo, a wife who overindulges, and a house mortgage I can't afford." He's trying to justify his actions to seek sympathy. It won't work. "I needed the money. I'm sorry...I'm so sorry."

I frown at the broken man in front of me and turn around. I find my dad's furious gaze when he asks, "What do you think?"

"I don't think he's lying. Not now anyway," I say with absolute certainty. I've seen my fair share of interrogations, most done by my hand, others by observation, and I know when a man is broken, and Dr. Murphy is broken. A man tormented by a terrible decision he knew deep down would come back to haunt him in ways he never imagined.

Uncle Leo approaches and hands Dad a piece of paper. He skims the paper, his face turning red in anger before he hands it to me. It's the actual result. The un-doctored one. I should know. I studied the vile piece of paper long enough that I can recite every word verbatim.

"We found this among his things when we grabbed the doctor from his office. The dumb fuck had it in his desk drawer," Leo explains. "We have his computer and phone, and we'll do what we can to trace the caller and payments."

I hand the damning proof back to my uncle. "Anything else?"

"He speaks the truth. He's got kids in college, a gold-digging wife, and a heavy house mortgage."

"What now?" Enzo asks, coming to stand next to me.

Dad sets his hand on my shoulder and squeezes. I agree. The doctor knows too much now. He consciously decided to betray our family, which can never be forgiven. Believing we would never find out the truth was his fatal mistake. The damage he did, all in the name of greed and selfishness, is too terrible and far from over.

Judge, jury, and executioner. It's the way of our world. The punishment must fit the crime.

I turn around and stand behind the doctor. He's sobbing words of apology between mumbled prayers to his God. I hope he finds comfort in them and that God forgives him when he stands in front of heaven's gates. Because I won't.

I pull my gun from its holster, point it at the back of the doctor's head, and squeeze the trigger.

25

ROSE

Michael waits for me downstairs, and my mood lifts when I round the corner and he sees me. Over the past couple of days, I've quickly learned that little surprises Michael. Except for two things, that is. One of those is me and the other is being entertained by his aunt on the living room floor.

"Mommy looks beautiful. Doesn't she, sweet boy?" Gabriella asks Liam, pulling my eyes from the smoldering look Michael is giving me. I smile at my handsome boy and reach for him.

Holding him in my arms, I rock him back and forth, eating up his happy giggles. I was so worried that the time apart from me would negatively affect him, but I seem to be the only one suffering in that department. And that's fine by me. I would rather be the one haunted by those memories. Liam deserves to grow up happy and loved and safe. The last item is the most crucial and also the most concerning at the moment, with a blaring alarm that my time is running short.

"I think Mommy looks breathtaking," Michael comments, coming up behind me. He rests one hand on my waist and the other cups Liam's hat-covered head. Then he dips his face down to my neck and kisses the bare space my styled updo left exposed. "This outfit is begging to be ripped off you."

I hum low in my throat and lean back into his warmth. "Maybe I just might let you."

"There's no maybe about it, Rose." Michael nips my earlobe, and I swallow back a moan. Barely. "I hope you're not too attached to that outfit because it will be in pieces before the night's end."

"It better not be," Gabriella voices, her tone laced with annoyance. "I picked out that outfit."

"That you paid for with my money," Michael reminds his sister before he presses one last kiss to my neck and pulls away.

Gabriella surprised me with a mountain of clothes, and I've spent the past hour trying on different pieces for my date with Michael tonight. I eventually decided on a navy-and-white cami jumpsuit with a high-thigh split, cinched around the waist with a cute little buckle belt.

Michael's sister crosses her arms over her chest and frowns at her brother, knowing full well that he got her there. "Fine. Just be more gentle with the clothing. Please."

Michael smirks. "I'll try, but I can't promise."

"Whatever." She rolls her eyes and then steps forward to collect Liam. Gesturing for me to hand him over, I do after one last cuddle and kiss. "Get out of here, you two. Liam and I have a night of bonding and shenanigans to start."

Michael gathers our coats. "We won't be far. If you need anything—"

"You'll be down at the private beach, enjoying a night picnic under the stars. Yes, I know. Now go. Please. I'm begging here."

Michael leads me to the elevator, and I turn in time to catch Gabriella helping Liam wave bye just before the elevator doors close. I drop my head and take a deep breath. This is the first time being away from Liam since the kidnapping, and while I know he's safe in the penthouse with Gabriella and Enzo, I'm struggling to accept it.

I feel Michael's comforting presence a moment before he envelops me in a hug from behind. "He's going to be perfectly fine, Rose. I wouldn't let anything happen to him."

That's what worries me. I close my eyes and rest my head back on his solid chest. Michael doesn't know the truth about me and, in turn, Liam. My father is a powerful man with hands in deeper pockets than most dirty politicians. In fact, he probably owns the pockets those politicians play in. It's a silly, idealistic dream to imagine that Michael can stand against the leader of the Miami Irish mob, but I've always wanted to live with my head in the clouds.

And then there's the very real possibility that the truth may scare Michael off completely.

"Rose? If you're not ready for tonight, we can go right back up. We don't have to do this if it's too soon." Michael must sense my unease, but it's not about tonight. It's about everything else.

I turn in his arms and run my hands up his hard abs, over his muscular chest, and across his broad shoulders. He tenses beneath my touch, but not from fear or disgust. Pleasure has blown his pupils wide and swallowed the light. I meet his dark eyes and smile, knowing I'm playing with fire yet again and love the thrill of burning.

Michael's lips tease up into a knowing smirk. "Careful, sweetheart."

"What if I don't want to be?" I know I'm pushing his limits, but for the past few days, I've lived in sweats and oversized shirts, feeling every bit as unattractive as I thought. Even though it never seemed to bother Michael, it did me. But the way he's looking at me now brings back memories of the night we first met, making me feel like the same girl all over again.

Michael leans forward and whispers, "You should know that I don't put out on the first date."

"Oh, good." I press up on my toes and meet his playful challenge. "Then you should know that I don't put out until the third date." And then I kiss his cheek and smile like a cat that has just gotten into the cream.

"We'll see. You'll find that I can be very persuasive."

"And I can be very stubborn."

Michael nods as if processing that bit of information for later before he suddenly grabs my wrist and pulls me straight into his chest. Gripping the nape of my neck with one hand, he brings the other to settle on my cheek. His mouth is on mine before I can say a word. His tongue dives in and tangles with mine. It's a sensual dance to which only we know the steps. When I push forward for more, he chuckles against my lips and pulls back, leaving me breathless and incredibly frustrated.

"Still feeling stubborn?" He runs a finger down my cheek, tracing the curve of my neck and brushing over my pounding pulse before stopping right above my neckline.

I swallow, unable to form a single word. The smirk on his face tells me he knows my threat holds no weight.

Michael leads us out of the elevator, through a private, empty hallway, and out the door at the end. He takes my hand the moment we step outside and guides me through a richly lit stone path surrounded by thick shrubbery and flowers. The air is alive with the sounds of insects and the distant roar of crashing waves. As we get closer to our destination, the smell of salt water grows stronger, reminding me of better days when Mom was alive and the afternoons we spent along the shore.

We round a corner, and the stone path empties onto the

white sands of the beach. The moon is full and high in the black night sky, illuminating the water below like a dark mirror. Fairy lights twinkle along a veranda's high exposed wood beams, creating a magical atmosphere for the space below where a picnic mat has been stretched out, complete with throw pillows and blankets.

Michael helps lower me to the blanket and sits next to me. He reaches for a wicker basket, pulls out a red rose, and hands it to me. I make a show of smelling the delicate fragrance before setting it down beside me with a murmured thank you.

I watch as Michael dishes dinner and fills two glasses with red wine. "Rose, we did things completely backward. And I don't know about you, but I want to give whatever this is between us a chance. I'd like to see if there is something more between us than just raising our son together. I want us to be a family."

The truth slips free before rationality can stop my mouth. "I'd like that too."

"Good. Then I have a serious question."

I eye him warily, not sure if he's about to pull a ring out. "Okay."

"What is your favorite color?"

What?

"My favorite color?" Did I hear him correctly?

"Yes. Mine is red if that helps break the ice."

"I guess then mine is purple, but not the deep color, the lighter shade of purple like lilac."

"Favorite food?"

"Anything. Everything. But I really love anything hazelnut, like Nutella, coffee creamer, dessert, and so on."

"I'll put it all on the grocery list, then."

It's nice to talk about things I don't need to lie about. Yes.

I'm hiding who my family really is, but not who I really am. Because to me, Rose Bennett and Rose O'Leary are the same person. We share the same interests and passions, the same favorite things. My past doesn't define me as a person. Liam is my future, and I want Michael there with us. If it's possible when the truth is finally revealed.

"Can I ask another serious question?"

I nod because all we've been doing is talking about our favorite things. None of which I'd define as serious. "Do you want to know what my favorite movie is now? It's *Beauty and the Beast* if so."

Michael drowns the rest of his wine, and when he takes my glass from me, I know he means it. "Why did you leave that night at the club? Why didn't you stay for me?"

I had been expecting this question for a while now. "Honestly? I got scared. I wanted the memory of our time together to remain perfect and was worried that I...that I wouldn't live up to your expectations. That you would regret what we did, and I—"

Michael cups my face between his hands and quiets my words with a crushing kiss. I'm breathless when he pulls away, momentarily forgetting what we had been talking about to begin with. "I don't regret a single moment of our night together. It's all I think about. You are all I can think about. I have no expectations for you to live up to because you are perfect the way you are."

I press forward and kiss him lightly on the lips. "I'm sorry I left."

"Just promise me you won't leave again," he whispers.

I shiver, but not because of his hot breath brushing against my mouth. But because he's asking for something I don't know if I can give. I'm so tired of all the lies, and to avoid making up one more, I ask, "Can we take a walk on the beach?"

"I'd love to."

We slip out of our shoes to enjoy the warm sand beneath our bare feet. The breeze coming off the water is cool enough that I wrap myself around his arm to seek the warmth he provides. Like a beacon of light, the moon illuminates the beach, and the rhythmic crashing of the waves offers a soothing soundtrack for the night. We kiss the edge of the tide as we walk, and a sense of calm fills me with each wave that washes over my feet.

He stops and turns toward me, doing it so abruptly that he takes me by surprise. Swallowing hard, he leans forward to rest his forehead on mine.

"Where have you been all my life?" he whispers, barely audible above the roaring ocean beside us.

"Waiting for you."

ROSE

At my answer, he inhales sharply before his mouth falls on mine in a frenzy of sweet passion. His fingers slide into my mass of silky auburn hair and grip my face tightly. He nips at my bottom lip, and I moan into his mouth before his tongue dives back in. Michael's hand slides down to grab the zipper of my dress and tugs slowly.

I pull away. "Wait. We're on the beach, outside."

"And?" He tries to kiss me, but I stay back.

"Someone might see us."

"Okay." He tries again and frowns when I deny him once more. "Rose, I reserved this private beach for the night because I wanted it to be just the two of us. No one else is here but you and me."

It's crazy. An insane idea. But something in his voice sounds so sure, so confident, that my resolve falters.

"Tell me yes, Rose," he begs against my mouth.

"Yes," I breathe out with no hesitation because I'm so completely lost to him.

Michael bends down, places one arm behind my knees and slips the other around my waist before he picks me up in one sweeping movement.

"I want you, Michael. Please, don't make me wait." I plead, trying to appease the throbbing ache growing in my pussy.

"Patience, *rossa*." He chuckles as he walks us back to the picnic area.

Setting me down on the blanket, he rises and slowly strips for me. I want to touch him, help him undress, but I'm too caught up in his show to move. My eyes follow each article of clothing he removes and eat up every inch of smooth bronze skin he reveals. His chiseled abs, his defined chest and shoulders, his muscled arms...every inch of him is hard and perfect. He drops his pants, pulling his briefs with them. My eyes trace that delicious V of his hips that points to the most impressive part of Michael. His cock juts out, long and thick, flushed a dark red, and already leaking pre-cum. I lick my lips at the sight and slowly raise my eyes to find him staring down at me with a hunger I can't explain.

"I've been waiting for this for so long, Rose." His voice is so deep, so primal that I moan just hearing him. He falls to his knees and leans over me, his face thrown in shadows.

I reach up and kiss him softly. "We have all night."

He growls against my mouth and dives upon my neck. He bites and sucks the sensitive skin over and over until I'm certain I'll be covered in fresh marks. Something I know will please him to see. Something I want to see too. For some reason, I want others to see the evidence of our passion and desire for one another. Just like the first night we met.

Michael helps me shed the jumper, and I watch the black of his pupils overtake the gorgeous amber. Pregnancy did a number on my body, and I move to cover myself, embarrassment overtaking the need.

Michael pulls my arms away and pushes them into the blanket covering the sand above my head. "Don't you dare hide a single inch of your body from me. Seeing the evidence of when you carried my child is the most erotic sight to me."

My body flushes at his words, and I nod silently, letting him know I understand. He releases my arms, but I keep them there as he skirts down my naked sides until he reaches for my panties. I lift my hips up to help him guide them down my legs. He holds them up to his face and inhales deeply, his dark eyes meeting mine.

"You smell divine, Rose. I need a taste. I want to drown in it."

Holy fuck.

He travels kisses down my chest, showing each breast attention before he continues down my body. His breath is hot against my bare pussy, and I cry out when he parts my lips with his fingers and runs his tongue straight up my slit. His lips latch onto my clit, pulling the tender bundle of nerves free as he sucks. He feasts on my pussy like he's a prisoner and I'm his last meal before execution.

I run my fingers through his hair, holding him between my legs as I grind shamelessly against his face. My orgasm gathers at the base of my spine, the warmth spreading forward as it consumes my entire being.

Michael slides up my body as he rolls my clit with his thumb and scissors my pussy with two fingers. "Come for me, sweetheart."

I explode at his command. The orgasm crashes over me, setting each nerve ending on fire. My body locks up, and I see stars.

"I could watch you fall apart all day, every day. It's my favorite thing to see," he whispers before claiming my mouth in another soft yet dominating kiss as I come down from my high. I taste myself on his tongue, and it's like a powerful aphrodisiac.

He grabs his cock throbbing against my inner thigh and runs the head up and down my soaking slit.

"Ready to play with fire again?" he asks me, capturing my eyes with his.

"Always."

Michael leans in for a kiss as he positions himself at my entrance and slowly pushes in, fitting so perfectly as if we were made for each other. The pressure is intense and stings moments before my body begins to give way, remembering how it feels to have a man inside.

"Are you okay?" he asks me, worry clear on his face that this is too much, too fast. I grab his face and bring our mouths together in a brutal kiss.

"If you don't fuck me right now, Michael," I warn him, "I won't let you touch me again for weeks."

At my words, I watch the beast break free. He tightens his hold, curling his body over mine until not a single inch of space remains between us. The air fills with the sound of our moans and grunts, and the sound of our bodies slapping together with the natural sounds of the ocean behind us. It's carnal and hot, and I can barely hang on.

"You're so fucking tight, Rose," Michael groans in my ear, peppering my neck with kisses and love bites. "I can feel every time your pussy clenches down on my cock. She was thirsty for me, wasn't she? Thirsty for my cock?"

"Yes." I've missed this...missed him. "Oh God."

"He's not here, darling." Michael chuckles, and I feel the vibration from his chest resonate through mine. "Your pussy is mine. Not God's."

"Yes. It's yours." I run my hands up and down his back, my nails digging in hard enough to leave thin scratches. Michael hisses at the pain and drives into me deeper and harder. "And your cock is mine. Only mine."

Michael's breaths are choppy in my ear, and I know he's close. I'm not far behind him. I hold Michael tight as the dam breaks and the pleasure crashes down around me, pulling me under the water until I'm weightless in its depths.

Michael seizes and groans low and deep into my neck as he releases his hot seed in me. We probably should have used protection, but I couldn't give a single fuck right now. Let me get pregnant again for all I care.

Michael buries his face in my neck, his hot breath caressing the thin layer of sweat that coats my skin, sending a shiver down my spine. "I think I'm falling for you, Rose."

My chest tightens painfully at his confession. He's falling for half of a woman. Will he still feel this way when he knows the truth? I hope he does. I need him to because I'm not falling for Michael.

I've already fallen.

27

ROSE

"What do you think about this one?" Gabriella points at another glider.

I shake my head, giving the colored trim a single look over. "No."

Gabriella sighs and turns toward me. "Rose, this is the fifth glider you've said no to, and you're not even looking at them. Where is your head at?"

I can't very well tell her the truth. That I'm deeply terrified someone will recognize me here in this baby boutique store, putting Michael and his family in immediate danger.

"I'm sorry." I study one of the glider chair tags, reading over the safety stats and details. From the corner of my eye, I wait for Gabriella to move on, but she stands there staring at me instead. I drop the plastic tag and meet her eyes. "What?"

"Did I push you to come out with me too soon?"

Yes. "No. You were right. I need to choose some things in person for Liam. I'm just distracted." I smile at her before dropping her gaze, focusing back on the glider.

"Okay. But if you're worried about anything, don't be. Enzo's with us, and he won't let anything happen."

I peer over my shoulder at our "bodyguard." When Michael couldn't join us, he sent Enzo instead, and I think the Viking wannabe regrets his eagerness to come now. Watching

Enzo attempt to navigate the cramped aisles distracts me from glancing endlessly at the front door every time the bell chimes.

"This one looks nice." I point at a light gray and white glider with a matching ottoman. Sitting down, I glide back and forth a handful of times, just to appease Gabriella more than anything. "I like it."

Enzo grabs a huge box from under the display with ease, like it weighs lighter than a feather, and takes it to the front counter for us.

"How are things going with my brother?" Gabriella asks, following me as I grab more diapers and wipes.

"It's been going really well."

We've been in our own little world since our date a few days ago and can hardly keep our hands off each other. So much so that we were recovering earlier this morning from the most delectable wake-up call when Gabriella surprised us by arriving unannounced. Michael quickly threw on some sweat-pants, then politely advised his sister to text before coming over next time. As soon as Gabriella saw me in panties and an inside-out shirt with sex-tousled hair, she understood.

As if she's remembering the same thing, Gabriella tosses me a knowing smirk over her shoulder. "Mm-hmm. How about the family dinner tomorrow?"

I pause, my hand hovering over a cute winter coat. Michael only told me about this dinner last night, after ensuring I was so utterly spent from several orgasms that my only answer could be yes. To say my anxiety is high would be an understate-ment. It's so high that bitch has jumped into the next galaxy.

"I'm nervous."

Gabriella snorts. "I'd be surprised if you weren't. But don't worry, our parents are great. They're going to love you."

"I hope so," I admit. I'm still uneasy about meeting them.

The more people I lie to, the more people at risk from my father.

"And they're not going to judge you about what happened, okay?" Gabriella adds, reminding me that Michael told them about my ordeal in Italy - being kidnapped, sold, and eventually rescued by him. Lies aside, what happened to me doesn't say much for first impressions.

"Are you sure you're okay watching Liam? Again?" I ask, changing the subject.

Gabriella nods. "Of course. I love that little boy. And if babysitting gets me out of family dinner, I love him even more."

I toss a baby blanket at her face, which she catches with a laugh. "Traitor."

We're checking out when I notice a woman watching us from the corner of an aisle. I don't recognize her, but that doesn't mean she doesn't know me. As soon as she notices me looking at her, she quickly turns away, focusing on Enzo instead. To be fair, he does stand out in the cute shop, his tattoos a startling contrast to the pastel colors of the boutique. The lady was probably just shocked by his appearance and was wondering what the hell he was doing in the store in the first place. Still, my heart races and stays like that until she finally leaves the store. Only after she disappears do I take a deep breath, struggling to calm my pounding heart and thoughts.

We're loading our haul in the back of the Rover, when a gust of wind sends a chill down my spine and makes the nearby palm trees rustle ominously. I can't help but feel like I'm being watched, causing the little hairs on the back of my neck to stand on end at the eerie feeling. I don't see anyone, but it leaves me wondering if it's a sign of something far worse to come.

MICHAEL'S FAMILY'S home is impressive and a little overwhelming. I know Michael's wealthy, given his state-of-the-art penthouse, but it never occurred to me that his parents are too. The security cameras and the number of guards patrolling the property catch my attention as we drive through the iron gates. My gaze cuts to Michael, wondering if there is something more about him I missed. Like illegal more.

Michael mistakes my apprehension for fright and squeezes my hand. "Dad likes his privacy, and the excess security comes with that. Don't be scared, though. You won't even notice they're here."

I most definitely will, but I appreciate his effort. "Will you give me a tour later?"

"I'd love to." Michael kisses our clasped hands as he parks the car on the circular driveway. "Ready?"

I nod even though my stomach is in knots. Michael climbs out and comes around to open my door. He offers me his hand to help me. What a gentleman. Until he pinches my ass.

I squeal and playfully smack his chest, but before I can move out of his reach; he pulls me toward him and kisses me thoroughly until the knots ease.

Looking up at the house, I immediately feel a sense of warmth emanating from its white stucco walls and red-tiled roof. Taking my hand, Michael leads me through an adorable outdoor garden and into the house. The atmosphere of the house immediately envelops me like a warm blanket. From somewhere in the house, soft classical music plays. The foyer is airy and bright, with the fading sunlight streaming in from the second-story windows and reflecting off the dazzling chandelier hanging high above. A grand staircase stretches upstairs to a landing that reminds me of a balcony with an open column-designed banister.

"This way." As I follow Michael through the house, the enticing aroma of lasagna grows stronger, filling the air and making my stomach growl.

Michael glances at me. "Hungry?"

"Starving," I toss back.

"Michael, is that you?" a woman's voice calls from an open doorway ahead.

"Yes." Michael squeezes my hand before he drops his voice and asks me, "Are you ready?"

"Hurry up, son. We're hungry." The familiar deep timbre sets off a warning bell in my mind.

Like I've heard it before.

My steps falter, and Michael senses my hesitation. "Everything okay? You have nothing to fear. They're going to love you."

I want to tell him that isn't what's bothering me, but I don't even know how to put into words what is. My mind screams at me to turn around and leave because nothing good awaits me around that corner.

"If you're not ready, though, just say the word." Michael searches my face for an answer I know he won't find because I don't have one for him.

The warm caress of his fingers on my cheek helps clear my mind, and I shake my head. "No. I want to meet them."

Surely, I'm just being paranoid. The encounter with the strange woman yesterday has me shaken up, making every unknown voice sound like danger.

Michael drops a kiss on my lips and then smiles before we continue down the hall. Each step feels heavy, like I'm being walked to my execution.

I tell myself that I'm being silly. That I'm letting my past control my present. But a little voice returns with a vengeance and screams at me to turn and run.

I should have listened.

We round the corner and step into the dining room. My eyes immediately land on the man sitting at the head of the table, an older carbon copy of Michael and his brother. I freeze and ignore Michael's attempts to pull me forward because my world is crashing down all around me. All the sense of safety and love I have found since Michael rescued me is shattered.

Because the man sitting at the head of the table is Dante DiAngelo, don of the Italian Mafia, leader of the High Table... and my godfather.

28

ROSE

Does God hate me? Did I do something to offend the universe? Because it sure feels like fate has paired up with karma to play with my life like I'm their new shiny toy.

Because Michael is not Michael Gallo. He's Michael DiAngelo.

The eldest son of the most powerful crime family in Miami, next in line for the seat as head of the High Table...and my son's father.

If the situation wasn't so fucked up, it'd be comical.

I was a child the last time I saw Dante and his wife, Alice. My mother's funeral, to be exact. Before then, Mom never allowed me to attend any High Table functions. She claimed I was too young. So I never met Michael. And even if I had, I'm ten years younger than him. He wouldn't have given a gangly preteen the time of day.

How could I have been so blind?

The signs were there, and I foolishly ignored each one instead of questioning them. I could blame my overwhelming concern about reuniting with Liam for my blindness, but that's no excuse.

From our mysterious first meeting, to my rescue, to his lavish penthouse and guarded family home, every moment replays in my mind like an endless movie reel. Only this time, I watch with clear eyes and not through rose-tinted glasses, seeing the truth in each moment.

I've heard the rumors, the stories about the DiAngelo brothers and how together they're known as the twin Grim Reapers, with Michael being the more deadly of the two. I'm certain now that my buyer didn't die in the car accident. There's no way Michael would have left him alive for long after what he did to me.

How could I have fallen for the one man in all the world I should have stayed clear from?

How could I have been so stupid?

My entire world has flipped on its axis, and all I can think about is getting out of here because I'm scared of what Dante might do if he discovers who I am. He has an alliance with my father. Even if he doesn't want to hand me over, he could be forced to. And then there's Liam to consider. They could take him from me, use him as a bribe or as a way to control me.

All I can think about is running. So I do just that. I turn and run.

———

"ROSE?"

I tense at the sound of Michael's voice.

"Rose? Are you okay?"

When he sits beside me, it takes everything to keep my eyes focused on the setting sun. I forgot the DiAngelo estate sits on an island. It's the worst place to be when all you want to do is run. I'm literally surrounded by water.

Michael reaches out a hand to brush my hair back, and I flinch. It's not intentional or because of who he really is, but it's more about taking my shot nerves by surprise.

"Rose, please." The plea is evident in his tone, which only makes this next part harder. "Tell me what's wrong. You promised me you wouldn't run again, and you did just that."

I take a deep, shaky breath and finally look at him. The sunlight catches on the gold flakes in his bright eyes, making him appear angelic when he's anything but that.

"I'm so sorry, Michael. I had no idea who you were," I whisper.

"What do you mean?"

It's now or never. "My name isn't Rose Bennett. It's Rosaleen O'Leary. My father is Patrick O'Leary, the Irish mob boss of Miami."

Michael's eyes fix on me, but it's as if he's looking right through me, lost in his own thoughts. My chest tightens with uncertainty. Did he hear me correctly? Do I need to repeat it? Or maybe I should say something else? Do something? Maybe he needs some space. Maybe we both do.

I shift backward, planning on at least climbing to my feet, when Michael reaches out and takes hold of my left hand with an ironclad grip that's borderline painful. Raising my eyes to his face, I find his has drastically changed. Despite the sun's setting rays, his eyes are in shadows, staring at me with no hint of recognition or compassion. It's like he's shut down. And I know now that I'm no longer looking at my Michael, but the man he portrays to the world.

The Grim Reaper.

Cold. Cruel. Ruthless. Unforgiving.

"Are you a spy?" He pronounces each word slowly like he needs to make sure I hear him clearly.

"No. Not at all."

"Did you know who I was when we met at the club?"

"No. The night we met was my first night back in Miami after ten years away."

"And when I rescued you? Did you know who I was then?"

"No."

"Then how long have you known who I am?"

This feels an awful lot like an interrogation, and I almost wish he would just yell at me. Any kind of emotional reaction will be better than this robot-like attitude.

"Tonight. I swear." There. A small flicker of emotion crosses his face, like my answer surprises him. "When we walked into the dining room, and I saw your father. I recognized him as my godfather, but I don't think he remembers me." It has been over ten years since he last saw me, and back then, I was a gangly preteen with braces and wild red hair.

"Why did you run then? How long were you planning to keep this quiet?"

I don't like how he's looking at me now. I want the other Michael back, not this dark mirror image. When I try to free my hand, he tightens his hold. If he doesn't let go soon, he's going to break something.

"You're hurting me, Michael," I tell him in a small voice.

"You know, I have to give your father credit. It really is a genius plan. Hide you away just long enough until everyone forgets what you look like. Then he brings you home and has you seduce me. Did your father know about the fake result? Was the plan always to get pregnant then?"

"Michael, please stop."

"Were you going to just run away and go home to Daddy as soon as you could? Leave my family to be torn apart by your deceit? Forcing me into breaking the fucking marriage contract between you and Igor? Is anything you said true? Were you even kidnapped? Is Liam even mine? You were so quick to fuck me that night, after all. Makes me wonder how many other men you have spread—"

That's enough. I slap him hard across the face. His head snaps to the side, his eyes blown wide in shock and surprise. The urge to end the poison spilling from his mouth is so intense that I didn't bother stopping myself.

"You bastard," I snap and glare at him through blurry, furious eyes. "I didn't lie to you that night, and I'm not lying to you now. I hate my dad more than you could ever imagine. He was the asshole who sold me when he found me with a baby in Italy. I was sullied goods now, but I could still fetch him a fraction of what Igor was paying at least." Tears fall down my face, but I'm too angry to wipe them away. "You know, I waited out here on this beach, waiting for the moment I'd feel scared of you. Because I should be. You represent everything I hate, everything I ran away from...but it never came. For whatever fucking reason, I have felt safe, and warm, and loved with you because you have always made me feel like that. From the very start. But this?" I gesture to the space between us, my left hand still held hostage in his iron grip. "This isn't safe, Michael. You're hurting me. And right now? You're just as terrible as my dad."

Michael's eyes fall to our hands, and he flinches as if he suddenly feels the ghost of my slap. He releases my hand, and I quickly pull it away, cradling my throbbing hand to my chest. A few heartbeats later, Michael rises to his feet and takes a staggering step back. I watch him with careful eyes as he pulls out his phone and pops off a text. The sudden change in his behavior is jarring, as if a switch has been flipped, and it leaves me feeling uneasy. Did I get through to him? I know what I said was harsh, but he said and acted much worse than me.

Afterward, he crosses his arms over his chest and turns his

back to me. He stares out over the horizon. A storm cloud is rolling in and the wind has picked up, bringing with it the smell of rain and the sound of distant thunder.

I don't know how long we wait there, but the silence stretches until it's almost suffocating. His rejection stings worse than I thought it would, and I hate that it does. He doesn't get to be the only one hurt or upset here. Never once did the idea cross my mind that Michael has some sort of secret agenda. Not to mention, the bastard told me his last name was Gallo. So if he's going to point fingers, he better point one at himself too. Hell, he better point a whole hand.

"Boss?"

I turn my attention to the walkway and see Enzo stop at the edge where wood meets sand. His eyes dart between Michael's stiff back and my weeping form, cradling a throbbing hand.

Finally, Michael turns around. Fighting the urge to look at him, I focus on a piece of tree bark buried in the sand instead. I refuse to give him the satisfaction of seeing me cry. Right now, he doesn't deserve a single thing from me. Except maybe another slap or two.

"I need you to take Rose back to the penthouse immediately. I'll have the doctor meet you to examine her hand," he orders before he walks away.

Because I'm apparently a glutton for punishment, I watch him go, wishing he would just look over his shoulder once at me. I don't care if it's with anger or regret because if he just looks at me, it means he still feels something, and anything is better than watching him walk away as if I mean nothing.

With a heavy heart and tears in my eyes, I watch him disappear around the corner and out of sight, never once looking back.

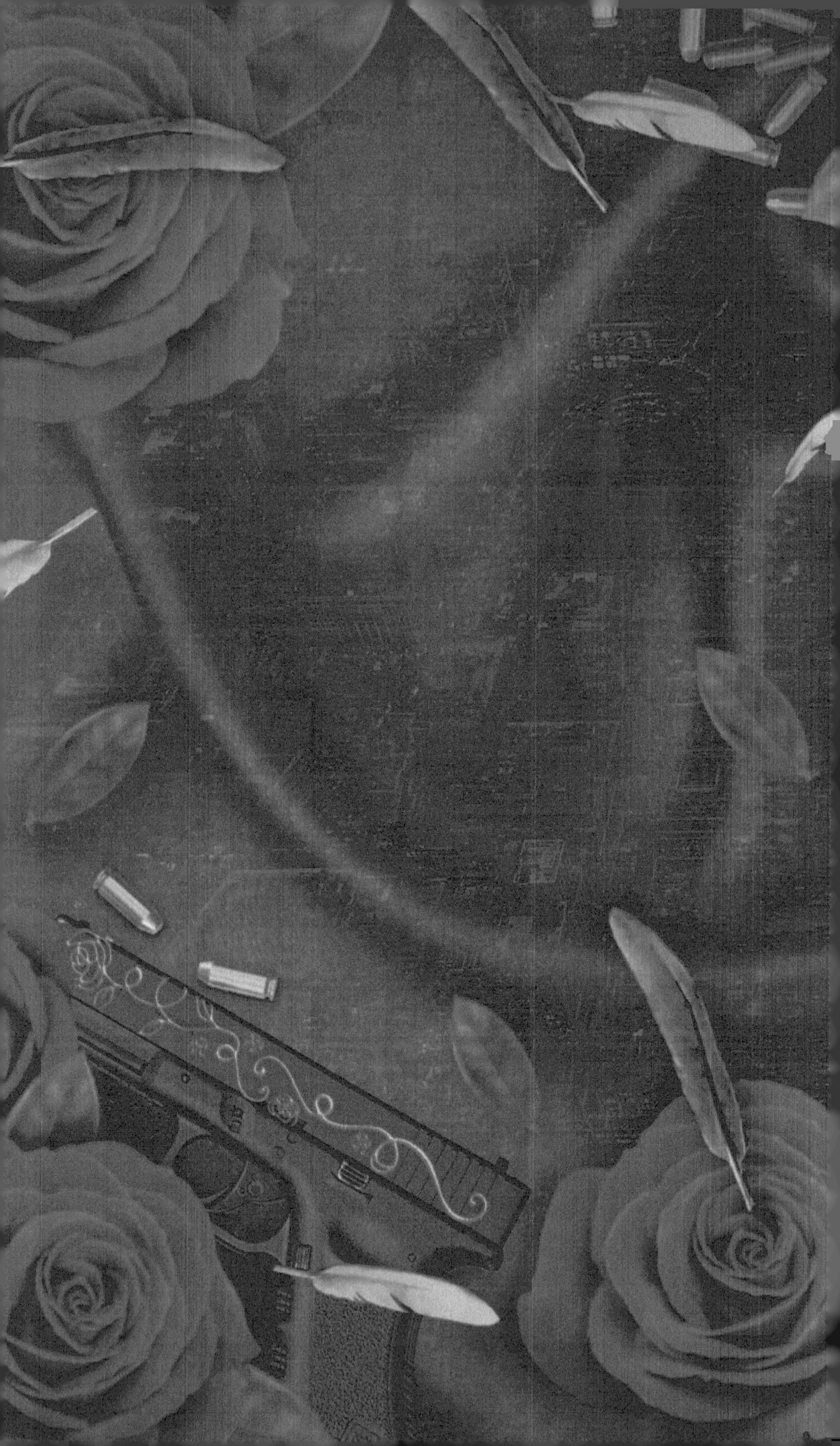

29

MICHAEL

I watch Enzo leave with Rose.

Rose...short for Rosaleen.

Rosaleen O'Leary.

Fuck.

The mysterious Irish mob princess, who vanished from her sister's wedding, is engaged to Igor Mikhailov, and the mother of my son.

FUCK.

I turn away, my anger boiling over, and punch a hole in the drywall. Pain explodes in my hand, the skin of my knuckles splitting and bleeding. I welcome the hurt because it drowns out the chaotic noise of my demons and helps me to focus with a clearer fucking mind.

Her confession took me by surprise, and instead of just listening, I lashed out and accused her of scheming with her father. Then I attacked her character and her virtue, which had been like throwing gasoline on a smoldering fire. Something I'm extremely good at tonight. Honestly, I deserved that slap and more. Rose was right to compare me to her father. Because at that very moment, I was no better than him.

Only when I was stunned into silence did I finally listen, and the more I thought about it, the more it made sense. Rosaleen O'Leary left Miami over ten years ago, and no one has seen her since. We never met before she left...and why would we have? She's ten years younger than me. She was getting her first training bra while I was busy taking them off.

This isn't safe, Michael. You're hurting me.

Rose's words echo over and over in my mind, making me feel worse by the second. As much as I want to chase her and fix this mess before it gets even worse, we both need some space, and I need to talk to my dad. This revelation isn't something that can wait.

I stop in the nearest bathroom and bandage my bleeding hand before leaving in search of my dad. I'm passing a room that hasn't been used since Gabriella was a baby and stop, opening the door to reveal a nursery. The staff keeps the room clean and organized even though it hasn't been used in over two decades. My eyes scan the room before fixing on the crib, and an image clear as day comes to my mind, like I'm seeing it play out right before my very eyes.

Rose stands next to the crib, rocking our newborn daughter as she hums a nursery rhyme. Liam sits at Rose's feet, flipping aimlessly through one of those pop-up children's books. Our little girl is bundled up, wisps of brown hair poking out from underneath the cap she wears. Her eyes slowly close as she drifts away, happy as can be after a bath and a warm bottle. Once asleep, Rose kisses her forehead and lays her in the crib. She watches our daughter with a loving smile before she turns and aims the same smile at me.

I want that moment and every moment after. Suddenly, nothing else matters. Not who her father is or what her last name really is. None of it matters because I've gotten to know Rose as the person behind all of that. She's the woman who somehow captured my dark heart. I need her to be my calm amid my rage, my constant anchor in the chaos when it threatens, and the light that guides me through the turbulence of my life. Knowing the truth about her past doesn't make any difference in how I feel about her.

Because I love her.

My breath catches and my heart skips as the realization washes over me. I fucking love Rosaleen O'Leary.

My phone buzzes in my pocket, and I pull it out to find a text from Enzo.

Enzo: The doctor just left.

Michael: What did he say?

Enzo: Some serious swelling and bruising, but nothing's broken.

Thank God. I'm relieved, but it doesn't excuse my behavior since I'm the one who hurt her.

Enzo: Except maybe her heart. What the fuck did you do? And yes, I'm assuming it was your stupid ass that did something.

Michael: Has she said anything?

Enzo: Not yet. You gonna tell me? Or do I need to come beat it out of ya?

I'm not ready to talk about any of it. Especially not over text.

Michael: You can try.

Enzo: If this shit wasn't so serious, I'd be happy to take you up on that challenge. We both know I'm the better hand-to-hand fighter.

Michael: Because you cheat and bite.

I have the scar on my leg to prove it.

Enzo: You spelled scrappy and smart wrong.

I roll my eyes because while annoying, those traits make him such a valuable asset in a fight.

Michael: Make sure she eats something. She didn't get to eat.

Enzo: You should be here. You need to apologize for whatever you did.

Enzo: No. You need to grovel at this woman's feet and beg for her forgiveness because she and that adorable kid are the best damn things to have ever happened to you.

Irritation grows in my stomach.

Michael: You don't think I know that? I fucked up, and I feel terrible.

Michael: Just take care of her for me. Both of them, please.

Enzo: Come home, Michael. Communication is the foundation for every successful relationship.

Michael: Says the man who has never been in a successful relationship.

Enzo: Ouch. You're extra mean when you're upset, and it hurts.

Enzo: How's that for communication?

Enzo: And by the way, asshole, you also have never been in a successful relationship. Your marriage to the Ice Queen doesn't fucking count as "successful" by any means except for maybe the day you signed those divorce papers.

He's not wrong. Before Sophia, finding a woman or two to bury myself in for the night wasn't difficult. But that's all they were. A means to an end that never went beyond a single night.

Enzo: Michael?

I look down at my phone, my mind narrowing down to one truth. Until Rose, I never gave a woman a second thought. And now she's all I think about.

Michael: I love her. I think I have since the moment I saw her that night in the club.

I didn't mean to type that, but for whatever reason, I want him to know. Maybe somehow Rose will hear it.

Enzo: 😒 I think you should lead with that when you come home.

Michael: I'll be home soon.

DAD IS in his office nursing a scotch. Alone, in the dark. Something he often does on the nights when storms roll in over the bay, enjoying the show as Mother Nature intended. One of my fondest memories as a child included sitting on his knee, watching the storms roll in with him. He would say it's nice to be reminded that as powerful as you may think you are, there are elements far more powerful that cannot be controlled by anyone.

"Father."

"Michael. Come in."

I step in and close the door behind me, knowing this conversation needs to be private. Fixing myself a drink, I take a long sip before sitting on the bay window and facing my dad.

From this angle and dim light, his age shows on his face, and my chest tightens at the sight as the reality of the situation bears down on my shoulders. Dad should be retired by now, enjoying his remaining years relaxing with Alice in the Italian countryside.

"Is Rose feeling better? I saw Enzo leave with her."

Before running after Rose, I made up the excuse that she wasn't feeling well. I drown the rest of my drink, savoring the burn down my throat. "She's fine, but I need to talk to you about Rose."

"What is it, son?" He sounds exhausted, and I hate how I'm about to add to it.

"Rose is not who she says she is."

"What?" Dad rests his glass on his knee and gives me his full attention. "Who is she ?"

There's no turning back now.

"Her name is Rosaleen O'Leary. She's Patrick O'Leary's missing daughter."

Dad stares at me, his mouth falling slightly open from the shock. "Holy shit," he finally breathes out. "Are you serious?"

"Yes."

"When did you find this out?"

"Tonight. She recognized you. That's why she took off. You're her—"

"Godfather," Dad finishes. "Yes. I am. How did I not recognize her?"

I shrug, unable to give him that answer.

Dad finishes his drink in one giant swallow before he blows out a heavy sigh. "I suppose it has been a while since I saw her last. God, it has to have been over ten years now. If I remember correctly, it was at her mother's funeral, and the poor girl was so quiet and sad. Not at all like the girl she was before the accident."

I stand and hold my hand out for his glass, offering to refill it. He hands it over, and I cross the room to the bar cart. Pouring a fresh scotch, I continue revealing more secrets. "She said it was her father who sold her into the sex trafficking ring."

"What?" Dad swings around. "Patrick sold his youngest daughter?"

I nod. "Her dad found her in Italy and claimed she was sullied goods now, so he sold her."

Dad places his hands on his desk, leans forward, and hangs his head. "Yes. From what I know of the contract, Igor was paying a hefty amount to marry a virgin." He looks up, seizing me with a glare. "Did you take care of that, too?"

I chuckle humorlessly and shake my head, handing him his refilled glass. "No. Not that I'm aware of, at least."

Dad snorts into his glass before taking a sip. "I wonder if Patrick knew that."

"Doubt it."

"Where did Enzo take her?"

I glance away. "She's back at the penthouse."

"That's good." Dad nods, and I know the wheels are turning in his head already. "Who else knows?"

"Just you and me, as far as I know. I don't know if she's told anyone else."

Dad nods again. "Let's keep it that way for now. We need to be careful here."

He's referring to the fact that Rose is technically still in a marriage contract with Igor, and I broke that when I slept with her and got her pregnant. "I didn't know who she was when I met her, Dad."

"I believe you. Even you're not that stupid."

"Thanks?"

He either doesn't hear me or doesn't care because he just barrels on. "Have Rose and Liam stay at the penthouse for now. I'll need to talk to Patrick and—"

My phone rings, interrupting Dad. I pull it out of my pants and say, "It's Gabriella. She's with Rose and Liam."

"Answer it."

I swipe the green button. "Gabriella? What—"

"Michael!" she shouts, her voice choked with sobs. I'm immediately on edge, and Dad mirrors my anxiety having heard his youngest through the speaker. "They-they shot Enzo. And they took them!"

"What? Who?"

"The Irish. They shot Enzo and took Rose and Liam."

30

ROSE

"The good news is that nothing appears broken." Dr. Gonzalez prods my hand, and for the second time tonight, I'm tempted to slap another asshole in the face. "Place an ice pack on it in twenty-minute intervals. Twenty on, twenty off until the swelling goes down. You can take some ibuprofen for the pain, and if it gets worse, I'd like for you to come in and get an X-ray done." He packs up his supplies before he smiles at me comfortingly. "Be careful, my dear, and try not to slam your hand in any more doors."

I nod to show I understand, feeling guilty for lying to him, but when he asked me how I injured my hand, it was the first thing that came to mind.

"Thanks, Doc," Enzo says before he walks the older man to the elevator.

"Here you go." Gabriella hands me a baggie of ice wrapped in a kitchen towel, two orange ibuprofen pills, and a glass of water.

I swallow the pills and carefully set the ice on top of my hand. "Thank you."

Gabriella watches me from the corner of my eye. She's curious. They both are. But I'm still reeling from Michael's reaction, and honestly, I'm scared they'll react the same way if I tell them the truth. And if they do...then Liam and I really will be alone.

My eyes focus on the sleeping infant tucked inside a cocoon of blankets on the couch. He's too young to roll over, but I don't want to take any chances. Besides, if he were to get hurt, Michael will no doubt blame that on me too.

Enzo returns with a glass in one hand and a bottle of scotch in the other. He wiggles them suggestively out to me. "Care for something a little stronger?"

Logically, I should say no because being inebriated is the last thing I need right now, especially after taking pain meds, but my heart and mind are too heavy and tired to say no. The idea of feeling numb is extremely tempting.

Balancing the ice bag on top of my hand, I beckon with the other. "Please."

Enzo fills one glass generously and hands it to me. The alcohol is a delicious and smooth burn down my throat. But to be honest, he could hand me home-brewed moonshine, made in the back country swamps, and I'd still drink it because I'm desperate for that numbing sensation.

"Anything else we can get you?" Gabriella asks.

A time machine, so I can go back in time and fix this shit show at the start. "No. I'm just tired."

Gabriella nods and hands me a blanket from the other side of the couch. I accept it with a polite smile and curl up next to Liam.

Enzo sits on the coffee table in front of me, sets the bottle of scotch down, and leans forward, balancing his elbows on his knees. Looking directly at me, he grows serious. I eye him warily and pull the blanket tighter around me. Just like with Michael, I've also heard the rumors about the blond reincarnated Viking at his side who is as crazy as crazy can be. But he's been nothing but kind to me from the start. It's strange. Perception vs. reality.

"Rose, I understand you may not be ready to tell us why you and Michael were fighting, but I need to know…was he the one who hurt your hand?"

Yes.

No.

"It's complicated."

Enzo's gaze drops to my ice-wrapped hand. "That's complicated?"

I swallow a large sip and look away.

"I knew you didn't slam it in a fucking door," Enzo growls. "I'll kick his ass."

My face snaps up. "No. Please, don't. It wasn't his fault."

"Don't make excuses for him. There is no reason to hurt the mother of his child," Enzo fires back, already reaching for his phone on the table.

Gabriella reaches out and snatches Enzo's phone, making the man growl his annoyance. She tosses him a narrowed-eyed look before turning to me. "I think you need to tell us what happened." Gabriella sets her other hand on my knee and squeezes gently in silent encouragement.

"I guess I should start by telling you that my name is not Rose Bennett. My name is…Rosaleen O'Leary."

And then I tell them everything I wanted to tell Michael, and they listen. Without judgment, without criticism, they listen to every detail, the good, the bad, the ugly, the beautiful, and everything in between.

Explaining the insanity of the past ten months is a roller coaster of emotions, but it's also incredibly freeing. Telling them is like having an immense weight lifted from my shoulders. Now that someone else knows the truth in its entirety, I feel lighter somehow.

"And that's it. You two know everything." I set my empty

glass down and rub at my face. The alcohol sits warm in my belly, and exhaustion sets in. I feel like I could sleep for a week. Maybe I should. Maybe it'll give Michael the time he needs. The time we both need.

"How much of this did you tell Michael?" Enzo's the first to ask a question.

"None of it. He wouldn't listen even if I had. He just accused me of being a spy for my dad and planning this whole thing. That I got pregnant on purpose and set him up." I sigh. "None of that is true, by the way. My dad can rot in hell for all I care, and I never expected or intended to get pregnant either. I didn't even know who he was that night. Mom kept me from all the High Table functions, so I never met him. Besides, he's ten years older than me. What twenty-two-year-old is going to care about a twelve-year-old?"

"You've met me," Gabriella reveals softly.

I look directly at her. "What?"

"It was at your mom's wake. I remember catching sight of this little red-haired girl around my age running up the stairs. I followed you and found you locked in a bathroom. You were crying and thought I was your dad when I knocked on the door. You yelled at me to go away, and it was the cutest thing ever. So much spitfire and sass on such a sad day. It reminded me a bit of myself, and I wanted to be your friend instantly. I even told my mom about you, but then you went away. I'm sorry. I totally forgot about that until now."

The memory is faint and tickles my brain as I struggle to remember. I spent most of that day in an angry, depressed haze and did my best to block the days after it in the years that followed. "I'm sorry too. I don't remember it either, but it does sound like me."

"Don't be sorry. You were grieving." Gabriella's logic is so simple and pure.

I study them both, looking for some kind of anger but find none. Still, I have to ask. "Are you two mad at me?"

"Why would we be mad at you?" Enzo asks incredulously. "You didn't know who we were, so it's not like you lied on purpose. And I actually find it admirable that you were trying to protect us from your father. Not that Patrick O'Leary scares me, by the way."

"I'm not mad either. I think it's all very romantic the way you and Michael have fallen in love without all the pressures of the family dynamics." Gabriella sounds wistful, like she's talking from experience.

"We're not in love," I argue rather pathetically, ignoring how the admission stabs somewhere deep in my chest. Like I don't want it to be true even as I say it.

Gabriella snorts and rolls her eyes. "Okay."

"Michael will come around," Enzo assures me.

I'm not so sure. "I don't know. I compared him to my father and said he was just as bad as him."

"Do you still feel that way?" Enzo asks curiously.

Reliving the memories with Gabriella and Enzo reminds me that there is good in Michael despite his behavior on the beach. One negative moment doesn't define a person, especially when so many positive moments prove otherwise. I'm not the kind of person to judge someone on that. I don't have the right to, given my choices.

"No."

"Then don't worry." Enzo speaks like it's that simple and even shrugs a single shoulder for good measure.

"How can I not worry?"

"Because of this." He holds his phone out to me so I can read a series of texts between him and Michael that started when we first got back to the penthouse.

My eyes blur as I read the texts several times over. He loves me. Even after everything, he loves me. And I love him.

Overwhelmed by a sudden realization, I collapse into Gabriella's embrace as emotions crash over my battered body and soul. The tears return, and I do nothing to stop them. Because I'm not sad. I'm not scared. I'm loved. I'm free.

And I know then that whatever consequences might come from this choice to love Michael, we would survive it. Together.

LIAM WIGGLES BENEATH MY HAND, pulling me from my sleep. The familiar smell of a dirty diaper greets my nose, and I sit up with a grimace. The living room is dark except for the muted light and sound coming from Enzo's phone. He notices me and sets his phone down.

"Everything okay?" Enzo asks, his voice quiet to avoid waking Gabriella, who's fast asleep on the other end of the couch.

"Liam just needs a diaper change."

Liam tells me a story in a rush of babbles as I change his diaper. The familiar sound of the elevator doors opening echoes down the hall. My heart lifts at the idea that Michael's home, only to be shattered by the sound of shouting followed by a ringing gunshot.

"Where is she?"

I freeze as my father's voice drifts down the hallway. A

dozen questions race through my mind, each one as terrifying as the man responsible for raising them. How the hell did he find me? How did he get into the penthouse? What about Gabriella and Enzo? There was a gunshot. Are they okay?

"Who?" Enzo asks. He sounds a little too casual and cheeky, but alive.

"Don't play dumb with me, boy," my dad snaps, his anger pushing through his tone. "My worthless daughter."

"Oh, her? She's not here."

"She's with Michael." Gabriella's voice is like steel and sends relief through me, knowing she's okay, too.

"See, now I know you're lying. I know for a fact she's here," Dad seethes. "One more chance."

"You've made a big mistake," Gabriella warns my dad with the fire the DiAngelos are known for fueling her threat. "My father—"

"Your father will be dead by the end of the night or under such a tight leash, he'll wish he were dead. Now answer the fucking question. Where is Rosaleen?"

They both stay silent, and my stomach sinks because my father is just crazy enough to do something cruel. The bang of a second gunshot cracks through the air, and I jump at the same time that Gabriella screams.

I glance back at Liam resting in his crib. He's a little fussy, but the pacifier in his mouth is keeping him quiet. For now. My feet are moving before I can second-guess my decision. I can't allow Gabriella and Enzo to pay for my secrets, and I'll do anything to keep Liam safe.

"Tell me!" Dad shouts. "Or the next one goes through his fucking head."

"Stop!" I cry as I walk into the main living space. The sight before me guts me. Gabriella is cradling Enzo's limp and bleeding body in her arms. She looks up at me in panicked grief, and I rush over. Enzo's blood soaks my pants when I kneel beside them, but I don't care. I place two fingers on Enzo's neck, searching for a pulse. It's faint, but it's there and steady.

"Well, well, well," Dad drawls. "There she is."

31

MICHAEL

I burst through the hospital doors and shout, "Gabriella!"

"Michael?"

My eyes immediately zero in on my little sister curled up on a seat in the corner. Climbing to her feet, she runs toward me and crashes into my chest. I hold her tight as she cries hysterically against me, her small frame shaking from her sobs. After a moment, I gently grasp her shoulders and push her back to get a better look at her. Dry blood covers the front of her clothes and cakes her arms and hands. I hate knowing the blood belongs to my best friend, but I'm also relieved that my sister is not hurt.

Dad appears beside me, and when Gabriella sees him, she lets go of me and falls into his arms, seeking the comfort only a father can provide. My heart squeezes painfully at the sight. I may have only known I'm a father for a week now, but the time didn't make the truth any less real. And seeing Gabriella with Dad is a harsh reminder of that.

"Has she said anything more?" Dad directs his question to me, and I shake my head. We only know that Enzo was shot when that bastard Patrick O'Leary broke into my home and that he took Rose and our son with him when he left.

"I can help fill in the details."

I turn toward the voice and lock eyes with a familiar pair of icy blues. "What the fuck are you doing here, Dimitri?"

The stoic Russian gestures toward Gabriella's crying form. "I brought your sister and friend to the hospital."

Confusion washes over me. "What? Why?"

"Because she asked me to."

My eyes flick between my sister and the pale, dark-haired Russian looking at her in a way that's a little more than mere acquaintances. The memory of their encounter at Grace O'Leary's wedding flashes across my mind. Immediately, my temper flares, and I storm over, grabbing the soon-to-be-dead man by the lapels of his jacket. In one swift movement, I shove him hard against the stark white hospital wall. The commotion draws the attention of the emergency room occupants. I have maybe a couple of minutes before the sorry excuse for security guards shows up. "What the hell is going on between you and my sister?"

I can feel the tension building in his body, winding up like a toy, ready to explode, but instead of breaking free, he levels me with his eerie bright blue gaze and says in an irritatingly calm voice, "Let me down, DiAngelo, and I'll explain."

"The fuck I will, Volkov."

"Do you want me to answer you or not?"

"You can answer from where you are just fine."

Suddenly, Gabriella stands beside me, her blood-caked hands digging into my arm that holds the Russian captain to the wall. "Let him go, Michael."

Dimitri glances at Gabriella, and I growl under my breath at his audacity to even put eyes on my sister. "No. I'd rather not."

"Please," Gabriella pleads. "He helped us. He's the only reason Enzo is alive right now."

"Michael." Dad's tone leaves no room for argument. "Let the man speak. We don't have a lot of time."

Begrudgingly, I release the bastard and step back, folding my arms over my chest to keep from strangling the man more than anything else because Dad's right. Every minute that passes is another minute Rose and Liam are forced to spend in Patrick's hands.

"Gabriella and I are—"

"Friends." My sister cuts in, her eyes as sharp as her tone.

Dimitri's lips thin as if he doesn't care much for her answer, and honestly, I don't care much for his reaction.

"Right. We're...friends. She called me when they broke in, and I rushed over when I heard what was happening. But by the time I arrived, Patrick was gone along with Rose and the baby. I took care of the men he left behind and brought Gabriella and Enzo to the hospital."

"I just received word that our guards on patrol tonight were killed, including the Doc. From the looks of it, they tortured him to get the override code to the penthouse elevator. That's how they got in," Dad says, answering my next unspoken question.

I bow my head and take a couple of deep breaths to calm the rage spiraling out of control in my mind. Doc was a good man who loyally served our family for decades. It would take a lot to get the code from him, so I can only imagine the pain he must have been in at the end.

"Enzo's in surgery," Gabriella says, her words pulling me from the red haze that clouds my head. "He lost a lot of blood, but the doctors are confident he'll be okay."

Relief floods my system at the news of my friend, followed by the guilt of his situation. If I had just stopped and listened to Rose, he would never have taken her home. He never would have been at the penthouse. He would be safe and not here on death's door at the hospital.

"There's more," Dimitri continues, his voice annoyingly calm. "Patrick plans on marrying Rose to Igor tonight at midnight at St. Paul's Church."

"And how the hell do you know that?" I demand, my anger surfacing again, driving my body forward. My knife flicks open, and I'm ready to bury it in Dimitri's belly when Gabriella steps between us, holding her arms out like a barrier to protect the bastard from my demon-fueled anger.

"Move."

"No," Gabriella snaps, not frightened by the fire in my eyes or the knife in my hand.

"Why are you protecting him? Because you're fucking friends?" I hiss.

"No, you jackass," Gabriella spits out the words.

I raise my eyes to Dimitri. He has his hand wrapped around Gabriella's wrist, almost like he's ready to pull her away in a heartbeat. "Are the Russians behind this?"

"Unclear," Dimitri answers. "I was with Sergei earlier this evening, and he didn't mention anything about his brother or O'Leary. If he knows something, he didn't share it with me."

His tone slightly changes at the end, and I latch on like a hound would a scent. Someone's upset at the idea of being left out. "Trouble in paradise there, Volkov?"

Ice-blue eyes narrow at the insinuation. I wait for him to unleash his anger, to strike me, to do anything, but he remains fucking silent. It's incredibly frustrating. One day, I'll break through his icy shell and figure this asshole out.

"So how do you know where they went?" I ask.

"Because Rose's dad bragged about it before they left," Gabriella answers me.

"That bastard is not her dad," I growl. "A dad doesn't sell

his daughter into the human sex trade when she's no longer worth a dime to him."

Gabriella lowers her eyes. She knows.

"She told you?"

My sister nods. "She told us everything tonight. Michael, he was going to kill us if she didn't go with him. She doesn't want to marry Igor. You know that, right?"

The hidden innuendo in my sister's words is not lost on me. Rose really did tell them everything. Including my behavior on the beach and my cruel, naive accusations. Shame washes over me, dousing the flames into submission. "I know."

Dimitri meets my eyes behind Gabriella's shoulder. "Midnight is in less than two hours."

"Michael, we need to move," Dad says, placing his hand on my shoulder and squeezing gently. "Think of Rose and Liam."

He doesn't have to tell me that. They've been the only ones on my mind since barreling back into my life. I snap my knife closed and step back, taking a deep breath to refocus my mind and concentrate on what's next. "Gabriella, stay here for Enzo. I'll send men to guard the hospital." I shift to look around my sister and narrow my eyes at Dimitri. "You should probably stay too. You don't want to be at that church tonight. I may mistake you for the enemy."

"I assure you, I am anything but that."

"That remains to be seen."

We turn to leave the hospital when Dad stops and glances behind his shoulder at Gabriella and Dimitri. "Volkov?" The Russian raises his head expectantly. "Don't think we won't be having a conversation about how exactly you are friends with my daughter."

32

ROSE

"Get out of the car."

Staring daggers at the guard, I don't move from my seat. "Not until I know if Enzo and Gabriella are okay."

"Who?" The man smirks like he's just told a joke.

My face twists into a scowl. "That's not funny."

He shrugs just as my father's booming voice fills the night air. "What is taking so long?"

"She won't get out of the car, sir," the guard calls back over his shoulder.

"Rosaleen, get out of the car this instant, or I will call my men and have Gabriella shot next!"

And he will. Because he's just crazy enough to go through with his threat. But at least I know Gabriella hasn't been hurt...yet.

The guard levels me with a look and a raised brow like he's actually daring me to make any other choice. I shove him to the side as I climb out and glance around the empty street and sidewalk, searching for my son. Some bastard guard ripped him away from me when we left the penthouse, and I don't know where he went. For all I know, he could be halfway out of the city by now or sleeping in the other car idling at the curb, completely unaware of the danger. Either way, he's not in my arms and at my father's mercy.

"I want my son. Where is he?"

"Safe," Dad answers vaguely. "So long as you do what you're told, he will stay that way."

"How do I know you're not lying?"

"Because that baby is more useful to me alive than dead. But if you do not fulfill your end of the bargain, you will never see that boy again. Do you understand me?"

He means marrying Igor Mikhailov. That was the agreement. Leave the penthouse with him, marry that sick old man, and he wouldn't hurt my son or my friends.

"What about Enzo and Gabriella?"

"Maybe if you hurry this along, I might just feel grateful enough to send an ambulance." Dad's phone pings. He checks it and then turns to one of his men. "Igor's arrived. Let's get this show on the road."

Dad has me backed into a corner with no way out, and he knows it. I'm completely defenseless when all I want to do is fight. And I will because I'm not helpless. I'll bide my time, and when the moment's right, when I know my son and friends are safe, I will escape or go down fighting, taking as many of these assholes as I can with me.

WHEN I PICTURED my wedding as a little girl, I always imagined beautiful flowers, billowing fabrics, and a room filled with our closest friends and family. I would walk down the aisle of scattered rose petals toward the love of my life. His face was always a mystery, but I remember his warm presence. The calm that settled over me was like a heavy blanket of comfort. The peace in knowing I was right where I was always meant to be, with the man I was always meant to find.

And for a brief time, I dreamed Michael was that man. Despite all the secrets and the unanswered questions, I still want him to be. I want Michael to be waiting for me at the end of the aisle. Not this piece of shit, perverted man, grinning at me like he's won a prize. Which, I suppose, I am to him. Because for my entire life, that's what I've always been. Something to be bought, to be owned, to be controlled. Until Michael, that is. He's the first to see the real me. To see the girl hiding behind the name. To see the girl trapped in a dark cage, craving to be set free and feel alive again.

"Move," Dad snaps as he shoves me forward.

I stumble a few steps down the worn-out rug and sneer over my shoulder at my father. "Mom would be ashamed of you."

Dad reaches out and grips my hair with his fist, pulling my head back with one hard yank. I can't help but cry out before swallowing the pain down. His eyes are livid, and his teeth clenched as he spits in my face, "You brought this on yourself. I'm practically paying Igor to marry you."

"Then why bother?" I pull free of his hold and twist around to face him. "Marry me to Michael instead. That's what you want, right? A powerful marriage between the High Table families? Who better than a DiAngelo?"

Dad barks out a laugh. "You think I want to be tied to that family? The DiAngelos are a sinking ship; they just don't know it yet. And now with your son in my possession, they'll just sink quicker."

"What the hell do you mean by that?"

"Can we hurry this along, Patrick?" Igor barks down the aisle.

Dad grips my arm tight and practically pulls me down the aisle. He shoves me forward in front of Igor and a clammy-looking, pale priest. It's clear he's as much of a prisoner here as I am. He clears his throat before glancing at the shaky Bible in his hands and reciting, "Dearly beloved, we are gathered here today to—"

"The short version will do, Father." Dad cuts in, gesturing with his free hand not holding me captive before the altar.

The priest clears his throat again, tugging at his collar as he does. "Right. Of course, Mr. O'Leary. Do you, Igor Mikhailov, take Rosaleen O'Leary to be your lawfully wedded wife to have and to hold from this day forward, for better and for worse, till death do you part?"

Igor licks his lips as his dark eyes skirt up and down my body. "I do."

"Yes. Good." The priest turns to me with a sympathetic gaze before he looks away. "And do you, Rosaleen O'Leary, take Igor Mikhailov to be your lawfully wedded husband to have and to hold from this day forward, for better and for worse, till death do you part?"

Dad's grip on my arm tightens to the point I whimper from the pressure. I'm trapped. Even if I say no, it won't make a difference. If anything, my stubbornness will only anger him, and put my son and friends in danger for sure.

"Yes," I hiss. That single word sounds like a guillotine blade slamming down on my neck.

"Excellent. Then, by the power vested in me by the State of Florida and our almighty Lord, I now pronounce you husband and wife. You may kiss your bride."

Igor steps forward, his beefy, sweaty hands reaching out toward me, but just before he reaches me, a loud explosion breaks the silence and all hell breaks loose.

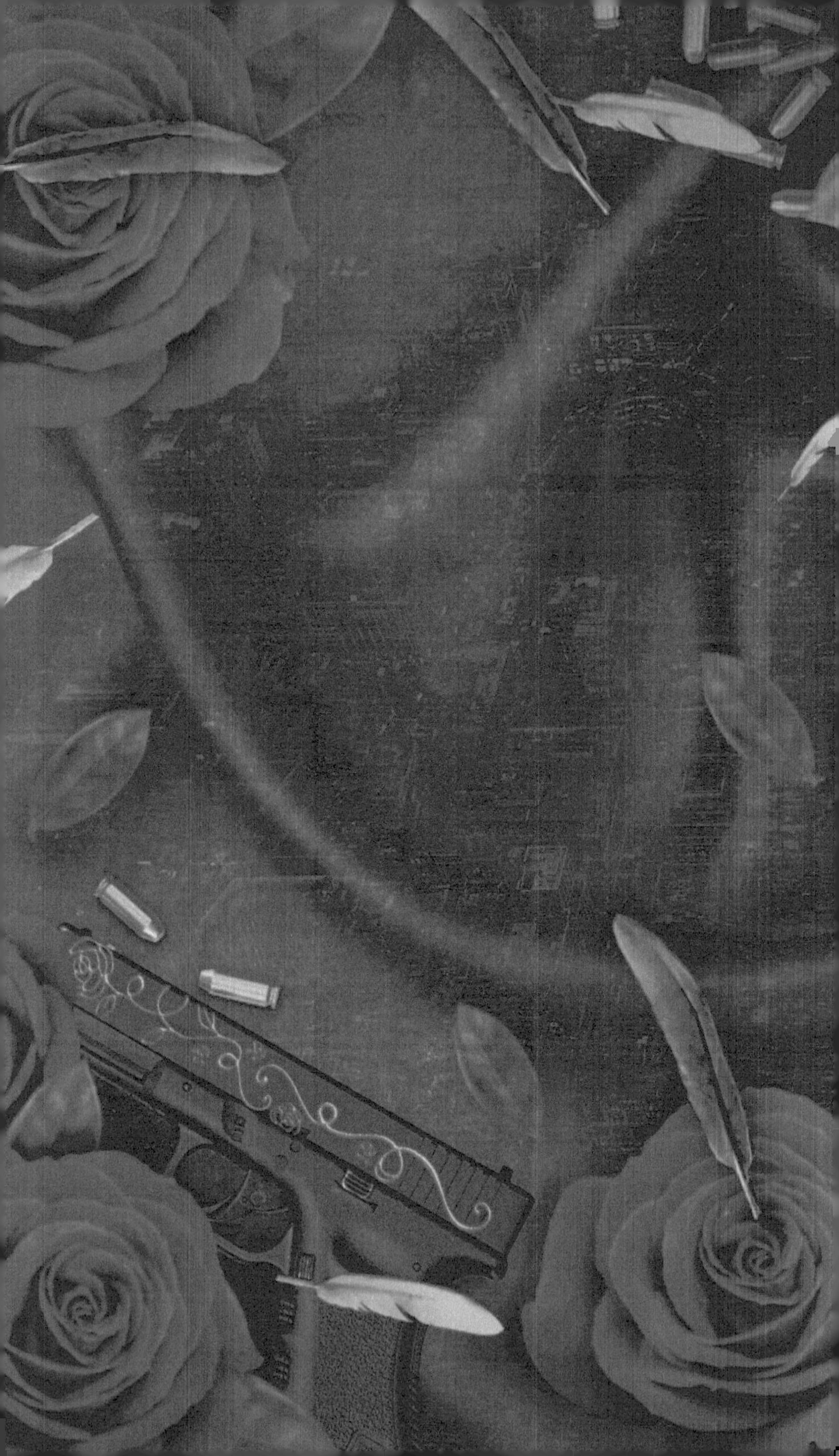

33

MICHAEL

"I still can't believe that your Rose is Rosaleen O'Leary." Dominic whistles low as he straps a string of flash grenades to his chest. "Talk about coincidence."

"Or fate," Raphael adds, slipping two extra clips into his vest and holding out another pair for me.

I store the clips and ignore them both, focusing on the task at hand. Which is to get Rose and Liam back, safe and unharmed, and put Patrick O'Leary six feet under.

Beside me, Dad also gears up while Uncle Leo stands in the doorway with his arms crossed over his barrel chest. He's upset, watching each of us like a hawk. "You need all the help you can get, Dante. I don't understand why you're not taking me."

Dad looks at his brother. "Because I need you here, guarding Alice and the estate in case Patrick has something else up his sleeve."

"You're taking my son with you. I should be there."

"And I'm taking both of mine."

Uncle Leo scowls but says nothing back. Mom appears behind his shoulder, and when he sees her, his scowl deepens into a frown before he walks off in a huff. Dad watches him go with a dark look, but it's fleeting and gone the second he turns to his wife.

She reaches up and cups his face. "You come back to me

tonight. Do you understand me? The devil does not own your soul. I do."

Dad pulls Mom close and proceeds to devour her mouth in a way that leaves Raphael and me exchanging an awkward look. But if Rose and I can look that happy together, with that much passion after decades of marriage, then I too will happily kiss her in front of our kids.

Kids.

The idea makes my heart skip at the thought of that kind of future with Rose. Tonight, we're fighting for more than the present. We're fighting for the future.

As EXPECTED, Patrick and Igor did not come alone.

"I count at least a dozen outside," Dominic announces as he scans the front courtyard of the church through night vision binoculars.

"Body armor?" Raphael asks.

"Standard stuff," Dominic answers. "Nothing we can't handle."

"Patrick is not stupid. He knows we're coming. Which means the element of surprise is not on our side," Dad says. "Still, though, stealth is our best option until we can make our way inside the church. We don't want to risk Patrick harming Rose or Liam."

My eyes remain trained on the church. Somewhere inside is Rose and our son. I can feel them close by as if my body is tuned into theirs. And maybe it is.

"I'll get him out, brother," Raphael assures me with a squeeze on the shoulder.

I nod. Raphael is to find Liam and get him to safety immediately while Dad, Dominic, and I rescue Rose. The strategy sounds simple enough, but nothing ever goes to plan.

I move like a shadow through the night, bringing death to every enemy in sight.

The first slice of my blade into an unsuspecting guard's exposed neck sets the demons in my soul loose, and I let them run free. Each kill feeds them into a frenzy, narrowing my focus to the main objective. The only thing that matters.

Get to Rose.

She is my salvation. I know that now. I'm an addict, and she's my favorite drug. She's the only one who can quiet my demons and soothe my soul. The only one who can bring me peace among the chaos. Like the eye of a hurricane, she's where I find rest when the storm rages on outside.

The last Irish soldier falls to the ground. I stand panting above him as the life drains from his eyes. My hands are wet from the blood of my enemies, and my soul darkens even more from each kill, but it makes no difference. I was doomed long before tonight.

"The door's locked," Dominic whispers when we approach the church doors.

I peer over at Dad, who appears deep in thought. We don't have long, and every second we wait is another second Rose has to spend in this torment.

"Raphael, you take the back entrance and find Liam," Dad orders. "Meanwhile, we'll cause a distraction to draw attention away from you. When you have Liam, you get out, no matter what. Do you understand?"

My brother nods solemnly. He doesn't like the idea of leaving us behind very much, but knowing my brother, he'll send in the cavalry to help us if it comes to that.

"What did you have in mind?" Dominic asks his uncle.

Dad reaches behind his back and pulls out a grenade. Holding it up, he smiles. "Let's ring the doorbell, shall we?"

It's chaos the moment the explosion goes off. Bullets fly through the lingering dust and debris cloud, but we expected that. We wait for a break in the fire and slip inside while the soldiers reload. Now that our presence is known, stealth is no longer needed. We make quick work of the handful of soldiers inside, then I'm standing in the middle of the aisle with a gun in each hand, pointing them at the two men the devil waits to welcome.

Rose stares at me, her beautiful face blotchy and red, and her eyes a cascade of emotions. Terror, relief, and anger all flash across her emerald orbs. She's wearing a simple white dress, which only angers me more. Her bastard father went as far as to even think about a dress for the ceremony.

With a quick scan of the cathedral, I know Liam isn't here in the main space. This means he's either not here at all or in the back, where hopefully Raphael has found him by now.

"Well, if it isn't the DiAngelos." Patrick smirks, his tone even and unimpressed, like he's not scared of the gun pointed at his head. He should be. My trigger finger's feeling a little bit twitchy this evening. "Come to congratulate the happy couple?"

"Let her go, Patrick," Dad orders, coming up beside me.

"Gladly." Patrick releases his grip on Rose's arm and shoves her directly into Igor's embrace. "She's no longer my problem."

Rose cries out when Igor grabs her, his meaty hands all over her body. "I'm looking forward to our wedding night."

I catch on to his meaning, and then all I see is red.

I fire, and a bullet clips Patrick's shoulder. With a curse, he staggers backwards and swiftly retaliates by drawing his gun and firing. I move at the last second but not before a burning sensation explodes from my thigh. I fall to the ground, my breath coming in short hisses between my clenched teeth. I'm already losing a lot of blood. I can feel the slow but steady stream of life flowing out from the wound. The bastard must have nicked an artery. I don't have much time, but I'm determined to finish this. Because if I'm to die tonight, it will not be before Rose and Liam are safe. The devil can wait to collect my soul.

"You fucking bastard!" Patrick shouts, his heavy Irish accent echoing through the cathedral. A second later, I hear Rose cry out and fight through the pain to stand, immediately training my gun on Patrick. He holds Rose in front of him like a shield, his uninjured arm tight around her neck while he struggles to hold his gun in the other to her head. "Surrender now, or I will kill her. I swear I will."

Even with a gun pointed at her head, Rose fights hard against her dad's hold. I'm insanely proud of her and the fire burning inside her, but I also know that it will only take one slip of his finger to end her life.

"This wasn't part of the deal, Patrick," Igor spits, his face flushed red with anger. "She's my wife now. If you kill her, the deal is off."

"What deal is that?" Dad asks, turning his gun on the Russian.

Igor eyes my dad warily. Before he can answer, though, Patrick interrupts. "I want your seat, Dante. I want to be Head of the High Table, and Igor is going to help me get it."

"And how's that exactly? Igor doesn't speak for the

Mikhailovs. Unless you're telling me that Sergei is in on your little scheme too?"

"My brother doesn't know shit," Igor reveals.

"So how is Igor supposed to help you, Patrick?" Dante asks.

It all suddenly clicks in my brain. Marry his daughter to the Russians, the daughter who has a son fathered by the eldest DiAngelo. "Liam."

"That's right." Patrick smirks. "Use that bastard son of yours to force Dante to give up his seat."

"So what? Marrying Rose to Igor was just a conciliation prize or something?" He could use my son with or without Rose married to the pig.

Patrick snorts. "Igor wanted the girl."

"Part of the deal," Igor adds.

"And selling her into the sex trade?" I snap. "Was that part of the deal too?"

Igor narrows his eyes on Patrick. "You did not tell me this."

"It makes no difference now." Patrick waves away the comment like a bothersome fly. "You wanted a virgin wife. She was soiled goods when I found her in Italy. Had I known Michael was the child's father, I wouldn't have been forced to sell her."

"You wouldn't have had to marry her to Igor either," Dad voices. "We could have discussed a wedding between Michael and Rose."

Igor narrows his eyes at our dad but stays silent.

Patrick scoffs. "You wouldn't have given my demands the time of day. I want your seat. Do you not understand that? As if you would give that up without a little...persuasion."

"I'm listening now."

Patrick pauses, seeming to actually consider Dad's offer.

Igor notices and growls. "The hell you thinking, O'Leary? The girl is married to me now."

Patrick tilts his head in the Russian's direction but keeps his eyes trained on my dad. "Not until that license is filed, she isn't. What did you have in mind, Dante?"

"Marry Rose to Michael. Make their son legitimate and heir to both of our families."

"And your seat?"

Dad clenches his jaw; the pain on his face is clear as day, and I know he's going to say yes.

But before Dad can surrender, Igor rushes forward, the steel blade of a knife in his hand catching in the fluorescent lights.

Time slows as a few things happen all at once.

Rose lets out a scream as Igor plunges the knife into her side. I shout and push forward, desperate to get to her side. Blood instantly stains her white dress. Patrick subconsciously releases her, and she falls to the ground, her hands clenching her side where blood seeps through her fingers like water through paper.

Patrick swings his gun at Igor and fires. The Russian stumbles backward, knocking into a table holding dozens of ceremonial candles. It crashes to the ground, and flames ignite the lace curtains, climbing high to the ceiling in mere seconds.

A second gunshot rings through the air, and a body falls near me, but I can't tell who it is. I focus solely on Rose, who lies only a few feet before me. I reach out for her. She sees me and tries to reach me too. Tears cascade in twin currents down her face as she mouths my name.

The edges of my vision are fading to black.

God, I really do love her. I want the chance to tell her that every day, if given the chance, but there's no redemption for me. No miracle to bestow on me. My wicked life has come to a close. My dark choices have always led to this point. I'm just happy that, for a moment, I was blessed to know an angel and be loved by her.

"*Mia piccola rosa*," I whisper on an exhale. *I love you, Rose.*

My soul feels at peace. Even my demons fall silent as a heaviness I've never known falls over me, stealing my breath. Darkness swoops in, dragging me down, and I know no more.

34

ROSE

"He looks like Aiden did as a baby," Grace admires her nephew in her arms.

I peer at Liam's sleeping face and smile, seeing the resemblance to our little brother. "I was thinking the same thing the other day. Until he opens his eyes, that is."

That's when he looks like his dad.

My sister's hand lands on my knee. She squeezes it gently. "Michael's going to be okay."

It's been one week since the wedding and fire at the church. One week since Michael was placed in a medically induced coma from complications of the gunshot wound my father gave him. But he's alive. Something everyone reminds me of several times a day because it's something I need to hear often.

I lean back in the hospital chair and swallow back the painful groan when my stitches pull on my side. If Grace sees it, she'll go tattle to Gabriella, who will then tell my doctor, and I refuse to spend a day longer than necessary in this bed.

Turns out, Igor did more damage than a simple stab wound. He nicked one of my ovaries, and while the doctors fought hard to save it, they were forced to remove it. I'm coming to terms with the knowledge that I only have one ovary now. It will make conceiving in the future more difficult but not impossible.

If I still have a future with Michael, that is.

Grace eyes me, noticing my stiff movement. "Rose—"

I frown. "Don't even think about telling Gabriella. Today is the first day I've been able to walk on my own to the damn bathroom."

Grace holds her hands up in surrender. "Fine. Just don't come crying to me when you pop a stitch from pushing yourself too hard, too fast."

"I won't because...I won't," I reply childishly, earning an eye roll from my big sister. I reach out, take her hand, and squeeze it. "I'm so glad you're here."

Grace is about to reply, but her phone buzzes, interrupting her. She pulls it out and checks the screen. The sight of her pink cheeks and sparkling eyes makes me smile. I know who it is before she even says his name. "It's Connor. His plane lands in a couple of hours. I'm planning to surprise him with his favorite dinner at home."

When I woke up, Grace was there by my bedside. It seems Gabriella called her following the incident, and since then, she's only gone home to sleep and shower. But now Connor's returning after being in Ireland for the past few days, meeting with our uncle James.

Because our father is dead.

It still doesn't feel real. For ten long years, that man controlled my life. It may have been from a distance, but his presence was always there like a constant noose tightening around my neck. When something that powerful, that large disappears... the relief isn't sudden. It comes in stages, moments when you still feel like they're there, ready to punish and control you, and when they don't...that's when the relief comes. That's when you start to believe they're gone. That's when you know you're free.

The memory of his death is a blur and something I'm in no hurry to remember. Connor explained that after Patrick shot Igor, which set the church on fire, he turned his gun on me. That's when Connor arrived, and he didn't hesitate to save my life.

Don't get me wrong. I'm thankful he did, but Connor is... no, was, Dad's right-hand man. Killing him was an act of betrayal, a treachery of the worst kind.

Our uncle James had every right to call for Connor's death, but...he didn't. Instead, Connor received our uncle's support as Miami's next Irish mob boss. It seems Mom's and Aiden's death broke Dad more than we realized, and he slipped further into a state of madness that blinded him from protecting and properly running the business. Connor saw it, the men saw it, even his brother saw it from across the ocean. It wasn't much of a stretch for Connor to take control. The men already respected him, so it was an easy transition.

When I spoke with my uncle yesterday, he apologized profusely for my father's actions. He told me about everything he did to protect me from my dad's poisonous reach growing up. How it wasn't until he spoke to Evie that he learned Dad lied to him about my disappearance and that I wasn't on some extended vacation like he was told.

I always knew Dad and his brother weren't close. That he agreed to take me in after Mom's death out of respect for her but not his brother. Needless to say, there was no love lost between the two brothers before the shooting occurred. The straw that broke the camel's back was when Connor told him what happened at the church. Had Dad survived that night, I doubt he would have lived for long.

Connor and I spoke at length before he left, too. Turns out, he was the one who sent Michael the anonymous email instructing him to save me. When he heard a rumor from the men that Michael was going crazy over a mysterious woman he met in January, a woman he'd been unable to find since, he remembered picking me up outside of Sinners and put it all together. I understand now why his hands were tied that night in Italy. It was impossible for him to save me at that moment without endangering himself, me, and Grace. So he did the next best thing and sent Michael the anonymous email about the auction's location.

I owe Connor more than I can ever imagine, and for that, I forgave him for his part in Italy. But despite having that, Connor still asked how he could make it up to me, and I simply said to love my sister with everything he had for the rest of their lives.

Speaking of forgiveness, I tried apologizing to Grace, but she refused to hear a single word. She admitted that she was hurt at first, but then she revealed how she had secretly contacted Evie a few months after I disappeared. My best friend never told me Grace did, and believe me, I gave Evie an earful when I finally got the chance to talk to her. But she helped give my sister peace of mind, so I couldn't stay mad at her for too long.

And speaking of Evie, after hearing what happened, she hasn't left either. A certain six-foot-four reincarnated Viking god developed quite the crush on my hot British friend, and from what I've seen, Evie feels the same, but she won't admit it. Not anytime soon. She likes to be chased, and Enzo is more than happy to oblige, even if it means doing so in a wheelchair while he recovers from his wounds.

Grace's phone buzzes again, and this time, her face goes as red as a tomato. It doesn't take a genius to know that this newlywed couple is still enjoying the honeymoon phase.

Jealousy rears its ugly green head, and I do my best to shove the greedy bitch back down because it's unwanted and unnecessary. Of course, I'm happy for my sister, but...I miss Michael.

I miss hearing his voice. I miss the way he holds me close, craving that physical connection. Whether it's a warm touch on my knee or a tender hand caressing through my hair. I miss the comforting scent of sandalwood and warmth that used to surround him, instead of this sterile hospital smell that now lingers on him. I miss the intensity of his eyes, like twin suns ablaze, setting my heart on fire with a burning passion.

He should be awake by now, and I'm tired of hearing the dozens of reasons he isn't.

The door opens, and Michael's nurses walk in, wheeling his bed behind them. My eyes go immediately to his prone figure, my hope further crushed when I find him still lying unconscious in bed.

Gabriella arrives as they're connecting Michael back up to his dozens of machines. She's typing away on her phone, smiling as she enters the room. I hear the familiar whooshing sound of a text being sent before she sees us. She looks almost embarrassed like she's been caught red-handed.

She clears her throat and asks, "Hey. How are you feeling?"

"Better than yesterday." It's the truth.

With Grace's help, I climb to my feet and settle on the space beside Michael. I brush strands of hair from his forehead before kissing the area, savoring the warmth of life on his skin. I take his big hand between mine and ask the doctor, "Any updates?"

"Results are better than last time. There's more brain activity. The swelling has all but subsided, and the—"

"So no big change, then?" I cut in with a heavy sigh.

Gabriella frowns at me. "That's not what he said."

"I can read between the lines."

"Well, you need to be listening instead of reading, then," Gabriella flings back, narrowing her eyes to go along with her frown. Behind me, Grace snickers, and I resist tossing her a look over my shoulder. Gabriella and Grace know each other from family functions but were never really that close. Until now, it seems. The pair of harpies enjoy teaming up to torment me. "Sometimes pain medication can act as a suppressant. We've reduced those along with the others keeping him under. Once the drugs leave his system, we'll know more."

"Thank you, Doctor," Grace says as his team leaves us alone in the room with Michael's sleeping form.

I lower my gaze to our hands and squeeze his gently, willing him to squeeze back, but he doesn't. A wave of guilt rushes over me. I'm letting my anger and bitterness and pain get to me...again. "I'm sorry, Gabriella. I didn't mean to be rude. I know you're just trying to be helpful."

"It's okay. The stress is getting to all of us. If my stupid big brother would just wake up, it would do all of us a world of good." She gingerly nudges his sock-covered foot poking out from under the blanket.

"He will." I swallow back a hard lump of doubt in my throat and say it again, so that maybe I will even believe it myself. "He will."

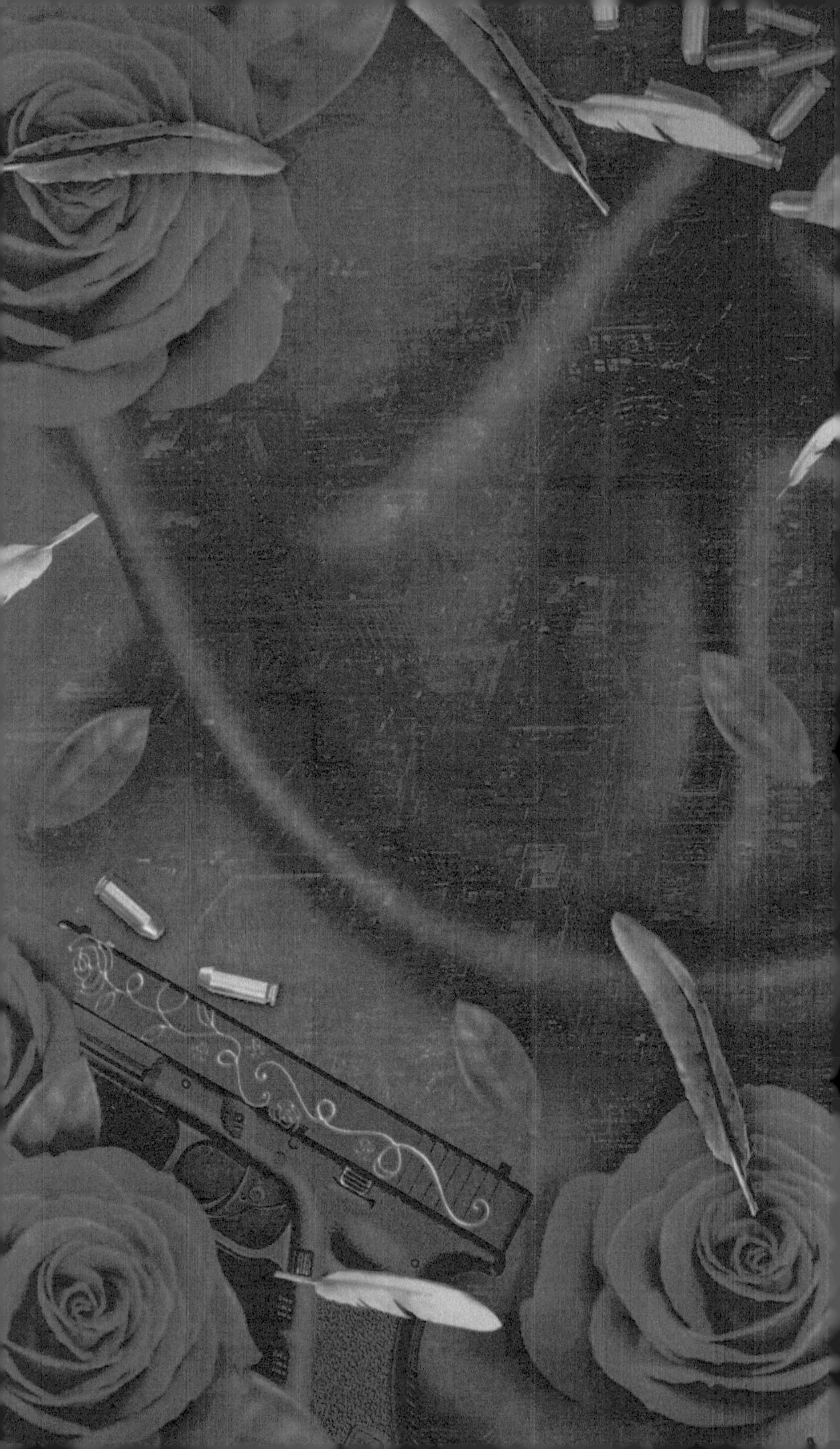

35

ROSE

I've just finished feeding Liam the following morning, settled in the chair next to Michael's bed, when Dante and Alice DiAngelo walk in, followed by Raphael.

"Good morning." I offer them a small smile. I'm still a little unsure how to act around them all, but we're making progress. Raphael getting my son out of that church helped significantly. Something I'll always be eternally grateful for.

Alice approaches, carrying a caramel latte and a brown paper bag from my favorite bakery. She offers them to me, and in exchange, I hand her Liam. Once he's settled in her arms on the couch, I dig into the muffin and sip on the sweet, warm drink, fighting the temptation to chug the entire thing.

"How is he? Any change?" Dante asks, standing on the other side of Michael's bed.

The head of the DiAngelo family is a difficult man to read, but I see so much of Michael in him, and for such a powerful man, he's a complete golden retriever when it comes to Alice.

"His doctor weaned him off the pain meds as well last night. He said they can sometimes act as a suppressant."

Dante nods. He moves to sit beside his wife and gently cups the back of Liam's hat-covered head. He stares down at the baby with a strange look.

"What is it?" I ask.

Sighing, Dante leans back against the couch. He meets my eyes for a moment before he suddenly sits up and leans forward, his elbows resting on his knees. He's on edge about something. "I have to apologize to you, Rosaleen."

"It's Rose. Please."

"Right. Of course. I have to apologize, Rose."

"You have nothing to apologize for." I mean it. He did nothing wrong, as far as I can remember. "I'm the one who should be apologizing."

Dante chuckles lightly. "For what? For making my son the happiest he's ever been and bringing this sweet angel into our family?"

"I guess that and the huge headache my identity brought. We almost lost Michael..." I lower my head and voice. "We still might."

"None of that talk now." Alice interrupts. "Michael is strong, and he will wake up because he has a lot to live for. There's a whole future ahead of him."

Dante kisses his wife's head. "You're right, dear." He looks back at me, and I meet his eerily familiar gold gaze. "I'm sorry for failing you when you were a child. I'm your godfather. Your mother was a close friend growing up. She trusted me to look after you no matter what, and I failed her too. A regret that I will take to my grave."

"You didn't fail me or her. You didn't know what was going on. There's a difference," I tell him. A truth I've been trying to accept for the past week.

Dante smiles softly. "You're so much like your mother. Wise beyond your years. Did you know that before the accident, we were in talks about arranging a marriage with you and Michael? When you graduated from university of course."

"I didn't know that."

I turn my head and look at Michael, studying his quiet and still face. He has a couple of days' scruff growing on his face, making him look ruggedly handsome. I kind of like it. Maybe I can convince him to keep it. At least long enough to know what it feels like running kisses up on my neck, down my chest...between my legs. I want that chance with him. I want every chance we can get.

"Do you think he'll forgive me?" The question has been a constant concern lingering in the back of my mind.

"Forgive you for what?" Dante asks. "Keeping your identity a secret? You didn't know who Michael was. You haven't from the beginning. I can't fault you for being protective of Liam and yourself. If anything, I'm proud you did."

I chew on my bottom lip. Logically, his words make sense. Of course, they do. But that small part of my mind that feeds my anxiety perks up. "I should have told him the moment he rescued me. I wanted to. But I didn't want to put his life or anyone else's in danger because of who my father is...who he was. I was scared of what he would do if he found me again."

"If Michael had told you his real name instead of our mom's maiden, would you have done the same?" Raphael asks, taking Liam from Alice when he gets a little fussy. The brothers are identical, but Liam doesn't know any different, and without Michael awake to hold him, Raphael has stepped in to help.

"My entire life, I've only ever known one truth. And it didn't matter if I was here in Miami or over there in Dublin. I am an O'Leary. Dante is my godfather, but he's still a DiAngelo." I turn my eyes to the patriarch of the Italian family. "You're still the head of the High Table and, as such, an ally to my father. When Michael rescued me from that car, I was terrified.

My father had just torn me away from my son and then sold me like I was nothing more than a piece of meat. So if Michael had told me who he was then, at that moment? Knowing what I did at the time?" I look away and cover Michael's hand with mine. "No. I don't think I would have. To be completely honest, I probably would have tried to find a way to run." I chuckle under my breath, but it holds no humor. "That's probably not what you wanted to hear."

After a moment of silence, Dante says, "This world we live in, it's not always black and white. Take it from someone who knows that better than anyone else. Sometimes, the gray is the better path to take."

"As a fellow mother, I admire what you did. How hard you have fought, and no one can judge you for it. No one should, anyway," Alice assures me with a genuine smile.

I don't know why, but hearing her approval means more than having Dante's or Raphael's. Maybe it's because she's a mother, so she understands my reasoning a little better than anyone else. Or maybe it's because there's been a hole in my life where my mother used to be, and it has ached to be filled ever since she died. Whatever the reason, though, I'm happy to have Alice in my life and in Liam's.

"I have one last question," Raphael says, patting Liam on the back and getting a loud burp from the baby as a reward.

I hand him a blanket to wipe Liam's face. "Okay."

"Do you love my brother?"

"Yes."

There's no hesitation in my answer. The single word comes straight away, clear as day to the front of my mind. And there's no regret, no second-guessing, or uncertainty. Because I fell in love the moment I saw him on that dance floor. It was like every sappy love song, dreamy movie, and romantic book suddenly made sense. That the instant connection and the idea of a soulmate existing out there isn't just another impossibility. It's real. And it happened to us.

"I loved you first."

I swing my head around and lock eyes with the man from the dance floor and fall in love all over again. Michael's awake.

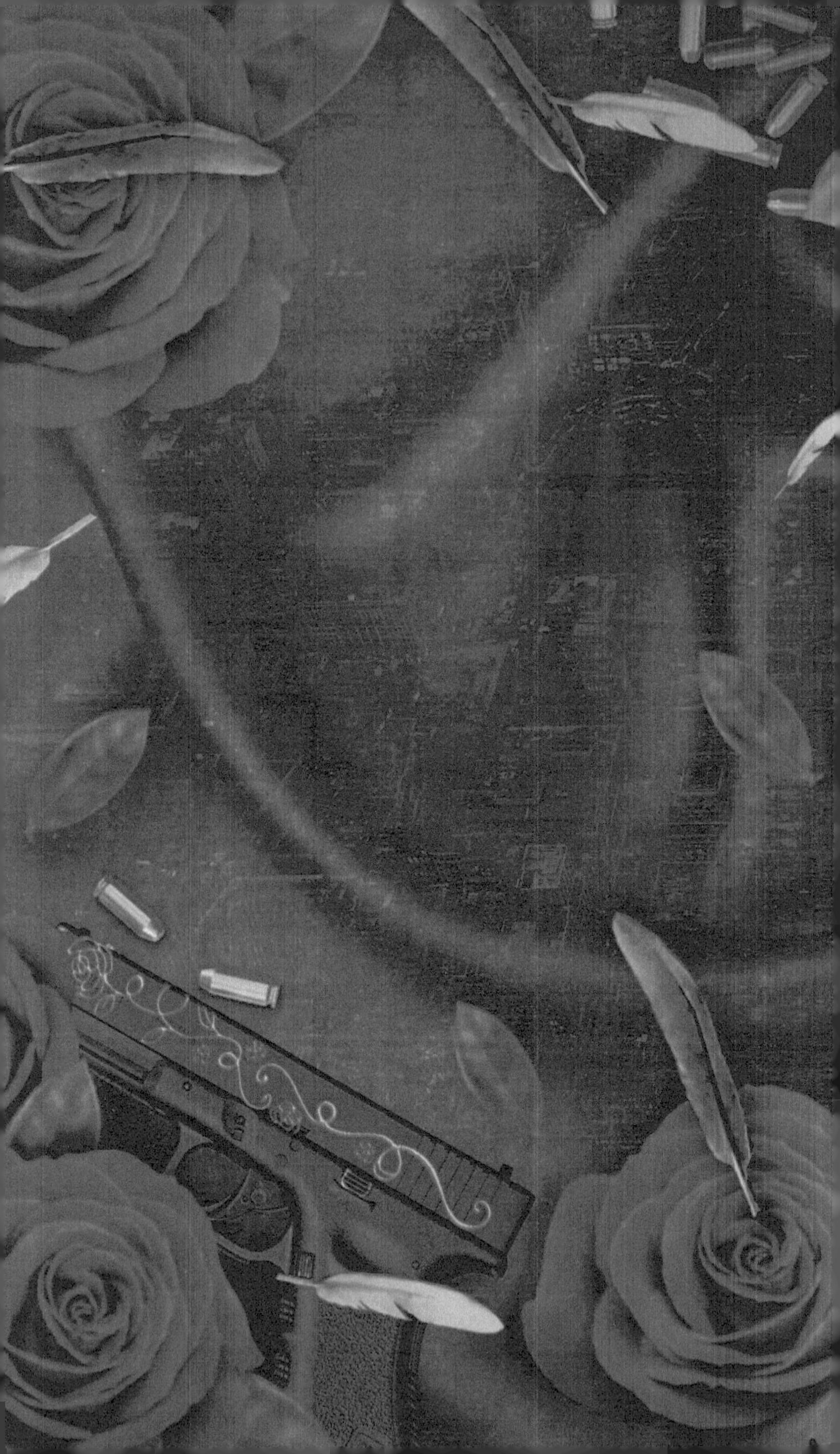

36

MICHAEL

Pain.

Every inch of my body burns and itches and aches with it.

It's all I know among the endless darkness surrounding me.

If it wasn't for the pain, I would think I'm dead and that this is hell.

Maybe it is.

I can't tell any longer.

I drift in and out of consciousness, lost in the numbing void that surrounds me, suffocating me.

How long I float is unclear. Has it been a day, a week, a year? There's no way to measure time here.

Exhaustion tugs at me. I try to fight it harder than ever before because I don't want to fade back into the void. I want to stay. I want to wake up.

But I'm too weak.

Just as the darkness looms, I hear a whisper. I follow it like a string until I finally hear a voice. Her voice. An angel's voice.

"I love you, Michael."

Like a siren, she calls to me from somewhere in the darkness, luring me away from the black depths and toward the surface, toward where I want to be.

She's everywhere. Her warmth surrounds me the closer I get to *her. Above me, a small light pinpricks the surface of the dark, and I fight my way toward it.*

"Come back to us. Please."

I'm trying, Rose. I'm trying.

Something's different about the dark this time. I'm aware of my other senses instead of the constant feeling of floating. The smell of lavender vanilla body wash, the steady cadence beeping of a machine, and the warmth of a soft, familiar body pressed close to me.

Rose.

"Do you love my brother?"

"Yes."

Her single word is my salvation. The light rushes toward me, and I finally break through the heavy surface. I open my eyes, and her beautiful face is all I see.

Mia piccola rosa, my Rose. Words I didn't get to say before, but need to say now.

"I loved you first."

Everyone swings their heads toward me simultaneously with the same shocked expressions. And then Rose crumples. She sobs uncontrollably and crawls farther up the bed. The moment she brushes the bandage on my thigh, a sudden pain flares up, making me hiss, which causes her to climb off the bed quickly. No. I don't like that. Not one bit. I try to reach out to stop her, but my arms feel incredibly heavy.

"Don't go," I croak out, my throat dry and scratchy.

After a moment of brief hesitation, Rose carefully perches back beside me on the bed. I manage to flip my hand, palm side up, on the bed for her. She immediately slips her hand in mine and squeezes it gently. I try to return the favor, but every move-ment feels weighed down, like gravity pushes against me, making it harder than normal to do even that simple thing.

"How long?" I clear my throat and accept a sip of water Rose holds out for me before continuing. "How long have I been out?"

"A week."

The events of the night at the church rush forward like a movie reel sped up. "Liam?"

Rose looks over her shoulder as Raphael approaches with the wiggling baby in his arms.

"Hello, brother." His eyes are glassy as he looks at me.

"Raphael."

Rose takes Liam from Raphael and perches him up on her lap close enough that I can see and touch him. I reach out my fingers, and Liam immediately latches on to one.

"I'm going to go get the doctor and let him know you're awake." Raphael wipes his eyes before he walks to the door, giving me one last look before he leaves.

Dad and Mom approach next, and I'm happy to see them both.

"Michael!" Mom sobs, her face a mess as she cries against my shoulder. "I'm so happy you're okay."

Dad squeezes my hand. "Glad to see you awake."

"Glad to be awake," I tell him. "What happened at the church?"

"When Patrick turned his gun on Rose, Connor arrived at that moment and put him down." Dante's eyes flick to Rose, and I follow.

Rose bows her head, kissing Liam's crown, and I shift to lace our fingers together as a sign of silent support. I'm sure she's feeling some level of guilt over her father's actions and maybe his death, but Patrick is responsible for his own actions. None of what happened was her fault, and I need her to know that. I need to tell her that I'm sorry for everything I said on the beach. That when I said I loved her, I meant it. I love every single inch of her. The good, the bad, the ugly. The black, the white, and the gray.

Another memory flashes across my mind, causing me to jolt upright. The sudden movement sends a sharp pain shooting through my body, preventing me from attempting any further. Hands reach for me as if to stop me, but it's unnecessary. I collapse back on the bed, and my eyes travel to Rose's side.

"You were stabbed."

"Yes."

"Let me see."

"Michael—"

"Rose." I interrupt and leave no room for argument. I may be laid up in bed, but I'm still me. "Let. Me. See."

She rolls her eyes with a heavy sigh. If I wasn't laid up in bed and she wasn't hurt, I'd have her over this bed right now, punishing her for that little act of sarcastic rebellion. Rose hands Liam to Mom and then slides off the bed. Her movement is choppy and slow, and if she thinks I missed that little grimace just now, she's mistaken.

Rose rolls her shirt up to reveal a large white bandage wrapped around her midline.

Before I can speak, she quickly says, "I'm okay," but I detect a hidden meaning in her words and notice the sadness on Mom's face before she averts her gaze.

"No, you're not," I say, and when Rose's expression falls, I know I'm right. "What else happened?"

"There was damage to one of my ovaries from the knife, and they couldn't stop the bleeding. They had to remove it, but I still have one of my ovaries and my uterus." Rose reveals the truth without meeting my eyes.

I reach out carefully with a shaky hand, place two fingers under her chin, and lift her face. The pain is clear in her eyes, but so is something else. Something like guilt. Oh, for the love of...

"You're alive. That's all that matters to me."

"But I might not be able to get pregnant again. One ovary makes things much more difficult, and I've always wanted a big family like you and—"

"Rose." She stops abruptly and waits. "There are other ways to have children of our own. Surrogacy is an option. Right?"

"Right," she agrees after a long second.

She may agree with me now, but I know this conversation is far from over. The guilt she feels is something we need to address because it's unnecessary.

A knock on our door interrupts our conversation. Raphael returns with the man I presume is my lead doctor.

From the sound of the doctor's report, I'm lucky to be alive. A gunshot wound to the upper thigh that nicked my femoral artery caused an excess amount of blood loss, which led to my heart stopping twice during surgery, forcing my doctors to put me in a coma so my body could recover without interruption.

I don't remember much about my time in the coma. It feels like a faint dream, like a long sleep that has left me tired still. I look over at Rose, and she lifts her eyes to mine. She's the reason I'm alive. Rose and our son. They gave me something to fight for while I floated in the never-ending darkness.

Begrudgingly, the doctor puts me through a string of tests, much to my immediate disappointment. When we finally return from having every inch of my body poked, scanned, and prodded, my room is full. Only now Gabriella is there along with Enzo and a strange woman I've never seen before.

My best friend is bundled up in a wheelchair with an IV pole set beside him. White gauze wrapped around his chest pokes out from his sad mint green hospital gown. He's pale with bags under his eyes, and his blond hair is tied up high in a very messy bun. Rose updated me that he ended up losing a part of his liver from the gunshot he sustained while protecting the most important people in my life. I owe him more than he will ever know.

"You look terrible, Enzo," I remark with a teasing smile.

"I can still kick your ass," Enzo tosses back.

I turn serious, my mind shifting once again to the reason he's in the wheelchair to begin with. "Thank you, Enzo. I could never repay you."

Enzo bows his head and nods, understanding the gratitude behind my words. "And you never have to."

I lift my eyes to the blond woman behind him. "Who are you?"

"That's Evelyn," Rose introduces the woman. "She's my best friend from Europe. She's the one who helped me escape when I found out I was pregnant."

So now I owe another person. "Thank you for helping Rose and our son."

"My pleasure," she replies.

Gabriella wipes her eyes and smiles at me from where she stands next to Raphael. "I'm just glad everyone's okay."

I look around the room, noticing one absentee. "Where's Uncle Leo?"

"He and Dominic are representing our family at Igor's funeral today," Dad answers.

Mom shifts on the couch, clearly uncomfortable as she mumbles, "Our family shouldn't even be there."

Dad places his hand on his wife's knee. "We had to send someone. Leo offered."

I'm torn because I agree with Mom but understand Dad's point of view politically. Regardless of the grievance against our family, the DiAngelos still rule the High Table. If we're not there in some form or capacity to show support for another High Table family's loss, then it looks bad to other crime families in Miami.

"How angry is Sergei?"

"He's upset over the death of his brother but has extended his apologies to us and the O'Leary family. He claims he had no idea of his brother's actions."

"Do you believe him?"

"No," Dad answers honestly after a long moment. "But I have no proof otherwise, so we're forced to keep watch for now. Connor has offered to help in any way he can."

I like Connor. He has a strong, solid head on his shoulders and being married to Rose's sister will help grow the bonds between the families.

"What about Dimitri?" I ask, catching the way Gabriella tenses her shoulders. I still don't like that the man is on a first-name basis with my baby sister.

"Sergei assures me that Dimitri didn't know anything either."

"What do you think?"

"That Dimitri didn't know about Igor." Gabriella interrupts our dad before he can reply. "He wasn't lying."

Dad and I exchange a look. Neither of us is sold on the Russian, and if he's covering for his boss, he's as good as dead anyway.

A nurse enters and gasps in surprise at the crowd of people in the room. Her eyes zero in on Enzo.

"Mr. Accardi! You are not supposed to be out of bed," she reprimands him.

Evelyn smacks his shoulder, ignoring his tiny cry of pain. "You said you were cleared to be in the wheelchair."

Enzo hisses and glowers at both women. "Well, excuse me if I heard my best friend woke up from a weeklong coma. I had to come see him."

"Well," she mimics his condescending tone. "Now you have. Back to your room."

Enzo groans and grumbles his goodbyes as Evelyn pushes him out of the room. Dad and Mom leave next, taking Raphael and Gabriella with them. Once the nurse leaves after administering a pain medication I tried hard to refuse, it's just Rose and Liam with me.

My gaze moves to Rose. She's still holding my hand, but her head is bowed, her hair hiding her face from me. Unacceptable.

"I'm so sorry, Michael. Please don't hate me for lying about who I really am and for keeping it a secret. Because if you do —" She raises her face, and the tears streaming down her cheeks fall on our clasped hands. "I just...I can't. So please, don't hate me."

"I could never hate you," I tell her honestly. "I just told you I love you, remember? And I'm sorry for all the horrible things I said on the beach. I didn't mean a single word of it and regretted my behavior the moment you left. I jumped to conclusions and pushed you away in anger, which set off this entire domino chain of a shitstorm. This is all on me and only me. I'm sorry. Can you ever forgive me?"

She reaches over and cups my cheek with only love in her

eyes. "I really do love you, Michael. You never need to ask for my forgiveness because you already have it. You always will."

"I love you too."

I must have horrible breath after being unconscious for days, but she leans in and kisses me anyway. My body might be weak, but one particular part is fully awake and excited. Only my attempt to relieve the pressure backfires when my leg rebels, forcing me to groan against her mouth. Rose pulls back and looks down at my blanket-covered legs. Her blush when she sees the obvious bulge is enough for me to say fuck it and push through the pain.

"I'm so sorry. Did I hurt you?"

"Sweetheart, if you don't climb on top of me right now, I might just die," I tell her, enjoying how her blush deepens in color, and I know she's envisioning the idea.

Rose looks over her shoulder at Liam's sleeping form in his mobile crib before she turns back to me with a sly smile. Carefully, she swings her body up and over, mindful of our wounds, and settles down on my lap with a content sigh as if she's finally coming home after a long time away. She leans forward, that playful spark I remember so vividly from the first night we met dancing in her eyes.

"Tell me what you want, sweetheart." I tease, nibbling at the corner of her lips. "Use your words."

"I want to burn."

And we did...

...until the nurse came back for night rounds, that is.

37

ROSE

I once thought of Miami as a pretty prison. Funny how a person's view can change when the ugliest part is removed and replaced by something far more beautiful.

Life over the past month has been a whirlwind. Once released from the hospital, Michael and I barely had a moment to ourselves. There seems to always be someone at the penthouse. It was nice for the first week. Now, it's getting a little too crowded.

I was trying really hard not to complain, but after Alice walked in on me laid out on the kitchen island, naked and covered in ice cream with Michael enjoying his "Sunday Sundae" between my legs, I gave Michael an ultimatum. He changed the door codes that same day.

Evie hasn't left either, but a certain blond reincarnated Viking may have something to do with that more than her best friend and godson do. I've never seen her act this way around a guy and I'm happy for them both. But they're not just fooling around, which there's a lot of, apparently. They're also working together to track down and gather information about the masterminds behind the human trafficking. So far, it's been quiet on that front. Which is a good and a bad thing. Because there's no way a business that sophisticated happens only once.

Whoever is behind it knows the High Table is on to them and is staying below radar on purpose.

Michael comes up behind me and wraps me in his arms, pulling me flush against his solid, warm chest. "What are you thinking about?"

Tonight is our first time away from Liam since returning home. We've both been officially cleared by our doctors with no restrictions...not that we've been very good at obeying a certain few of them.

But what can I say? The man is sinfully gorgeous, and I'm addicted.

To celebrate, Michael surprised me with a date away on his parents' beautiful three-hundred-and-fifty-foot yacht. We're anchored out in the bay for the night, and the setting sun has thrown the sky into a painting of the most gorgeous hues of red and pink and orange. The clouds will clear soon after the sun sets, and being this far out, we'll be able to see the stars tonight.

Michael dips his face and kisses the side of my throat. He hums low, the sound vibrating like an electric shock straight to the space between my legs. "You going to tell me?"

I contemplate staying silent if it means he'll continue his current path, but then he nips at my skin, and I blurt out the first thing that comes to mind. Something much more pleasant than the human trafficking ring haunting us. "I was thinking about Liam."

"Hmm." Michael hums his agreement, and then he lightly rests his chin on top of my head. "He's grown so much in the past month."

"He rolled over in front of Gabriella the other day. I've never seen her so excited. She wanted to stay all evening just to keep watching him."

"She's welcome to stay if it keeps her from that Russian bastard," Michael grumbles.

I playfully smack his arm. "They're just friends, Michael."

"I don't want them to be even that," Michael argues.

"Well, we can't always get what we want. Now, can we?" I know I'm poking an angry Italian bear, but I like playing with fire. Remember?

Michael growls and then spins me around, pinning me against the yacht railing with his all-consuming body mass. I rest my head back on his shoulder and peer up into his handsome face, smiling innocently, like I don't know exactly what I've done. When he sees the gleam in my eyes, he understands right away and leans down to nibble at my bottom lip. "You'll find, sweetheart, that I always get what I want."

He captures my mouth in a claiming kiss that leaves no question about who owns my body and my pleasure. Michael presses into me, and when his cock twitches in his pants, I push back against him with a small giggle.

"Do that again, and I'll fuck you right here, right now."

"Promise?"

With a growl, he grabs my hand and pulls me away from the yacht's edge and into the primary suite. He locks the door behind us, and the energy in the room is charged and ready to explode.

"What about dinner?" I ask as he slips off his jacket and tosses it onto a nearby chair.

He crosses the room and presses his entire body up against my back. Nuzzling his nose into my hair, he raises his hands to my shoulders and brushes his fingers down my arms. Goose bumps rise at his touch, and I lean back into his chest. He caresses a hand around my hip and skirts his way up my body, pausing only to squeeze my breasts, which entices a moan from me.

His hand wraps around my throat and tightens ever so slightly, guiding my face toward his. His bright eyes are blown black, lost in the throes of passion and desire, and I've never seen something so fucking beautiful. To be wanted with such intensity should be frightening, but it's intoxicating.

"Are you hungry?" he whispers.

"Not for food," I confess.

He growls against her mouth before kissing me breathlessly. "Good girl. Now, get undressed."

38

MICHAEL

I wonder for the millionth time how I got so lucky. I'm not a good man by any means, so what I've done to earn this angel's love and affection is beyond me. I'll burn the world to ashes if she asks me to. I'll deliver her the heads of anyone who has ever harmed her and lay them at her feet. The hold this woman has over me makes no sense, but whatever it is, it's ours. Because without her, I'm just a shell of a man over-taken by the darkness inside him and the demons that call it home.

"On the bed," I tell her and watch as she obeys without question, pleasing a side of me I may explore with her later.

She props up on her elbows to watch as I undress. We've seen each other naked a hundred times by now, but every time feels like the first time. I grab my briefs and tug them down, my cock springing free, the tip already leaking pre-cum. Rose sits up and wraps her small hand around me, leaning forward to run her tongue along the slit. She opens and swallows me down her throat before I even know what's happening.

Holy mother of...

She feels incredible. She always does. Rose sucks my cock like it's the only thing that can save her. She fondles my balls with her free hand, and I nearly come right then. But no. Not yet. I reach down and pull her away from my cock. The pout on her face is fucking adorable.

"You're too good at that, sweetheart, and you know it. But I don't want to come down your throat. The only place I'm coming tonight is inside you." I kiss her deep and groan at the taste of myself on her lips. "I want you pregnant again and need to fill this sweet, sinful body every chance I can get."

"Then hurry up and fuck me," she growls against my lips. "Make me scream loud enough they hear it on the island."

Now that's a challenge I can win easily. Rose meets my lips in a soft kiss and gasps when I run a finger through her slit. "You're soaking wet, little rose."

She practically purrs her agreement. I swallow her moan when the tip of my cock nudges her entrance. "Ready for me?"

"Always. Fuck me hard enough that I feel it tomorrow."

I slam forward and resist kissing her so she can scream loud enough for those on the island to hear, just like she asked. Being buried in her slick heat is like coming home. Every thrust pulls another scream from her throat, and I already feel my balls tightening from the impending release it craves.

"Ride me, baby." I wrap my arms around her and flip us in one quick movement. Rose straddles me and peers down at my cock covered in her juices, and Lord help me, the devilish gleam in her eyes when she looks back at me is enough to make my demons question what's about to happen. She takes my rock-hard cock in her hand and lowers herself excruciatingly slow on it.

She sighs when I bottom out, and she just stays there for a moment. Her head is tossed back, her mouth wide open to the ceiling, unable to voice the way my cock hits all the right angles in this position. I wish I had my phone nearby because this picture deserves to be my wallpaper forever.

"Fuck me, sweetheart. Take your pleasure." I grab her face

and pull her down to seal my lips over hers, diving in deep to claim every inch of her mouth as my own.

Rose moves, finding her rhythm quickly. Placing my hands on her hips, I help guide her as we climb higher and higher, chasing the crest of that wave we lust after.

"Holy shit, Michael." She leans forward and runs her nails down my chest. I growl at the sensation. "I'm so close. Harder, baby. I need to come. I want to come all over your cock. Please. Fill me until I'm still dripping tomorrow."

I lean forward and slide one hand up her back to grip the nape of her neck, holding her close to me while I keep the other glued to her hip. Burying my face in her neck, I suck and bite at the soft sensitive skin there, knowing full well that there will be a mark in the morning. Good.

With the proper leverage, I angle my hips and thrust up into her wildly until her walls clamp down on my cock, and she cries out louder than I've ever heard. I can't hold back any longer. I explode with a roar, my seed flooding her greedy cunt as her walls milk me dry.

"Fuck, Rose," I groan into her neck, my heart racing.

"I know." Rose chuckles into my hair, her voice slightly hoarse from all her screaming. "I think you won the challenge, by the way."

"I aim to please." I collapse back into the pillows and take her with me.

We're covered in sweat, but I don't care, and neither does she. She curls up on my chest, and I run my hand through her hair.

A wave of peace washes over me, and as I hold the woman I love, the mother of my child, I'm overcome with emotion. I planned to do it at dinner, but there's no better time than now.

It might be a little unconventional, but when have we ever done anything by the book?

I kiss the top of her head and reach for my jacket, which luckily ended up on the chair right next to the bed. Rose is so exhausted she isn't even bothered by my slight movements. I find the small black box and pull it out. My throat suddenly closes up, and my heart races. The nerves are back, which is ridiculous because I have no doubt of her answer.

Lying on my chest, Rose immediately notices the change in my breathing and heartbeat. She picks her head up and stares up at me in concern. I'm not sure what she sees on my face, but it's enough to have her pulling back completely. When she tries to climb off me, my hand unconsciously grips her hip to keep her in place. My cock may be spent, but it's still semi-hard buried inside her, and it isn't ready to leave her warmth yet. Not when round two is knocking.

"What is it?" Rose furrows her brow as she studies my face and body for any signs of trouble. "Are you hurt?" Her eyes fall to the bullet wound on my upper thigh and the pink flesh covering it. "Maybe we should have waited a little longer for you to recover more."

"I'm fine. Never felt better." I run the back of my hand down her cheek. My eyes follow my fingers as they move down her neck. She swallows beneath my touch. "I love you, Rose. I—"

"I love you too." She interjects immediately, and I don't miss the hint of fear that creeps into her voice.

I trace the line of her collarbone before I move down her arm. She shivers at the sensation of my light touch. "I'm not a good man, Rose. I've done and seen things that are the stuff of nightmares. I have demons that never rest. Demons that live off the fire that rages inside me." I run my fingers back up her arm, then repeat the same process down her other side. "But one touch from you is all it takes to smother that fire and quiet the demons. I've been lost for a while, Rose, a shell of the man I once was, but you've made me feel alive again. You've given me everything I always thought I would never be worthy of."

Her eyes are on me, but I know that if I look at her now, I'll stop, and I need to get this all out.

"I've often thought back to the night we met, and I realized that a series of choices led to us meeting. If I had made just one choice differently, we wouldn't be here right now. Liam wouldn't be here. That night was the culmination of choices I made for myself, with no goal in mind. For the first time in my life, I threw caution to the wind."

My hand travels down her breastbone before I circle each breast, mesmerized by the sheer size and beauty of them. My hand falls to her stomach next, still slightly round from the proof of life we created together. I can't wait to see it swollen with our next child. "And then I saw you, and I made the best choice I will ever make in my life. I stood and said hello to a beautiful angel."

"Michael," Rose whispers, but I shake my head.

"Let me finish." From the corner of my eye, I see her nod. "And now I'm hoping that together we can make one more good choice because I want more. I want more chances of throwing caution to the wind, more choices. I want it all. And I want it with you."

Finally, I raise my eyes and find her staring directly at me with tears streaming down her face. The loving emotion on her face is enough to give me the confidence to move forward. I bring my other hand up and reveal the black velvet box. I flip it open and unveil a stunning vintage engagement ring with vinelike patterns on the sides of the band that lead to a diamond resting like a flower open in bloom.

Taking a deep breath, I continue, "Marry me, Rose O'Leary."

Rose covers her face with her hands and sobs. For a second, I fear she may say no, but then she lowers her hands and smiles through her tears. "Of course, I'll marry you. Yes. A thousand times, yes. I love you so much, Michael."

I pull the ring free and slip it on her hand, pleased to see that it fits her finger perfectly. Rose breaks into another sob as she stares at the ring in astonishment before she smiles again and grabs my face. She pulls me forward, and our mouths crash together. When I pictured tonight, I didn't expect I'd be proposing naked in bed with my cock still buried inside her. But as far as choices go, this is a damn good one.

Our story may have started out strangely and took some unexpected detours. We may have gotten lost on the way back to each other, but I don't regret a single choice because each one led us to this moment.

And if I had the choice to do it all over again, I would.

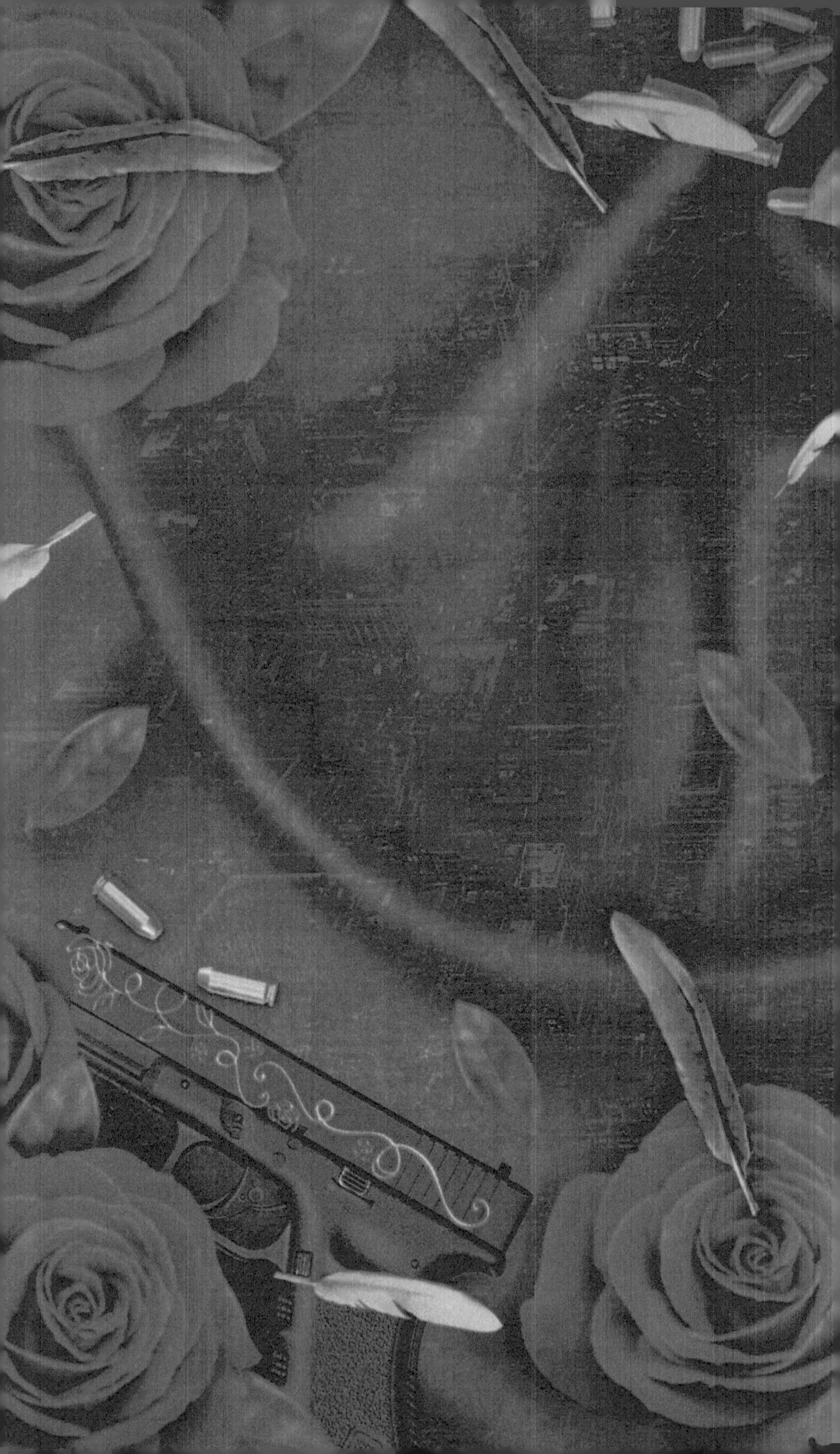

EPILOGUE

LILY

COLUMBIA

Another monstrous mosquito lands on my arm. One so large, I can actually count the stripes on the blood-sucking dinosaur as I watch it stick its needle into my flesh.

Bastard.

I would smack the damn thing and send it back to the hell it came from, if I wasn't busy helping keep a man's intestines inside his body.

As painful as the sting the bug leaves behind on my body after it drinks its fill and flies off to find its next victim, it's nothing compared to how our tent of war-torn patients feels. I gaze at the overflowing cots and makeshift gurneys with an inward sigh. Another attack on a helpless village has left dozens of innocent men, women, and children dead or injured. So many families have been torn apart as a result of a war they never wanted. So many lives destroyed...

I was an emergency doctor in Chicago for a couple of years and saw it all. At least, I thought I had. Bullet holes and stab wounds are elementary when faced with full-body chemical burns and partial disembowelment. I once saved a man who came in with a knife sticking out of the side of his neck, but here...I'm losing patients left and right because there's just not enough help, medicine, or technology.

Accepting and understanding the harsh reality around me is enough to make me ache for home, and I take nothing for granted anymore.

My current team and I have been in Columbia for a few weeks now doing relief work. This is my third rotation over the last year. It's not always like this—no, that's a lie. It is. I like to think my presence here is helping, however small or large that is, and for the most part, that's why I keep coming back. But to be completely honest, the pay for three months' work here is almost the same as an entire year's salary back home, and I have a mountain of student debt to pay off with big plans for the future. I want to buy a condo, get a new car since my old beetle is on its last leg, and take a really long vacation where I spend more time in a bikini than scrubs.

"He's crashing! Get the paddles!" the lead doctor shouts. A moment later, she's yelling, "Clear!" We all step back with our hands in the air.

My eyes lock on the black computer screen, willing the green line to correct itself, but it remains flat.

"Again! Clear!"

I glance at the patient, and my heart sinks at the sight. His face is pale, and his lips are turning blue. He's gone. It's clear as day, and the lead doctor knows it too because after one final attempt, she calls time of death.

"Dr. Song!"

I raise my head and turn in the direction of the person who called my name. It's Dr. Cole, and he's waving me over frantically. I snap my gloves off and tug my protective apron off, tossing both in the trash bin, and hurry over. When I step up, a nurse hands me a set of new gloves and an apron.

"What do we have?"

"Six-year-old girl with an open compound fracture to her left arm. I need to set it, but she only speaks Spanish and won't calm down."

I lean forward and give the terrified girl a kind smile before asking her in Spanish. "What is your name?"

She whimpers in loads of pain but latches on to the familiar language. "Louisa."

"Hi, Louisa. My name is Dr. Song, but you can call me Lily. All of my favorite patients do." I wink at her and earn a small smile and giggle in return. I glance over at my co-worker, and he nods. Turning back to Louisa, I try to assure her as best I can. "Now, I understand your arm hurts, right?" She nods meekly. "Well, my friend here will help you feel all better, okay? But first, tell me what's your favorite color?"

"Pink," she admits right away.

"Really? I like pink too. Okay, so once Dr. Cole has fixed your arm, we'll wrap it in a really pretty pink cast. How does that sound?"

Louisa nods before the brave little girl steels herself. I glance at the nurse beside me and ask in English. "Where are her parents?"

The nurse shakes her head solemnly. "She came in alone."

I sigh. It's unfair and cruel to leave an innocent young girl like this all alone in the world. An orphan in the blink of an eye. So many children have the same story, the same uncertain future, and I hate knowing the pain and fear they'll face in the coming days.

Of course there are programs to offer assistance for

orphaned children of war and extended families who may be willing to take them in, but that's not always the case.

I tried to keep up with the children during my first rotation, but there were so many that it became impossible. For my sanity, I lied to myself and imagined each one had a happy ending. Even though, realistically, I know differently. It's just easier sometimes to believe in the fictional.

By the end of my shift, it feels like I ran a 5k...in the rain and wind, through the mud and then up a hill...wearing a weighted vest and hung over. All I want is to soak in a tub and sleep for a week, but out here in the forests of Columbia, that's not an option. There is no Hilton nearby. We live in shared tents that make my camping trips as a kid look like a resort stay. Our showers are outdoors and no matter what time of the day, you're sweating even while you shower, making the entire effort pointless.

"Hey, there you are."

I look up and see Dr. Rodriguez approaching. The man gives me the creeps. And that's putting it mildly. It's my first rotation serving with him and hopefully my last. Something in the way he looks at me sets every warning bell off in my head. And I'm not alone. Several of the nurses and other female staff share the same opinion.

His eyes roam over my covered body, and I tighten my cardigan anyway, as if the thin fabric will somehow shield me from his lecherous gaze.

"How can I help you, Dr. Rodriguez? Did I forget to fill out a chart or something?"

He holds up a bottle of what I can only assume is alcohol of some kind. Alcohol isn't exactly forbidden since it's a favorite way for many team members to deal with the stress of the job, but I've never been a fan of the hard stuff. I'm a wine and spirits kind of gal.

"A little nightcap?"

"Not tonight, but thank you for the offer." I hate having to be polite, but he's technically my boss, and, like I said, I need the job.

He sighs like my rejection hurt him, and I can't find the energy to really care if I did. I'm exhausted, and if I can't soak in a tub, then I just want to take my sweaty shower and go to bed beneath my mosquito net.

"I heard about the guy and the kid whose parents were killed," he says. "Sounds like a tough day. Are you sure you don't want one little shot? It'll take the edge off and help you sleep."

I lean forward and rest my elbows on the wood railing, swallowing my groan of annoyance. Glancing around, I search for anyone who might help get me out of this awkward situation, but dinner is still being served, so this side of the base is empty.

"Come on. Just one shot?" Dr. Rodriguez pushes again.

"I'm really tired and just want to get ready for bed. Next time, swear."

"Please?" He pouts. "I promise to leave you alone afterward. Look. It's just, I had a bad day too and could use the company."

I take a deep breath and blow it out hard. Fine. A shot would help take the edge of the day off, and if it will at least make the man shut up and go away, I'll do the damn shot.

"Okay, just one, and then you really need to go find Dr. Cole or someone else to drink with. Deal?" I tell him and then turn away as he grabs two plastic cups to pour the alcohol into.

He holds one out to me, and the powerful smell of whiskey invades my nose. He clinks his cup against mine, like there's anything cheerful to celebrate in this war-torn country. In a hurry to get this over with, I toss back my glass and wince as the bitter taste slides down my throat. It's almost nauseating, but I manage.

"Thank you, Dr. Rodri—"

"Call me Joe."

I blink hard, my eyes suddenly tired from the day. I've always been a bit of a lightweight, but one shot is a little odd. When was the last time I had a drink, anyway? Back in Chicago? Or at Sarah's birthday party? That was months ago. No. It was the week before I came to Columbia. Right?

"Dr. Rodriguez, I think I'm going to call it a night."

"Joe, please."

I try to tell him it's not professional, but my face feels heavy. I take a step back and stumble.

"Whoa, my dear! Careful now." He rushes forward and wraps his arm around my waist, pulling me forward flush to his chest. I try to push back against him, but my arms won't work.

"Wha-what's-what's going on?"

Dr. Rodriguez brushes my light hair from my face, and there are two of him in my vision now. "You've been teasing me ever since you arrived."

No, I haven't. I've barely said more than six words to the man outside of a case.

"And well, I'm done waiting for you to make the first move."

He leans forward. Black rushes from the corner of my eyes. I try to resist its overwhelming force, but it's relentless, weighing me down, and I've never felt so helpless.

I'm trained to save lives...but who will save me?

EXTENDED EPILOGUE

MICHAEL

I pull up at the valet curb outside the club. The bright neon sign spelling out the name Playground through the windshield lights up the night. It's only eight o'clock and a line is already wrapped around the corner to get inside.

"The Playground?" Rose reads the sign. She looks over at me with a sly smile. "Where did you bring me? Is there an actual playground inside?"

"Something like that," I tease before opening my door and sliding out, giving the crowd and atmosphere one sweeping look before moving to the passenger door. Rose holds out her hand expectantly, and I wrap mine around hers before helping her out of the car. Her dress tonight is borderline revealing, and the last thing I need is for anyone to get a look at her. I'd hate to kill on Russian soil. Our alliance is too...fragile right now to tempt my luck.

I take a moment to admire Rose. All I told her about tonight was to wear a dress that's easy to access. That she chose a white dress similar to the one she wore the night we met is a sign too hard to miss.

She styled her hair in an elegant updo, exposing her neck, another sign of what she's hoping for. Her makeup is flawless, which is a shame because I plan on destroying all that hard work by the end of the night. And those heels? The sight of her is enough to make a blind man see and tempt a holy man to sin.

The guard at the door nods to me and mumbles, "Mr. DiAngelo, welcome," before opening the door. We pass and walk down the stone steps, illuminated by real fire burning in the sconces hanging on the wall. At the end of the steps is a ceiling-to-floor heavy velvet curtain. Sweeping it open, we step through the veil into another dimension, a world of temptation, desire, and sin. A world where a man or woman can explore that darker side of their soul they keep hidden behind their perfect houses and cookie-cutter marriages.

Here in the Playground, your inhibitions run wild.

Here in the Playground, you're free to unleash the animal within.

Here in the Playground, you're reduced to just your most primal, basic desires.

The newest addition to the private club is immediately when you walk in. A glass room rests on a raised platform that rotates to give the audience a clear view of the inhabitants from all angles.

Tonight, two men and one woman are inside the glass box. The blond woman is bent over an adjustable table, naked as the day she was born. The man behind her is tall with an athletic, thin build and the one in front of her is a larger, more weight building man. Both men are Hispanic and could be brothers. Hell, maybe they are.

The man behind slams into the woman's pussy with even, hard thrusts. He has his hands on her hips, using them like a steering wheel to direct their pleasure. The man in front wraps his hand in the woman's blond hair as he fucks her mouth. He barely has to move because his companion on the back end slams into her so hard, he moves her entire body forward each time, forcing her to take the larger man's cock over and over.

A little man-on-woman-on-man action is nothing new to me, but it is for Rose. Everything about this private world is new to her. It's one thing to watch this kind of sex in movies, in porn, or read it in those smutty books I've caught her reading before, but it's another thing entirely to see it in person, right in front of you.

I look over my shoulder at Rose and feel a rush of heat shoot directly to my cock. The look on her face is captivating. Her green eyes are wide and locked on the display in front of us. Her mouth has dropped open into the cutest little O. Her tongue darts out to run across her bottom lip before she draws it between her teeth. Never once does she tear her eyes away from the trio locked in the glass box.

Slowly, I move to stand behind her. I lean forward and whisper, "What do you think of your surprise?" I run the tip of my tongue down the shell of her ear before nibbling on the sensitive lobe.

Rose pushes back into me with a moan that I feel vibrate through my body with a direct shot to my cock. I know she feels it jump against her lower back, especially when she wiggles her ass like she's directing me with where she'd like it.

"Tell me, sweetheart." I turn my attention to her neck and pepper light kisses up and down every inch of skin I can reach. "Do you want to see more?"

"Yes." She breathes out before tossing her head back on my shoulder and to the side, giving me better access to her neck.

I caress a hand around her hip, skirting my way up her body, pausing only to squeeze her breasts before coming up to wrap around her throat. I tighten just enough to bring only pleasure and not fear. When Rose doesn't fight me, I use my hand to guide her face towards mine. Her cheeks are flushed even in this low light, and her pupils are blown. She's lost in her passion and desire, and I've never seen something so fucking beautiful.

I capture her mouth in a claiming kiss that leaves no room for question on who owns her body and delivers her pleasure. Our tongues battle and our teeth clash as we fight for the little air that exists between us. It's hot and wet...something out of a high schooler virgin's book, but we're so consumed in one another that we don't care how or what it looks like.

Fuck. I'm so fucking hard that it's beginning to hurt.

I break away only because I have more exciting things planned for us than kissing like a pair of horny teenagers. I lean my forehead against hers as we alternate sucking in gulps of air.

"Come."

"I want to," Rose mumbles before I take her hand and guide her to a set of stairs that lead to a long row of doors broken up only by a dissecting hallway. The rooms at the end of that hallway are for the entertainers, while the rooms surrounding it are for the spectators.

For tonight's purpose, I turn to the right when we walk up the stairs. From up here, Rose has a better view of the glass box and the couples watching from their own semi-private booths. If she's surprised to find the couples watching fucking their brains out in response to the live show, she doesn't show it.

My good, dirty, curious girl.

I open one door, and the low lights automatically turn on, activated by a sensor in the door. A leather couch is pushed up against one wall, and a table similar to the one in the glass box in the main room is on the other side. Beside the door are shelves with various products and toys to use and take home with you. The wall directly across from the door is made of one-way viewing glass. We can see out, but they can not see in.

The room on the other side lights up just as I close and lock the door behind us. Rose drops my hand to walk to the window. She sets her hand against the glass and presses forward as if she can see better if she gets closer.

The room in front of our window features a California King-size bed complete with four bed posts and a canopy above with several rings in different shapes and levels. The canopy moves down if desired, and many do. It adds another level of sensation to the sex when the partner hangs by their arms from the canopy but can rest their knees on the bed.

"What are they going to do?" Rose's voice is thick as the stars of the show enter the room.

A handsome blond-haired man and an equally attractive brunette walk in holding hands. They're clearly a couple, and by the comfortable ease with which they traverse the room, this is not their first time here. The room we're in is designed for couples who enjoy watching other couples partake in sexual acts. They're called voyeurs, and I suspect Rose is curious about the idea.

The couple on the other side is aware that they're being watched. It's part of the fun for them and makes them feel like they're putting on a show.

"Whatever they want." I approach her and place my hands on the glass on either side of her, caging her in but not quite touching her.

Already, I can feel her breath quicken as her chest rises and falls rapidly. Rose continues to stare at the couple as the man slowly undresses the woman until she stands in nothing but a pair of sheer lace panties. He then directs her to kneel at the bottom of the bed, facing it. He pulls two hair ties out of his pocket and quickly styles her hair into two pigtails.

Once done, he strips to only his boxer briefs. He says something to her, prompting Rose to ask, "Can we hear them?"

I reach over to the control box by the window and click a button. Immediately, soft, sensual music fills the room, and we catch the man say, "On the bed, face down."

She complies, and her partner wraps a soft red rope around her ankles, pulling tight enough to where she can't escape but loose enough where he can still maneuver her as he sees fit. He does something similar to her wrists, only this time he pulls the rope tighter, forcing her to rise up on her knees as her arms are stretched out in front, unable to rest on the bed.

Satisfied that she's in the position he wants, the man runs his fingers over a selection of crops hanging from the wall. He selects a short riding crop that's no more than eight inches long.

The woman shivers as he caresses the milky white skin of her bare ass with the tip of the crop. She's so into what the couple is doing that she doesn't even notice that I've undone her zipper until the cold air hits her bare back.

Rose peers over her shoulder. "What?"

"Shhh." I console her before placing a kiss at the base of her neck.

"Oh my God, Michael." Rose moans just as the sound of a crop meeting flesh fills the room, followed by the small cry of surprise by the woman.

"Do you like what you see so far?" I whisper as I move down her spine, placing kisses in even measurement.

"Yes." She moans.

I slip to my knees behind her, but I'm still tall enough to reach the top of her dress. I lightly pull at the sleeves, encouraging gravity to take over. When it does, the white dress falls to her feet in one glorious swoop.

The man in the room delivers two more consecutive slaps to the woman's ass, her skin turning bright pink.

"Do you want to be spanked?"

Rose groans as I run my hands up her sides and then to the clasp of her strapless bra. With skillful fingers, I undo the clasp, and her bra joins the dress a second later on the floor.

"Do you? Remember to use your words."

"I don't know," she admits with a groan. "I'd like to try it, though."

I smirk against her bare skin before standing. I pull her away from the window and over to the couch. Sitting down, I motion for her to lean over my knees.

"Good girl," I praise her as she listens without question. "I'll use my hand this time, but if it's too much, you need to tell me."

"Like with a safe word?"

"Yes. What's your safe word, sweetheart?"

She's silent for a long moment before saying, "Kiwi."

"Kiwi?"

"Yes. I don't like them, and if I need a safe word, then it should be something I don't like."

"Kiwi it is."

Rose wiggles on my lap, and I bite my bottom lip to prevent the moan, but it does nothing to stop my cock from twitching. When Rose feels it against her stomach, she giggles and wiggles again with more intention this time.

"Do that again, and I'll fuck you right now."

Rose lifts her head and turns her face toward me. She winks and counters, "I wouldn't complain."

I don't wait a second longer. I peel down her sheer white

panties, raise my hand, and bring it down on her blemish-free skin. She shrieks in surprise, and I enjoy watching her skin turn pink. Her other cheek looks lonely and begs for a matching mark. So I do it again and again until she's writhing and moaning beneath me in desire. I bet her panties are soaked, and I decide to test that theory.

"Jesus, baby. You're fucking drenched. Does spanking make your tight little pussy drip?"

Rose can only moan in response.

"Use your words," I order before I raise my hand to deliver another quick smack, not as hard as the others but enough for her to cry out, "Yes!"

"Look at our friends," I say, and she raises her head.

The man has finished stripping himself naked and has pushed his girl's panties down her legs. He moves to stand behind the bed before he reaches forward, grabs her hips, and maneuvers her to her knees. Because of the ropes on her wrist, she can only lean forward, trusting the ropes to support her entire weight. The man fists his cock and runs it up and down her slit, lubricating the tip with nature's perfect lubrication before he thrusts forward.

The motion pushes the girl forward, and when she clamps down instinctively on his cock, he shouts from the pleasure it brings.

"Holy shit. I want to try that," Rose admits, her cheeks flaming red as the man fucks his partner. The sound of their skin slapping fills the room. Rose rests back on her knees and looks up at me. We both share the same thought and move. I grab her upper arms and pull her up as I stand. Our mouths meet as she tears at my suit. She's so overwhelmed and hyper-sensitive from pleasure that her movements are jerky.

I pull back to help speed up the process. I slip out of my

shoes and unbutton my shirt. Rose pushes the shirt off my body, making sure her bare hands follow the lines of my body as she does. I undo my belt and pants, raising an eyebrow at Rose to see if she'll finish for me. She doesn't disappoint me.

Falling to her knees, she grabs my pants and pulls them down along with my briefs. My cock springs forward, leaking with pre-cum. Rose licks her lips before wrapping her small hand around the shaft and runs her tongue along the bottom to top, before she opens and swallows me down as far as she can. I'm so large that even when I feel myself hit the back of her throat, she still has room to wrap her hand around the base.

I bury my hands in her hair, effectively ruining her updo as I take my time fucking her sassy mouth. She does something with her tongue and throat at the same time, a favorite move for us both, that has my balls tightening. No. Not yet. The only place I'll be coming tonight is inside her.

I lean down to pull her to her feet. My cock slides out of her mouth with an audible POP, and the pout on her face is fucking adorable. Like I just took away her favorite treat.

As I lift her up, she automatically wraps her legs around my waist. My cock nudges her entrance, and she tosses her head back at the tease. I push her against the cool glass, and she hisses at the sensation as it contrasts with the heat from her skin.

I balance her against the glass with one hand and take my other to guide my cock toward her entrance and slam forward. Being buried in her slick heat is like coming home every time. Rose adjusts herself in my arms, and it causes her walls to clamp down hard around my cock.

"Fucking hell. Do that again."

Rose smirks and leans in for a hard kiss. "Then fuck me hard."

Each thrust pulls another scream from her throat, and I can already feel my balls tightening again, but I bite down on my cheek to distract my body from the impending release it craves. The room is filled with her screams, alternating with the woman being fucked by her boyfriend in the room.

I lean back to look at her and swear I see a halo surrounding her. I don't know what I did to deserve such a beautiful angel, but I will make sure that I spend every day of the rest of my life proving to her and everyone else how much I love her, how much she means to me, and how much I need her.

Because without her, I am just a shell of a man overtaken by the darkness inside him and the demons that call it home.

I angle my hips and thrust up into her until the feeling returns at the base of my spine and tingles down to my balls. Her walls flutter and clamp down on my cock as she screams louder than I've ever heard her. Loud enough that I wonder if the soundproof walls are thick enough or if our entertainers heard her.

I can't hold back any longer. I explode, shooting stream after stream of seed inside her walls, my cock spasming and thrusts growing less coordinated as I empty myself.

"Fuck, Rose. You're so perfect." I groan into her neck, taking deep breaths to calm my racing heart. "I love you."

"I love you too." Her voice is slightly hoarse from her screaming. "You know what, Michael? I think I like the Playground. Can we come again next week?"

ACKNOWLEDGMENTS

If I'm being honest, I am terrible at thanking people. I always end up leaving someone out, so if that happens, my apologies in advance. First, thank you to you, the readers, who took a chance on my debut novel. I wrote this book to get the characters out of my head and onto paper with the only hope of sharing their story with the world. Without your support, Michael and Rose's story would have forever stayed quiet. So, thank you again for taking a chance on a baby author. <3 I hope you continue on this journey with me.

A big thank you to my family for being my biggest fans and pushing me to follow my dream of publishing a book, even if it took me ten years and several story changes. To my dad and big sister for being incredibly supportive through the entire process. You're always willing to listen, and share your ideas and thoughts every step of the way. It means the world to me to know I have you both in my corner. To my mom for encouraging me to dream of love and magic and instilling in me the courage to never give up. I'll say it again...I hope there's a massive *Beauty & the Beast* level type library up in Heaven.

To my friends, Trina and Angie, for being there with me from the start of Dark Choices. You two are incredible women, soul sisters, and without your cheerleading, I don't know where this book would be. To Jenn, my sister from another mother, your passion and love of life is inspired much of

Evelyn, and I can't thank you enough for your unwavering support through the years. I promise my early stories will see the light of day...one day. To Robbie, for always answering my phone calls at midnight just to talk through a plot hole and helping breakthrough a problem that often led to a total rewrite.

To my editor, Jenny, you are a Godsend. Truly. I've learned so much from you and appreciate all your hard work turning my mess into a masterpiece. I promise, I'll eventually understand commas...and apologize for the grammatical errors in this.

To the Bookish Girl team and my PA Mandy Gray. There are no words for what you have done for me. No one tells you about all the little things that go into publishing a novel, especially as an Indie author. It can quickly become overwhelming when all I want to do is share my stories with the world. So thank you so much for taking a risk on me and believing in my books as much as I do. Buckle up! I've got a feeling it's going to be a crazy ride.

ABOUT THE AUTHOR

Connect with me
I love interacting with my readers!

instagram.com/author_k.boozer
facebook.com/author.k.boozer
tiktok.com/@authorkboozer

ALSO BY K. BOOZER

DARK ANGELS SERIES

Dark Choices

Michael and Rose

Dark Consequences

Raphael and Lily

Dark Truths

Gabriella and Dimitri

DARK ANGELS SPINOFF

Dark Memories

Enzo and Evie